# Each and Every Time

# EACH AND EVERY TIME

## NICK BLAKE

Matador
9 Priory Business Park,
Wistow Road, Kibworth Beauchamp,
Leicestershire. LE8 0RX
Tel: 0116 279 2299
Email: books@troubador.co.uk
Web: www.troubador.co.uk/matador
Twitter: @matadorbooks

ISBN 978 1838593 179

British Library Cataloguing in Publication Data.
A catalogue record for this book is available from the British Library.

Printed and bound in Great Britain by 4edge Limited

Matador is an imprint of Troubador Publishing Ltd

RIP Keith Flint
Who passed during the writing of this book.

# PREFACE

BY EVA HARKER, DAUGHTER OF DANNY-LEE HARKER,
AUTHOR OF *EACH AND EVERY TIME*

THIS BOOK WAS WRITTEN BY MY DAD, DANNY-LEE Harker, with the help of his wife, my mum, the journalist Marianne Harker; and his good friend, the DJ and producer, Zoe Marr. They completed a first draft sometime during 2008 following a series of often late-night discussions about my dad's experience of the early rave scene. These involved playing old mix tapes at high volume, tracking down rave footage on YouTube and exhaustive trawling through flyer memorabilia collected by my dad and his late best friend from the time, producer Rob Murgan. For reasons which are still unclear to me, they then did nothing. I discovered the draft from 2008 in a drawer last year and was determined to see it published. I worked with my dad on the editing, and *Each and*

*Every Time* is the result of that collaboration. I hope it gives you as much fun and understanding as it gave me – Hardcore, You Know the Score.

Eva Harker
2019

# PROLOGUE

Hardcore raving grew from the Acid House scene of the late 1980s and spread so rapidly that it seemed to appear almost simultaneously right across the UK. It was intense, viral and fizzing with the bottled-up creativity of a generation. Within a very short time, a complex network of operations evolved with the purpose of playing loud, drum-and-bass-heavy, sample-heavy, highly rhythmic electronic music to large groups of people who were buzzing hard on psychotropic drugs and stimulants. The intention was to have a laugh, dance for hours and otherwise contribute to, and be a part of, a communal ecstatic experience. During that time, a time before widespread mobile telecommunication and before the internet, a system and a culture sprang into being which, for a period of perhaps four or five years, delivered arenas, drugs, DJs, technicians and new musical content to thousands and thousands of people in venues and locations up and down the country each weekend. The scene, so rich and energetic, then diversified and evolved, and from it emerged several different and much-loved musical styles, and so it continues to this day. The music production side on its own is extraordinary; slice after slice of some of the most originally creative music ever made, often devised and produced in a handful of days by producers that were, at least in the beginning, essentially anonymous. These same tunes then, within mere days of production, went straight to the rave, identifiable only by a handwritten generic white label, where they were played by DJs who were also, at least in the beginning, fairly anonymous. None of this is to mention the flyer art, the pirate radio stations, the craft of the MC and, perhaps most importantly, the whole culture of shared manners, behaviour and values that grew up with the scene – being Hardcore, being Safe. It was maybe the last major youth movement of our times, the last shout of the analogue, and is certainly the biggest, the most phenomenal and, arguably, most influential such movement ever to occur in this country, if not the world. It continues to be an inspiration and creative source for many of those who did not enjoy it directly and, for those who were part of it, it invariably counts as the most positively formative time of their lives.

For my raving crew, past, present and future, each and every time.

Danny-Lee Harker
Essex Hardcore 1990-1994

# ONE

Danny-Lee Harker (commonly known as Lee) closed his front door and walked with intent towards the car parked just outside. With the hand which held his keys, he tilted down against the sun the peak of a creased and grimy Suburban Bass cap – one of several rediscoveries he had made earlier that morning while looking through a box filled with unexpected treasure; a box that had sat secretly in his loft for years, waiting like the seed of a desert flower waits for the touch of rain. With his other hand, Lee held, wedged against his ribs, more rediscoveries: a box of cassette tapes with a few photographs on top, a faux-leather-bound road map, a couple of old spiral-bound notebooks. There was also a slim A4 file, but that had not come from the loft. Lee leaned across and placed the file and the loft finds on the passenger seat of the car before getting in himself. He settled into the driver's seat, belted up and then, on the point of starting the engine, stopped in thought and lifted his face to the sky that lay beyond the windscreen. His eyes appeared to stare up and out but his whole vision was directed inward and its focus was the spirit of a time past, a wild and soaring thing within, a thing which now possessed him. Whatever the thing was, wherever it had come from, it felt like it had been waiting for him to arrive at just this moment; felt like it had been lying dormant in the box in the loft, lying low and quiet, just waiting for him to come to it in just the right way to bring it to life, to give it power.

Lee reminded himself of the disturbance the funeral had made in his head, reminded himself how he'd been transported by the Mangled mix, reminded himself how the last few days, and especially the nights, had been full of illusive dreams and odd sensations. The signs of something fucking weird were all there, he concluded, although, to be fair, what had gone on that morning had been altogether on another level of weird. He remembered how he had checked the kitchen clock on coming downstairs from the loft and how what it showed him had made him double-check it against his phone, his laptop and the little green lights of the clock on the oven timer. The devices all told him he'd been upstairs no more than a quarter of an hour, and yet he felt the time as a life of days, weeks, months; big things had gone off during it; images and sounds substantial remained of it, and tastes and sensations continued to swirl.

Safely down from the loft and sitting at the kitchen table trying to digest what had gone on, more and still more had come; stirring stuff, timeless, obliterating on the senses. And still more. *Just what the fuck is going on?* Lee demanded, interrogating himself. He repeated the words as he gently shook his head; *Just what the actual fuck...? Just what the actual fuck...?* Lee chanted the mantra softly to himself, let

2

his righteousness and resolve corral the skittish apprehension and confusion that threatened to loosen his uncertain grip. He returned himself to the purity of the decision that had come from the wild within; a decision that he should move with purpose, regardless of the lack of plan and despite the absence of clear understanding, to tell a story to the unseen world beyond the windscreen. It was such a story, he thought, a riot of circumstance, happenstance and myth, everyday epic, steeped and aglow, and he felt unknown pride in it. He would stand to shout it if necessary. The sense of purpose coursed in his chest then at the thought and it swooped to his guts the way it had in the loft and the way it had again as he sat at the kitchen table. It swooped and Lee gripped the steering wheel, breathless but upright, cognisant and strong but fully in the power of the drop.

## //

Coming down from the loft, it had been different. Danny-Lee had only managed the descent once he had drawn several deep breaths and reassured himself that he could manage to be steady on his feet. He then descended carefully, his head full of thoughts and his arms full of the things that had found him while he was up there amongst the rafters. He sat himself at the kitchen table, his body held calm but his head firing in all directions, hyped to the absolute fucking max, he observed, his synapses snapping like strings of firecrackers. Through the mental static he surveyed the artefacts he had laid out on the table like trial exhibits alongside the file binder, Baz's business card on top, already there where he'd left it on Thursday evening. These were relics of a life long gone, but not, it seemed, one that was ready to be over. For Lee, their power to show had been abrupt and direct; operating through

3

fierce flashback, dropping him entirely out of his continuum, exposing him to blasts of ultra-vivid and involuntary dream-memory. Like a trip. Had he been tripping? But it was not like any trip he'd experienced – and his experience here was deep and broad. And what had he been tripping on – dust and thin air?

Lee tried to think calmly, to view rationally what had taken place but couldn't get a real fix on any of it. Time had been loosened in his head since the events of Thursday, since the funeral; nothing since then had sat quite right; sediments disturbed still eddied in treacherous currents. He stared hard at the fridge in front of him, stared at its magnetic mementoes, school-art and scraps of domestic administration. It was another anchor to the real for him and he felt the assurance of it, like a chain fast to the seabed, moving ever so gently in the tide. It had been disorienting up there in the loft, freaky, a fucking weird one all told but, strangely, it left him feeling exhilarated; exhilarated and with a sense of definition, like you might feel as you finally embark on a major project that has been months in the planning. Except he hadn't been planning anything and he didn't know what he was supposed to be doing with this *definition*, this impulse, this resolve. But he did know that he could not stop thinking about that wild and uncharted time to which he had been transported by some wild and freaky magic. A magic he had unwittingly released. He'd had a flavour of the feeling driving home on Thursday, coming back from the wake listening to that Mangled mix; it had given him a draught of that time, a time that now seemed beyond possible, a time before things became pinned down, photographed, recorded, branded, registered, digitised and labelled; a time when things were out of sight until in sight; when there was newness to be made everywhere, when places lay untested, when scheme was absent. And above all, there was lack of awareness because how it was, was just how it was; it was just the state of things; it was just the usual because that's what was happening and that's what they were doing because that's what they did. When you're in something, Lee realised, when you're part of it, you can never properly see what it is you are actually in. When you're too close, what's immediately before you swamps your entire vision. In any case, he thought, it was all in process then, still being made, and you can't see all of something when it's unfinished. Only later, only after the event, can you really take stock, he told himself; only then are you really able to see things and describe them fully.

Yes, thought Lee, in qualified agreement with himself, all well and good, but once you can clearly see something, get hold of it from all sides, map it, it's gone. He'd never really thought about that; the idea was both a comfort and a source of regret. But it must always happen that way, he reasoned. It can't but be like that. And now, it seemed that maybe, if he so chose, he might really be able to see it all and feel a part of it again. He'd already had a glimpse and it had looked fucking magnificent, immense; it had also reared up, uncontrollable, unpredictable, full of hazard and the deep unknown, but still, always, truly, fucking magnificent.

It was in this frame of mind that Lee found himself as he sat at the kitchen table, safely down from the loft. The fridge, its magnets and mementoes, his anchors to the real, were in his line of stare and, on the table, the finds from the loft. He reached across and pulled one of the notebooks towards him, flicked quickly past the first few pages of sketches, lettering and stuck-in and folded event flyers. His shuttling eyes and quick hand told that he knew exactly what he was looking for. The page-turning stopped sharp and from the book he took a creased and much-handled flyer. On the front of the bill were two heads, indeterminate sex, kissing in a swirl of retro-psychedelic brown and orange hair. It was a picture of ecstasy and defiant abandon, of idealised love and sharp innocence. Lee turned the flyer over and read:... *we shall be giving you the chance to experience another night of ecstatic emotion.* That was it, he thought, that was what the image said. He flipped the flyer back over and looked again at the psychedelic kissing heads – the absolute figure of "ecstatic emotion" he confirmed. He turned the flyer again and continued:

> *40k of (ASS) sound * Multi-coloured laser * Projections * State-of-the-art lighting effects * Multi-dance platforms * Backdrops * Scaffold rig * Chill-out rooms * Balconies * Champagne bar * Ice bar * AND YES, BOUNCY CASTLES! This event will be nothing short of spectacular... From the branches of wisdom, stem the seed of truth, and from the seed of truth comes peace of mind... Bliss 1991.*

Lee turned the flyer once more to take in the full quota of wisdom and truth that remained in the arrangement of lines and colours, the creases and folds. It brought him back to the same idea: How can you understand something that you *are* a part of? Like knowing how you come across to others, you just can't. But, maybe, you can get close to something that you *were* a part of, that is past, because you find yourself a clear space from which to view it. Lee explained to himself: Ellis Dee and Mr C played that night at Bliss but he hadn't known at the time; he reckoned most of those there hadn't known, or even cared that much, as long as the music and the night delivered. But now, finding that out helped complete how he remembered. You couldn't get there 100% but, he reckoned, you might get close enough.

Lee looked down and the flyer filled with meaning until it crackled in his hand. The lines on it writhed and he marvelled at how the words, once read, took on life, had agency of their meaning and planted themselves into his story; the picture on the flyer only looked that way in *his* universe and only he could unlock *that* vision. Without him, without someone, it was all just marks on a piece of paper; a piece of paper in a box, in a blank space in the roof of a house amongst other houses in a street amongst countless roads in a part of a city... he let himself recede on the vanishing perspective of the idea.

Lee looked again at the kissing heads and offered the image to his memory and to his senses and to what was left in him of the wisdom of Bliss. He felt a slight lurch, like being on a plane which drops suddenly in turbulence, the onset of a rush. But it was not all-consuming this time as it had been in the loft. He could see its form and hold on to it. He could stay with himself this time. He had some volition and function. He could hear and feel the music of the event, the party, the rave, just offstage. He could smell the smoky venue and he keyed to the rise and fall of many voices working in emotion together. This time he could move on the wave of the trip, like in a flying dream where the soar and the speed are breathtaking but you still influence the movement. Lee felt ahead carefully into the darkness and the noise and sensed he could keep things just in abeyance if he wanted or, if he wanted differently, bring them on strong. In the loft, he had been tumbled and spun headlong into a vortex; no warning, no control, no up, no down, no floor, no ceiling. He had careered, turning end-to-end into a wormhole. The motion and the flux of his transport were total until he was spat out, on bended knees, gasping like a thirsty dog, his eyes wide at the location. No, this time he had some say in how it went; he could insinuate with his body, turn with imagination, with memory. It was not foolproof; not without peril, but he could pick a path of his choosing – or at least one that let him stay upright and let him keep his stomach and his head where they were meant to be. Lee eased back and relaxed along the length of his body, declining in a slow spiral through the strands and locks of psychedelic hair.

# TWO

Bliss was always a good night... Bliss at Kelsey Kerridge Sports Centre, Cambridge, June 1991. Big year in a big rave town. Cambridge? A big rave town? Lee laughed. You'd never think it now. He'd been there recently for work, walked around the Corn Exchange like a day-tripper, tried to work out on the satnav where some of the warehouse events had been. He eventually stood on Wheeler Street, still against the stream of tourists and po-faced shoppers, and looked back until he could make out a queue along the pavement, under orange lamplight, a line of ghosts fading away down the street. But Cambridge had been a centre. Mind you, thought Lee, everywhere started to become a centre once '91 got underway. Towns here, there and everywhere started to put on nights, to pull big crowds. But Cambridge really was at the heart then; big events, standard-setting events, thousands of people, mad fun, and every fucking week something somewhere. But that particular night in June wasn't so much about Bliss, or Cambridge, fucking wicked as it had been, and all respect to the Bliss crew; no, that weekend was all about the post-rave rave, the after-party the next day. They had been a big crew that night, remembered Lee. Donna and Danny and all the Cambridge crew they knew from Eclipse and other raves in the area were there, most of them coming straight on from Strawberry Fair. Insect Dave and the Colchester lot were in full effect and Ian and Faye and a big contingent of Clactonians. There were others there too from Braintree and from Witham, from Dunmow and from Chelmsford. Lee remembered them, brought them to full-colour life, as he pictured the clamour of the pub they were in before the rave. It was bursting with anticipation, loud with voices, impossibly primed and virtually no one drinking. The landlord must have wondered what the fuck was going on. Hardy anyone drank then thought Lee. Not like now. Raves rarely had an alcohol licence and no one wanted it anyway, not when you were on a New Yorker, taken in two halves, that kept you firing all night. Wicked little pills they were, he foot-noted, and, as far as he was able to tell that particular night, everyone else was on them too. The pub soon emptied and they joined the queue which, as usual, was way round the fucking block, and for forty minutes they shuffled their way to the front, joking and smoking. Once in, Lee got his bearings – toilets, water – checked the security – safe – settled, dropped a half, had to sit down for half an hour, lost everyone he had been with, lost most of the next four hours as he danced hard, tranced in his mind-space, and dissolved into the music and the lights and the committed exertion of the minds and bodies around him. The promise of the flyer was being fulfilled.

At some point in the midst of his bliss, Cambridge Danny found him: 'Lee, mate, listen up, when we're done here there's a big party at an old house in the country. It's pretty close, the sun's gonna shine 'cos I've ordered some on special, so, whaddya say?'

'Danny, mate, d'ya really need to ask? I mean, geeze, d'ya really come all the way out here just to ask me that?' Danny grinned at him.

'Right. Hook up in the car park after… follow us.'

'Sweet.'

'Yes, mate… and… you got any spaces in your car?'

'Could squeeze a little one in the back.'

'Right, safe. I'll get back to ya.'

Cambridge Danny was not fucking wrong, Lee affirmed, either then or, looking back, now. A big party at a house in the country was not the half of it. They'd travelled for nearly an hour in a mini-convoy, rolling quiet through the pre-dawn lilac-dark of the next morning to a run-down and abandoned farmhouse in the middle of fields and woods. They'd taken only one wrong turn, which Cambridge Danny, or his navigator – which must have been Donna – had quickly put right. You could just about see the house behind some trees down a track off a lumpy, subsiding single-track road that ran between steep ditches alongside wide open fields speared and leaved in green. The track opened into a large squarish yard of cracked asphalt and concrete and gravel. The sides of the yard were made up of scruffy hedges and trees, a row of stables and a collapsing cart lodge and one side of the house covered with ivy, which had almost obscured the only window in this elevation. Rusting ploughs and oil drums marked the point where the track entered the yard, and from here the lights of the cars swept the early morning half-light, projecting onto the side of the house and revealing a dark mullioned gateway where scruffy hedge met house; jittering tracks of green laser seemed to beam from the hedge-top and out up into the glimmerings of morning.

The mullioned gate led to the back of the house and what was once the garden. A once curving sweep of lawn, tall with weeds and poppies between overgrown flower beds, disappeared around the full and straggling bodies of untamed shrubs and flowed out of sight, down a slight slope. Back towards the house, the lawn went on to meet an area paved with stone, similarly unkempt and weedy, onto which opened a pair of large glazed double doors. The back of the house was more window than brick, huge sash frames sectioned into smaller rectangles, as if making up for the lack of window on the approach. The doors were open and an old kitchen table had been placed across the space. There were decks and other equipment on the table and behind it several figures, a couple of them bent over and busy with vinyl and labels, with faders and headphones. Speakers had been stacked on crates and giant cable-spools on either side of the double doors, along with lights and the lasers that could be seen from the yard. Lee could see makeshift lights and shadowy figures in other parts of the house, but most of the human activity was outside on the lawn. It was as if the dance floor at Bliss had been picked up and put down here, he thought. It was full of dancing people. Others sat around the house on makeshift chairs made from boards and blocks and bales, and off to one side in the shelter of a crescent of shrubs and small trees, a fire blazed in a pit. It was early June; the air was full of scent and the bright smell of new green growth. The music bounced in the retreating shadows of the night and uplifted against the still cold that comes at the end of a clear night in late spring. The sun was a promise in everything that was happening, and they had arrived with it.

For a while, the four of them stood and looked. They later agreed that they had all experienced the same feeling of revelation and arrival as they had walked through the gate in the hedge; the same sense of having entered into a secret world that lay behind the real one, a world that had always been there, would always be there, if you could just find the door.

'Fuckin' hell,' said Rob. 'Where are we?'

'I know,' said Zoe.

'I know,' said Lee and Kelly. They knew that Rob was not asking a question about geography or maps; he was asking about life, about time, about the cosmos.

'A'right?' said Cambridge Danny, joining them with a bounce and a sway of the shoulders.

'Fuckin' 'ell, Danny, what is this?' said Lee. Danny smiled and nodded.

'This,' he said, 'is fuckin' it! This is a party by the hardcore for the hardcore. This is a party for the fuckin' people,' and with that he put his arms around them and took them with him on a swerving dance into the crowd.

## //

Later into the morning, with the sun truly up and blazing hot-white and orange from a sky painted corner-to-corner blue, Zoe and Lee were sheltering in the shade on the far side of the house. They sat in a state of temporary physical and emotional exhaustion brought on by overwhelming feelings of extreme amazement caused by a period of roaming in the overgrown garden, commencing approximately half an hour after they had each dropped a Golden Ohm. To an outsider, it would have looked like a short, pointlessly meandering walk to one end of the garden and back, but for them it had been a saga of discovery, a poem full of the mystery of nature, deep with layers of cosmic understanding and replete with messages of love.

'Fuck me,' said Lee. 'I am buzzin' off my nut. The insects man... the IN-Sects...'

'I know,' said Zoe, 'I know... soil, soil, full of toil...' She paused, then turned to face Lee. 'Listen, man, you know that I know that it's all cool. It's all cool and too, too beautiful.' Rob put his arm round her and they shone with every living colour. They fused where they touched and at their backs the calm sympathy of minerals baked into the brick. It was in this state that they had belayed. It was to share a spliff, they had told themselves, but the logistics and hand-eye coordination required were way beyond the capacities of either of them. They accepted this reality easily and lay back on the cool grass that grew long where the lawn lapped up to the house. Lee opened his eyes and looked up.

'Check it out,' he said to Zoe, motioning up with his eyebrows. Zoe followed his look and noticed the aluminium ladder propped against the wall by the corner. It was positioned so that it could be used to get onto the small wrought iron balcony that jutted from the wall above. Some French doors led out to the balcony but looked sealed shut. The balcony and the doors quietly peeled paint and vibrated imperceptibly in the full sunshine of late spring and the early '91 Hardcore.

'I think we fuckin' well should,' said Zoe.

'I knew you could not say no to a ladder,' said Lee.

'Ladders, doors, holes in hedges,' said Zoe, 'take me, I'm yours...'

'Well, after you then, ma'am,' said Lee.

'Don't mind if I do.' And Zoe, after giving the ladder a firm shaking, began to climb. She went up steadily, feeling the aluminium flex more than she expected. It's just my heightened senses, she told herself, and fixed her eyes on the dusty brickwork. She could see when she did this that the brick and the mortar between the bricks were made up of lots of tiny individual granules and particles of stone and cement. She could see small holes in the wall filled with spider silk and others stuffed with tiny twigs and fragments of leaves. She was out of the angled shade now and the sun came back at her from the brick and made her warm.

'C'mon,' said Lee from below. 'You don' 'ave to give it a fuckin' inspection.'

'All right, Danny-Lee, keep ya fuckin' 'air on.' Zoe left the wall to its life in the sun and pulled herself up and over the faded black railings and stood looking back over the section of garden she could see and to the fields beyond. Lee quickly joined her, gripping an unlit cigarette in the corner of his mouth.

'Wow, nice,' he said as he took in the curves of the garden and the big blocks of green fields beyond, and more distant lines of hedgerows and pockets of woodland. He turned and looked towards the front of the house and the way they had come in, early this morning when it was still dark. A slice of old lawn and garden was visible at the front, then more hedgerow and fields and in the middle distance a continuous line of hedge which must be the road, he thought. There was a gap and it flashed shiny and black like tarmac. Lee tried to follow a line from the gap back to the large wood. He thought he could see where the road emerged. He was staring hard at the green and the black and the light and the shadow and the blue of the sky, and the heat haze was making everything dance.

''Ang on,' he said to himself more than Zoe. 'That's not the heat, there's something comin' up the road.' He looked hard now at the area where he thought the road emerged from the trees. There were cars moving there; he was sure of it. Quite a few of them.

'Zoe, look, can ya see that?'
'What?' she said.

'Look, there, where the big wood is. Where that tall silvery tree is droppin' down. There's cars. Loads of 'em.'

'Where… where… oh yeah. Fuckin' hell, there's loads of 'em. They're still coming. Is it the Old Bill?'

'No, it's not the fuckin' Old Bill. There's all different colours… heads out the sunroof. Music… there's music. I can hear fuckin' music too.'

'Yea, look, there's all heads and arms out the windows. Wave at 'em, Danny-Lee, wave at 'em.'

They both waved. The cars were too distant to tell for sure, but they felt that the people in the cars were waving back. The music from the convoy was louder now, and a distinct entity.

'They're still comin', said Zoe. 'Shit, there's loads of 'em. Who are they?'

The first of the cars was nearing the track and they clearly had directions and were clearly headed to the house.

'D'ya think it's the owners?' They both laughed uproariously at this.

'Oi, you two… wass 'appenin'?' It was Rob, with Kelly, standing down by the foot of the ladder in the shade and looking up at them; he shielded his eyes against the light with his hand.

'You not gonna believe this, mate,' said Lee, 'but there's a fuckin' convoy of people arrivin' right now. Loads of 'em. I know I'm trippin' but it is fuckin' amazin'. It is an amazin' fuckin' world and I don't believe I'm here. C'mon, Zoe… get down… less find out wass goin' on.'

By the time Zoe and Lee had got down, the first cars had pulled into the yard and were being welcomed by the organisers of the party. The yard was quickly full of vehicles and people and dust and sunlight slanting through the dust, and there was bird and insect noise and the sound of the party in the garden and sound washing too from the speakers of the cars in the convoy. Lee picked on a group who had just emerged from a blue Ford Orion. They were all grins and round sunglasses and bucket hats, dirty, fat trainers and fags.

'Where you come from?' asked Lee, 'Bliss, Cambridge?'

'Nah, mate, London, Labrynth posse... oi... oi.' And in a rush of triumph, Lee and the bloke – who became Stu – embrace like long-lost brothers.

'London... Labrynth...?'

'Yea, mate, Club Labrynth... Dalston Lane... only the happiest people innit...? Hardcore massive... We were out last night and this geezer says, look, how d'ya fancy a magical mystery tour and a party out in the countryside? Well, it's gonna be a sunny one and I for one ain't got no work next week... Well, fuck me, what could we do? And so 'ere we are, and right now you need to take me to your dealer.' Much laughter followed this.

Lee, Zoe, Rob and Kelly just stared mesmerised at Stu and his three mates – Sharon, Marky and Lisa – like they'd never seen other human beings before.

'Hey, stand there,' said Kelly, and she snapped a picture of them all, the blue Orion in the background.

'Right, this way,' commanded Zoe and led Stu and his mates across the yard to the gate in the hedge.

## //

'Nothing will be the same again,' said Zoe, looking round at the group of Bliss and Labrynth ravers sprawled around her on the weedy lawn, in the half-shade between the poppy-invaded flower beds. They chatted, smoked and listened to the tunes breaking across the space where the French doors opened onto the patio. The uplift they all felt was so extraordinary that they couldn't tell each other enough. In that light, in that time, in that noise, with the new smell and sound and sight of spring all around, everything became possible, everything moved within reach, every thought, each dream and idea flowed, floated out to welcome and encouragement.

'I mean, for me, nothing will ever be the same again,' she repeated. 'This has changed everything. Not just for me, though. Look at what's happened here. Just look. This thing is amazing, we are amazing and we cannot be stopped. We can do it all.' Zoe raised her arms in the air as she finished, and there were cheers and whistles. Zoe told them all in the car on the way back home later that day that she was going to learn to DJ. 'I mean, properly learn,' she'd said, 'get some decks, all the gear, start buying records. I'm serious… this thing is big. I said it before, didn't I, with the Prodigy and all that? But today has really opened my eyes.'

'I was thinking the same,' said Rob. 'I was talking with some blokes about makin' tunes. You don't need that much. I've got some of it already. I wanna give it a go. Let's fuckin' do it.'

'So, we going to Labrynth next or what?' asked Kelly.

'Oh yes,' was the unanimous response.

# THREE

'OH YES,' LEE FOUND HIMSELF SAYING AS HIS focus returned and he swayed against the current, held by the reality anchor of the fridge and its magnets and papers. He looked down at the Bliss flyer and the sketchbook it had come out of. On the page opposite where the flyer had been tucked inside, was a sketch in black biro. It showed the back of a house, big Georgian windows, trees and shrubs to the side; in the middle, figures, decks, speakers; in the mid-ground, heads and hands in the air; the foreground was long grasses and poppies, flowers and buzzing insects. In the distance, behind the view of the house, a wood out of which snaked a convoy of cars, one with a figure standing up out of the sunroof, hat, sunglasses, hands in the air. Lee looked at the sketch and inhaled. He could smell the sun and the grass, the hot brick and the cool on the breeze that rippled in from the shade of the woods around. He was still not sure, despite the reality anchor of the fridge, that he was not tripping, hallucinating, lucid-dreaming or something. These memories, these time-slips, felt as real as if he was right back there again. *Does it matter*, he asked himself, *the how and the why?* The startling and scary confusion of what happened in the loft had gone and was mostly now replaced by curiosity; he was having some kind of out-of-body experience, he told himself, calmed himself, out-of-body experience triggered by things from his past. No cause for alarm really and no harm done so far, he thought; if anything, he'd learned a few things and if nothing else he was having a good time. His instinct was to just go with it, see where it led. That's what the Lee who climbed the ladder in the garden of the abandoned house would have done, he told himself – that is exactly what that Lee would have done, maybe that is exactly what he should do here.

Lee pulled the box of tapes across the table. There must be at least fifty-odd tapes here, he thought, as he scanned the spines of the cases of those on top: *Top Buzz Coventry 1991, Mickey Finn Coventry 1991, Bukem Dreamscape '93, Seduction-Eclipse Weekender Bedford 1992.* The evidence of productive energy hit him again. Each tape a single set by a DJ playing on a night, or in a room that was part of a night, where there were maybe ten sets. And these events were going off every Friday and Saturday night all over the place for… well, for years. Lee looked again at the information on the spines of the tape cases:

*Unity at Hyperbolic Long Stratton, Ellis Dee at Fantazia Bournemouth, Lee Coombs & Stuart Banks at Eclipse Cambridge, Krome & Blackmarket at Labrynth Dalston Lane, Shaggy & Breeze at Eclipse Ely, Gappa G at Dance Paradise Great Yarmouth, Top Buzz Oscar's Clacton Pier, Clarkee and Bryan Gee Dreamscape Milton Keynes, Sy Mindwarp Colchester, Ratty Universe Big Love Warminster, Stuart Banks Ray Keith and Grooverider Eclipse Cambridge, Adrian Age & Vinyl Matt Labrynth Dalston Lane, Billy Daniel Bunter Labrynth, Carl Cox Sterns Worthing, Cuckoo & Manic Labrynth, Easygroove Dancefest Grantham, Slipmatt Double Dipped Bagley's Kings Cross.* Lee stopped. He could feel the rush again. The lurch of a pressure drop. The skin-creep phasing of a potent memory of music and unity and complete commitment to a scene created. It was like he was summoning power by reading the names and the dates; as if his contact with the latent information stored on the tapes was giving them life and that life was looping back inside him like a live current.

Lee pushed the tapes back across the table and cut the transmission. He thought about how Zoe, if she were here, would want to talk about the tapes as evidence of the staggering reach of the early Hardcore scene; the powerful self-organising principle behind it, the dedication of its followers to the movement. If she'd been tripping out with him just now, spun right back to the day of the Labrynth connection, well, she would have been unstoppable on the subject. He would have agreed with her too; have added in his ideas about the acid party pioneers in the '50s and '60s in the US; those US West Coast, Kool-Aid events of the '50s and '60s were, he realised now, basically, just raves – parties with lights and colours and visuals and music, parties designed around the effects of the LSD everyone had taken, parties that were all about the trip. The other thing Lee knew about that scene... yes, the other thing he recalled now was how they recorded the house-band doing their party set; at those events anyone could record the house band if they wanted. Like the rave tapes in front of him, the recordings became a thing in themselves. Audio quality was not the point; it was about having a direct copy of life, of an experience you had been part of. *Was it the same as recording every living moment on your mobile phone?* he questioned. He didn't think it was but… he'd have to think about that one some more.

Lee looked at the flyers and the notebook and the tapes, at the worn and weathered wild style lettering on the Sub Bass cap. Artefacts… records of life. He reached for the A4 folder and pulled it towards him; now what was in here was *about* the time, not *of* the time, he thought. Distillations. The sticker on the front of the folder read: *Zoe Marr: Zoe's Kitchen – Spin Junky Magazine.* Lee turned the cover. He'd already read the first two and flicked to the third, settled his eyes on the lines of type, stilled his teeming brain and read:

### Hardcore, you know the score – but do you?

Hardcore is a difficult genre to pin down and explain. In some ways it can be seen as the mystery at the heart of UK dance music. I've argued before in this column that the main streams of influence that fed into the homegrown UK sound of the early 1990s were Balearic, US House and Garage, and North European Techno and, also, a bit more under the radar, the hi-energy disco-house sound of the gay club scene. Hardcore was the UK sound that grew from these influences, following Acid House. As Acid House began to fade and a new wave began to gather momentum, there was only "rave". It was a term that reflected the wide spectrum of music that was played at "raves". But the term quickly began to refer to music that was being made in the UK for UK ravers to rave to. The homegrown "rave" sound reflected UK preferences and attitudes and incorporated the sounds and feelings of their experience. The music and the scene in which it was played were co-dependent and grew together. As the character and ambition of the music extended and developed, so did the parties and events at which it was played. And the more events that were held, the more impetus and energy was returned into the production of more music to fuel more events. It was a high-octane mechanism and the music evolved rapidly, as did the tastes and styles of the DJs that played it. You therefore had a situation where the "same thing", i.e. "rave", was being experienced in a multiplicity of ways simultaneously.

Also evolving with the music and the events where the music was enjoyed was wider "rave culture". A set of values began to emerge, as did a variety of uniforms, a language, and a broad pattern of behaviours that were recognised as "raving". At the heart of this were ideas about freedom, ideas given sharp definition by the Criminal Justice Bill which aimed to outlaw (and eventually succeeded in doing so) gathering in groups to dance to "repetitive beats". Ravers sought the freedom to dance how and wherever they wanted, to follow whatever music they wanted, to rip up what had gone before and reassemble it using new technology, to meet with like-minded individuals and to connect with them. The raver also sought to practise kindness, show compassion, and help others. They valued being "Safe". Being "Sound". Being "Hardcore". Knowing the coup. This was all super idealistic, but why not? Even if, in practice, ravers sometimes fell short of their own standards, most of them would, at the time, have signed up to those standards and meant it.

In the early days, at the turn of the decade, being part of this culture made you a "Hardcore raver". "Hardcore" described the attitude and outlook of the raver – their commitment to the lifestyle which they followed, and the purity and idealism of their "belief" in the scene. This culture and code grew with the music and informed its production, and "Hardcore" became a term which referred to the particular brand of homemade music that the "hardcore raver" favoured and followed. It also distinguished it from other flavours of rave music, in particular, "House" and "Techno", although Hardcore was not a jealous god and there was much cross-fertilisation. The music thus came to stand for, and to represent, an idealistic attitude and outlook on life, and so, for those involved, a "golden age" was born.

But, "Hardcore" as a style of music meant different things to different people at different times. You can see this in the way that music from the time is variously referred to as Rave, Hardcore Rave, Old-Skool Rave, Hardcore Breakbeat, Hardcore, Hardcore Jungle, and so on. There are probably almost as many views on what "Hardcore" is as there were Hardcore ravers enjoying the music during the period 1990-1993 – and even using these dates to define "Hardcore" invites controversy. Given the way the scene and the music evolved, those who experienced it first-hand are often fiercely wedded to their version and view of what it was, sometimes to the point of fundamentalism. For many old-skool ravers, nothing else compares, nor will it ever. But the music and the scene were nothing if not dynamic, and change and evolution were inevitable; from Hardcore came Happy Hardcore, Jungle, Drum and Bass, Hard House, UK garage, and so on. Whatever your take is on the music – and remember no one hates music like a music lover – Hardcore remains some of the most originally creative music ever made and is, undeniably, the source of a rich and varied range of musical styles. Over to you, Kitchen Crew.

Zoe E Marr/DJ Zoem, Spin Junky, February 2007

*No one hates music like a music lover... some of the most originally creative music ever made.* Classic Zoe, thought Lee as he flicked the folder shut and let the paeon to Hardcore filtrate. He sat like this, surrounded by his artefacts, unmoving for some moments. The fridge hummed and the house made small sounds as the day warmed up outside. Lee swung gently on the anchor of his reality until at the outer limit of one of these oscillations, as if snapping the chain, he stood bolt upright. He looked at the table critically and with visible determination began to gather his jacket, keys, wallet and phone, and to collect into one manageable pile the folder, notebooks, road map and box of tapes. He picked up the cap and snapped it back onto his head in salute. He felt like he'd volunteered for a dangerous mission, a hero about to undertake a quest for love, or for mercy, or for justice. He gathered his kit and accoutrements and stood tall. He felt like he was about to enter a zone of jeopardy but about to do so in the knowledge that he had everything he needed – knowledge, skills, courage, fortune – to succeed; had everything he needed and was sure of his ability to do so. He felt like he used to feel when he was inside a Hardcore tune. Like he would still feel inside a Hardcore tune, he was certain; a good slice of Hardcore, always full of moods of uncertain peril, malevolent intent, epic misadventure and manic ecstasy; but also laced with strident hope, seriousness, high purpose, insouciant defiance, miraculous discovery and success against the odds. It was all there for him; menace which lurked and rampaged and which could terrorise and dominate, but the tune always offering a path of ascension. The tune would always provide, Lee affirmed, would always show a way through for those willing to commit, to strive and to endure. That was the ride for Danny-Lee, rushing on a rhythm, taking everything on with a fat break, sub-bass and a safe and friendly attitude. The Hardcore hero vanquishes the darkness with his tales of rushing like a bad-boy, tripping out on a beat and dancing all night on a single Dove and half a gram of pink champagne. It was an adult retelling of an old, old fairy tale, and it was *once upon a time* as he headed for the door.

# FOUR

Danny-Lee (known as Lee), with clear intent but no plan, closed the front door behind him and headed out to the car. He settled into the driver's seat, placed his collection of finds on the seat beside him, turned, hands on the wheel, and stared out through the windscreen. The sun gleamed on the tarmac of the road. He looked across at the tapes and he thought about Zoe's magazine article, thought about what had happened in the loft and where this all might take him. So far it had been as far as Bliss and the after-party that had changed everything yet again. The whole Hardcore thing really took off then, at least for him and for Zoe and for Rob and Kelly. That was the weekend that they all committed their lives, as they then were, to the scene; the scene they were a part of and which had given them life in the midst of very little else. That was so true, he thought. Where would they have gone without the raving? Where did people like them go? There was a point back then in that old farmhouse, up a ladder on a dodgy balcony, when they were given a glimpse and they fucking went for it. What did any of them have to lose? Fucking nothing… and everything to gain. And that, by and large, is as it worked out, at least for the others and he supposed, eventually for him too. Who knows, maybe, probably, they would have got there anyway. Maybe? Maybe they would have made it to Labrynth anyway. Maybe? But that was the way it had happened at the time that it happened. That was the way it happened and it was fittingly monumental that it happened that way.

Lee became aware that he was exaggeratedly mouthing the word "monumental" and staring out through the windscreen, hands at ten to two on the steering wheel. He smiled as he pictured himself there in the car, then half-turned the key, checked the time. Just a few minutes. Was he remembering or spinning out and back into the past again? How would you know? Did it matter? In the loft, he had tripped within a trip, and if he hadn't come around in his own house and been able to anchor himself back to reality at the kitchen table, he would have testified that everything had been real. Well, it had been real, he countered. *What I mean is* – now actually arguing with himself – *it had been real then and it had been real as I remembered it just now*. Impossible bollocks he would have said only a few days ago, but these last few days had thrown him round a few unlikely angles. The stability of it all was up for question and he felt the press of a building tide. He was calm, though… he felt calm… calm and *prepared*? Was that the right word? *Prepared*? Yes, that is how he felt now. He turned his mind back a few hours. Back just as far as the hours when he had woken up this morning. Just back far enough to review what had happened since then. *Just back far enough*. He smiled at his deliberate naivety. Any distance back was all the way back now. Everything was becoming simultaneous. Back far enough to see all that happened past and present since now; he surrendered himself to however it would play.

## //

That morning, Lee had awoken from what had been a mostly disturbed night's sleep. The dissatisfaction of the night resided still in his bones and muscles and nagged behind his eyes. He felt different. Asleep in his body but his mind racing with tiredness and scraps of incoherent dreams. The day, the time, the air around him felt other and distinct. He was aware of himself and how he lay as if he looked down from above, his eyes moving under half-open lids, his torso twisted to one side so his face could look for comfort in the folds of the pillow. It was Saturday, and he luxuriated for a while, savouring the marvellous knowledge that he did not have to get up for work. Turning his head, he opened his eyes to stare up at the shadows thrown onto the ceiling by the sunlight that was coming through the gap between blind and window. Marianne must have done that, he thought, when she had got up; adjusted the blind to let the day in but not so much that it would wake him suddenly. He let that thought warm him. He shrugged; he usually heard her. Lee smiled at her quietness and allowed his eyes to take in the letterbox view of the gardens and the backs of houses created by Marianne's arrangement of the window blind. Lee stretched diagonally in the bed and thought about the day ahead and the shape it would take and tried to shake the strangeness of the feelings that had accompanied his awakening. He'd been like this since the funeral on Thursday. Out of sorts, agitated, a nervous pre-race kind of feeling. Unsurprising, he supposed; the funeral had dropped a big stone in the flow.

Lee pushed the strangeness away and looked at the straightforward day planned for him. A designated day of sorting and clearing out. Marianne called it *decluttering*. She wasn't in favour of *stuff*. He quite liked *stuff* but he got where she was coming from. They had been in the house a while now but had still not quite finished moving in. Lee was going to push for the finish; boxes, crates, tape and marker pens were ready; the garage and the loft had been scoped and his plan was to start with the former and, if all went to plan, then he would move on to the latter fortified by earlier successes. He shivered now at the thought of the chilly loft space and tuned himself back into the warm den of his duvet and to the smell of coffee and something toasted that rose up to him from the room below. Voices came up too; young and old, adult and child, mother and daughter, to and fro, too indistinct to catch any actual sense of the words. Saturday was a day of measured routines and there were schedules to be observed. But today, his was not the duty. Today he was on home guard, sorting.

Lee listened for the sounds of coats and bags in the hall, the sound of imminent departure, before he made his move for the toilet.

'We're off now, Danny-Lee,' came from below as he crossed the landing.

"kay, 'ave a good one,' he called back. 'I wanna see all the moves later,' he added.

'Okay, bye,' came back up the stairs, a perfectly layered sound of adult and child voices together.

'Bye, and the washing, when it's done, you can hang it? Tack,' she added, and Lee imagined her saying it with the pout she usually deployed when saying, 'Tack.' He let that warm him too.

'Yep, bye,' he said, without registering at all the task he had signed up for.

Then the solid metallic breech action of the front door closing and a rapid silence of empty house closing out the sound of footsteps and voices fading away down the path and out onto the road. The sound of the car leaving was lost in the flush of the cistern and the rush of the shower.

## //

Lee sat in the kitchen staring out over his coffee cup at the accumulation of experimental junior art, magnets, stickers and Post-its on the fridge door and the noticeboard. *Stuff*, he thought. He did love a bit of *stuff*. It was evidence of life being lived. *Stuff* was the trophies and the memorabilia of campaigns waged out there in the real world. Once in here, he concluded, it was like the real world was suspended, especially if you were on your own. He stared hard at the fridge and its display; without all that stuff, thought Lee, it would be just me in an empty house with the sound of a washing machine. There would be nothing to connect me to anything else. It is evidence that I am here. Lee focussed on the copied photo of Nanna and Grandad Swigler, next to the hand-drawn bird, held by a corner on the fridge door. Evidence of connection, he confirmed, and he thought how the path from the front door to the road outside still connected him to Marianne and Eva as they made the Saturday journey to the Dojo; there was comfort in that; roads were evidence too. He looked again at the photo on the fridge as he thought about the roads that could lead to and from his door; thought about Grandad Swigler and his talk of 'roads familiar and roads unfamiliar' and 'ones I like – as can bring a smile to ya face – and ones I don't much care for.' Roads, according to Grandad Swigler, could tell you who you were, where you had come from and where you were going; they could speak to you, help you on your way and tell you stories. Not like the roads to the funeral then, thought Lee, and shrunk from the recent memory; blank tarmac and concrete, silent and unconnected to him. And the journey back… weird… Lee shook himself. He was not prone to existential confusion and this kind of meandering. And there too, shifting about in the back of his head, that feeling he'd had when he'd first woken up; shadowy in the back of his mind, a haunting, nagging sensation a bit like you get when you wake from a dream so real you cannot be sure, sometimes for the whole day or longer, that it had not been, in fact, real. He was still dealing with the funeral, he told himself, and its aftermath.

Thursday, the day of the funeral itself, had been as difficult and strange as he'd expected it to be, especially the journey home and work the day after. That was only yesterday, he reminded himself. Fucking write-off really. His head had been all over the place and he'd come home early. No wonder then that he was having weird dreams. Just the mind's way of dealing with… *use the word*, Lee said to himself… dealing with the *shock*. The word itself sounded like a shock, he thought, briefly distracted by the onomatopoeia. But it *was* shock and there is no shame in that, he counselled. Even when it's someone not so close, a funeral is a shock, he thought. A funeral shakes you by the scrag, however you look at it. How can it not? It's a big deal. It's *the* deal. And the living, he thought, they say funerals are for the living, but no one ever really tells you what that means. Goodbye to one old friend but hello to all those other old friends and to a time you thought you'd left well behind. That bit had been more of a… well, more of a thing. You can't really leave time behind; there is no such option available really. Whatever happens, it is all still there. *Is that what they mean when they say the past always catches up with you?* he wondered.

He knew that a big part of what he now felt was his sense that he had not done that well with *the living* at the funeral. Except perhaps for Zoe. Zoe was definitely in the old friend category but... but nothing, he thought. Zoe was Zoe... and she'd given him that memory stick. Of course, she'd had to do that. She had to be the one to do that. And there was Baz. An old friend too, it could not be denied, and Lee smiled at the thought of Baz; brash, quick, handing him his business card. The "card" was made of metal, its surface printed, *Baz Murgan, Director, Each 'n' Every Audio.* You never know, Baz had said, and not much else. Lee grinned as he remembered and then winced as he remembered some more. It's the living that are the hardest part about it all, he concluded. Goodbye to an old friend, he knew where he was with that, but the living, what do you do with them? That's where Marianne was coming from when she had encouraged him to go. You'll regret it, she'd said. You go there to remember a time when you mattered very much to each other. When you experienced important things together.

Marianne didn't know much about that time in his life. He never really spoke of it, and she'd still been living in Sweden when Rave was going off in the UK. But they had gone out sometimes in a low-key way and she was an intelligent, well-informed person. She knew enough. He had looked at her then, considering her advice. She was wise, he had recognised; when they came to new territory in their life it was often like she had been there before and knew how to handle it, knew about his segment of the earth and how it worked for him. He had looked at her closely and directly and she had returned his gaze levelly and open with perhaps a hint of a question. He had continued to look at her as only someone can look at another they have been so close to and for so long, with whom they know they have nearly reached a point where what remains is that which they and no one else will ever know. He had looked at her as if he believed that by doing so he could absorb all her wisdom; and then he had looked again, this time wholeheartedly, believing he could absorb her wisdom. That took away some of his unsettledness, eased the knot in his chest and chased with light some of the shadows moving in the back. Lee's eyes found on the fridge his favourite picture of Marianne and Eva and he remembered how he had moved to her and how they swayed there within each other's arms as, in his head, he had begun to make the practical arrangements to go to Rob's funeral.

# FIVE

Everyone who lee expected to be there was at the funeral. There were plenty of others too, besides family, and this caused Lee to re-estimate Rob just a little, which had wrong-footed him. He had spent a lot of time before the service making understated nods across the car park and muttering low-voiced greetings to people in the shade of the entrance to the cemetery building, but now the service was underway he was feeling resistant and restless, unable to take in what was being said. We often find ourselves in these places because of what *was* rather than how it now *is*, he thought. At least that's why I'm here, he told himself. Because of how it *was*. Oh my, how it was… and for a split second he was dreaming. Lee pulled himself back and looked hard at the shiny coffin sat on rollers in front of the stiff square of blue curtain. I'd never have knowingly arranged to be this near him if he was still alive, Lee thought, and congratulated himself on his honesty. He doubted, though, whether he would share the thought with anyone later. The vicar, or speaker or chairman or whatever he was, was talking away: *father... son... brother... friend... music... commitment... creative... a reading from...* but Lee only registered noise and continued to stare at the coffin. In his peripheral vision, the speaker's mouth moved in well-rehearsed sequence. Lee glanced about him at the faces or, in most cases because of where he was sat, the backs and backs of heads, of those others from a place and time that *"was"*. It was as if they all trailed strings that wound and coiled back out of the building and disappeared in different directions to run back through the years, down countless roads to some lost point of common origin. Like evolutionary paths diverging from a common ancestor.

Lee leant slightly forward as if to feel the tension of the string that was his tie to the past. He rocked slightly on the balls of his feet as he sat, and became aware of the cold making its way up from the floor and into his feet through socks too thin for the weather and the soles of shoes he rarely wore. Quite possibly, he thought, I'll never see these same bodies alive – or even dead – again. Quite possibly this same bundle of strings will never again be gathered together in this way in the living, breathing world. Lee thought of those pictures and graphics of the world as a globe with super-scaled 3D-perspective buildings and people shooting out and up, from the surface, to mark significant features or places or events. That's how we are right now at this funeral, he concluded, an out-of-scale figure on a globe, standing way out from the surface of the earth to mark this occasion and to locate where, for the last time, probably, we will all stand together in one place. Lee was not sad about this. It was not a moment of sadness to him; it was a moment of inevitability. The strings which led back also led forward and there was no avoiding that. The others around him were not sad either. Lee could feel they were not sad. He could sense it in the square of their shoulders, the tilt of their chins, in the way they held the service paper at arm's length when they stood up – at about waist height as if they were about to let it drop into a blazing fire – that they were not sad. Sure, some of the close relatives, Rob's mum and dad, were doubtless sad. Maybe even more recent friends were sad. But for Lee and, he thought, those like him, it was something else, something other than sadness. The person and the time he remembered and was saying goodbye to, had passed a long time ago and this was… this was a formality really. An overdue act of paying respects, like burying the long-missing remains of a soldier from an old war.

Lee looked hard at the coffin, the rollers it sat on, the curtains, the hatch which led to the furnace. He watched as the curtains jerked back on their brass rings and he briefly saw a section of dark, orange heat as the coffin headed to incineration. Lee pictured them all in the pub afterwards, stood in protective formations; laughs, drinks, cigarettes in the wind outside. Old stories, favourite tunes, mad times… *do you remember… never happen now… never forget when…* And we never would forget, thought Lee, but it was nevertheless gone, and gone in the time and space it took for that curtain to go back and forth. There was sadness now and Lee felt it. A slight tension at the corner of the eyes, a tighter set to the lips and the jaw, but the sadness was uncertain and was not for the passing of his once friend but for the passing of their time, for the loss of the place that the winding, coiling strings led back to.

The coffin passed out of sight and the curtain stuttered back across the hatch, and the room was filled with crashing, epic, Hardcore-breakbeat. A Rob special, thought Lee, glancing at the service paper: *Ramos and Supreme: The Journey, 1993,* it said. There was no denying the tune and as Lee looked back up, the curtains over the hatch seemed to spin out towards him. The spinning curtains became a TV and on it a man in front of a map talking... *and these deposits, after millions of years, came to form the bedrock on which Northern Europe, including the islands which make up Great Britain...* Lee shook the spinning TV away and with an effort of will dismissed it. He opened his eyes. He saw now through a fish-eye lens of tears the backs of the heads of the mourners stood in front of him, circling like the heads of Queen performing "Bohemian Rhapsody" on *Top of the Pops*. The thought brimmed his eyes with more tears, making them compound and multiply the rhapsodic turning heads. Lee put out a hand to steady himself against the bench in front and listened hard to the music. He felt a succession of hands on his shoulder towards the end but he stayed until the tune finished. As it did, the music was replaced briefly by a low roar peppered with clicks and pops. Recorded from vinyl, thought Lee, through the tears he was finally getting the better of. When he finally looked up, normal vision had returned and the place was almost empty. Lee carefully made his way to the exit, Ramos and Supreme rolling and crashing in his head, and got into his car to follow the small convoy to a nearby pub for the wake. The after-party, he half-joked to himself, and felt a lift at the thought.

## //

The pub was noisy with the self-medicating roar of alcohol and reminiscence and Lee joined in, loosened by the up-welling of emotion. He contributed to the remembrance of old times and found himself pulling up stories that had lain untouched for years. In some cases, he had forgotten that he even knew them. He talked to Zoe, and Kelly and Baz and Jamie, Wayne, Adam;

took the card Baz offered – *Director of Each 'n' Every Audio* – and a copy of a photomontage that Kelly had made for the funeral. Lee met new people too, the others he had noted outside the building, friends from later times in Rob's life. All brought fuel to the fire and quickly the pub was ablaze with laughter and voices raised in competition, death the prompt to exaggerate the things that signal life. Everyone, it seemed, wanted to signal simultaneously that they did, indeed, live. It was exhilarating and exhausting, and after a while, Lee stepped back and watched it all from a distance, took in the rude assertion before him and nodded to himself. It's good, he thought. Rob would have been well happy with this. Of that much he was sure.

'Alrightee, Danny-Lee,' said Zoe, approaching.

'I'm good,' said Lee, kissing the woman who had approached him. 'And yourself?' Zoe nodded a bit too quickly to be convincing. The control he'd seen when they had said hello briefly outside before the funeral service had all but disappeared.

'No, kind of, you know. I can't believe it really. I only saw him the other week, for the first time in years. He seemed fine. Well, you know Rob.' Lee nodded. He hadn't really known Rob for a long time. They'd taken diverging paths. He'd seen nothing of him recently, although he'd heard things, and before that, only occasionally in the narrow lenses where their circles still overlapped. His death was like being told that you'd lost something that you thought already lost. Missing in action? Was it like that? Kind of, he thought, and pictured veterans round a grave.

'I knew him, Zoe... you know... I didn't really see him these last... well, you know, a long time really.'

'I know, Lee, I know. All of us really...'

'Different paths, I guess.' Lee looked at Zoe as the inadequacy of his words filled the space between them.

'But things like this make you think about stuff, don't they, Daniel-Lee? Make you re-evaluate. Ask yourself why you're going to the funeral of someone you didn't see or speak to for the last, what, seven, eight years of their lives. I mean, what happens?' Zoe began to cry. Lee put an arm around her and bit back his own tears. They stood close together for a few moments. Then, as if on command, they separated.

'I know you knocked it all on the head,' she said, 'but I knew you'd be here so I did this for you.' She held out a memory stick. It dangled from a small keyring shaped like a turntable. Lee took it and looked at it lying in the palm of his hand as if it might bite, or jump up and dance. 'Mixes...'90 to '94. Lots of them from events we were at, give or take, you know, and ones we used to play to death in the car. Loads of this stuff online now – you could write a book.' She laughed and sniffed at her tears.

'Thanks, Zoe,' said Lee. "preciate it,' he added, as if he was being prompted. Again, the inadequacy of the words hung between them.

'Fuckin' hell, Lee, I know what happened. I was there. We were kids. Look, I know you don't need me to tell you how it was when, you know, it all went wrong, and I can see, I think I can see, how it was for you, man, and I'm sure it still cuts you up, but there's a time for things and... well... shit. I don't really know how you feel, how could I? I suppose, you know, it is how it is. I know, I understand, I do, it's cool. But you have to know that for me and for the rest of us, those years and the few years that followed were, and always will be, the best years of our lives. Do you know? The best fuckin' years of our lives. Nothing was ever the same again.' Zoe laughed despite herself at these last words and paused and weighed the magnitude of those before. She looked at Lee, confident that her assessment was the truth. 'Anyway, whatever, I love you and that's a given,' and with that they hugged and the space between them filled with meaning and intent.

'I love you too, Zoe. I love you too.' They paused and their silence, now comfortable, was a quiet centre encircled by the noise of the pub.

'Oh, and the other thing is this…' and she passed Lee a slim white A4 folder. 'Some copies of the feature I do for the *Spin Junky*.'

Lee cocked his head to one side. 'What happened to the hardcore Drum and Bass DJ?'

'Well, yeah, obviously still that, but I do other stuff, you know… just a bit of journalism to keep me out of mischief, clear the head 'n' that…'

'Journalism?'

'Yeah, well, loosely called. It's near enough. The feature's called *Zoe's Kitchen*… inspired by kitchen chats at chill-outs and after-parties.' Zoe paused and looked hard at Lee. Was he getting this or was it all so far down, so deeply buried that nothing reached? This had been their thing; out all night, they'd invariably end up in a kitchen, on a beach, in a field, in a car, chatting bollocks and getting on one about music and rave culture and everything that came with it. 'Actually, the original idea was mainly inspired by those chat sessions we used to have at chill-outs, or in the car on the way home, tunes on, me skinning up and the lightweights passed out in the back of the car.' She saw him smile now.

'It's all about syncopation,' said Lee teasingly.

'It fuckin' well is,' came back Zoe with mock aggression.

'What did Frank Zappa say? – "Writing about music is like dancing about architecture".'

'I always took that as encouragement,' said Zoe. 'Fuck knows I've danced plenty about a lot of architecture.' They laughed in sync and for a moment, as Lee looked at Zoe, he did so from the driver's side of his old Polo, through wreaths of spliff smoke, tunes pounding, and them both chatting shit all the way back to Braintree. The skin of his scalp prickled with memory.

'So, anyway,' Zoe continued, snapping the old Polo back to its time, 'I carried on with that chat-attack stuff, even after you were gone – like I could stop.' They both laughed. 'I got it down to a fine art; really developed some ideas, read more, did a bit of research, listened to other people's bollocks too, and so on… I started writing it down for the fun of it really and then, last year in the studio, few randoms milling about, the subject comes up and it so happens I've got some stuff on the laptop. I read a little bit and, boom, few meetings, bit of this, bit of that, and I've got a magazine column, monthly. I've done four now. I do some kind of discussion piece based on chats I've had in kitchens and cars, at chill-outs or house parties, about music and music culture. Light-hearted, you know, but the ideas are kind of real and meant to start up a discussion. I invite people to send me their own chats too and I've started using some of those. Anyway, I thought you might be interested… and, I owe you for the inspiration. In fact, you should recognise some of the stuff. Let me know what you think… if you like.'

Lee looked down at the folder and then back at Zoe. As he did, he took in the slant of autumn sunshine that, breaking through the cloud cover outside, passed in dust-dancing clarity through the window and onto and over her shoulder. He could now see tiny individual stray fibres wriggling out from her jumper, dark and defined like the shadows on the edge of an eclipse. A few other heads in the main bar of the pub turned to the window, triggered by the light that had come pouring into the room.

'Great idea,' said Lee, tapping the folder, and he meant it. 'I'll have a look… once I'm in a kitchen.'

## //

Lee said his goodbyes and left the pub soon after that. He got into his car and put the folder Zoe had given him on the passenger seat, the little turntable keyring on top. Almost like she's there, he thought, and imagined her words floating up out of the envelope and around the car while Rob, Kelly and sometimes Baz, chimed in here and there from the back. Rob's hands are planted one on each of the front seats and his head hangs between the headrests nodding to the music. Lee looked squarely in the rear-view mirror to confirm that the back seat was actually empty and, in doing so, caught his own eye, unguarded and alone. He stared at himself quietly and watched, as in slow motion, a fat bright tear rolled out over lashes, launched off his cheekbone and fell splashing onto his leg. A few more followed, splashing in quick succession. *Those are for Rob and all of it*, he declared to himself. *I did love him, the fucking bastard that he could be.*

Lee grinned through the tears and shifted his eyes to look back into the car, and this time Rob is there, and Kelly and Baz, all asleep, crumpled together like a pile of rifled donations in a shop doorway. Lee smiled indulgently, paternally, pulled his attention away and forward, started the car and through the spinning and yawing lens of tears made it out onto the main road and began the drive home. It was hard going. Sighs welled up in him, which he expelled forcefully through puckered lips. He felt wired, charged with crackling, unpredictable, unearthed energy. He looked to the roads for help, but there was no solace there. No response. He did not know these roads and they did not know him. His own roads, the Essex roads and the roads of East London and East Anglia, spoke and reassured. Those roads offered things to him with the voice of his past; they spoke with a voice like that

42

of Grandad Swigler; Grandad Swigler who loved to talk about *his* roads. He could really do with some of that, he strongly, almost pleadingly, told himself. Someone to tell him the way, someone to point out the journey and why it mattered, would be no end of help right now. But this was not his country. He had no blood and no sweat invested in these roads; only a solitary thread of his story had come this way today and now he was following it back home. The tears brimmed again and collapsed his vision and he was forced to pull over. He just sat for a while breathing deeply. He opened the window to feel the air and let the world in. He followed his stare, unchecked, out from the velour space of the car through the air to the rubbish-ribboned hedge and fly-tipped verge of the lay-by he had parked in. Looking up, just beyond the hedge, high in the face of the wind, a kestrel hung, perfectly and totally, fixed on the wedge of ground beneath it.

Lee sat for some minutes staring at the bird, unmoving, his breath deep and his eyes wide. Then, without thought, he reached across to the passenger seat for the turntable keyring which held the memory stick. He leant forward and plugged the stick into the adapter and hit the "on" button as he leant back. The orange crystal display flashed on and he took in the names as he scrolled through the files: *Adrian Age... Bunter Labrynth, Carl Cox Unknown, Donnavon Bad-Boy Smith Dance Paradise, Dougal & Ellis Dee Helter Skelter, Krome & Blackmarket Labrynth, Bukem Dreamscape...* It was like an incantation. A spell to take him back in time, an enchantment. *...Frankie Bones & Lenny D Braintree Barn...* Lee paused and his head and eyes turned in thought and interrogation, up towards the open window. The bird was no longer there. Frankie Bones and Lenny D, he said to himself, nodding at the space in the sky. Frankie Bones and Lenny D at the Braintree Barn. I do not fucking believe it. Has she really found a mix of their first Mangled, his first raving experience, the beginning of it all, the one that kicked it off? Nervous, like a kid on Christmas morning, Lee selected the file.

Percussive piano, strings, 'yo yo mic, check one, two, Braintree in the fuckin' house or what?' – Was that Frankie or Lenny? He'd never known. In what Lee could only assume was a Brooklyn accent, the file spoke out: 'I don't hear no fuckin' noise, Braintree in the fuckin' house. I've flown five thousand fuckin' miles from Brooklyn to play to you fuckin' psychos and I wanna see you go totally fuckin' mental. 'Cos you people are like Brooklyn, you're like the fuckin' party animals in this fuckin' country and you're gonna go fuckin' nuts and you're gonna go fuckin' nuts tonight'. Cheers and whistles in the background, pause, 'Make Some Noise', big string stabs and it was off. Lee was in shock. His skin was tingling and covered in goosebumps and his scalp writhed. The excitement and anticipation of that night galloped through him and roared in his ears. He turned his main focus to the music and pulled out of the lay-by, back into the traffic, and drove. The music washed all around him. Muscular bass twangs, soaring piano, stabs of thrusting strings and disco-soul vocals. Cuts on the mixer – at the time he did not know that this was what was happening – snare-kick breakbeats, modulated and syncopated with piano, soaring stratospheric background strings, layers of instrumentation over repeated vocals, hip-house rapping. If he had been able, Lee would have stood on the seat and danced. He felt born again. Dry electro-typewriter snares, synth sounds of mystery edging out to the epic and touching on menace, scratching on voice samples, and open high-hats. Industrial noises with hissing open snare to bring in machines at work, cutters, sanders, hammers and whip, distorted and decayed vocals, utterance twisted beyond language.

Sense now in the words, almost admonishment, serious voices instruct to dance, to move, to groove, to rock your body. Yea, yea, yea, the noise of the analogue space age, video games, computer games, sci-fi FX and space battles to crescendo... drop out... flat dry pulsing kick drum return: decadent, demanding, decadent. Time-shifting stabs pull your body, shoulders dip, rolling the hip. Lee sang the drum part and moved his head backwards and forwards like a pigeon... *loooove*... Thumping 4x4 kicks, building, snare break building, drops and layers, flute response until industrial noise and distant whistle – original sound – drop... drop... drop... pushed beneath the beat, re-layer, vocal come forward, build and build again...

...build to meet the menace of outer space, alien planets we erupt, nebula of rolling keys scored by energy-beam, the breathing organ pipes and the steamboat whistle. The tuba, the gasp, the battered metal, the laser blast over strings in orbit. Snare, kick, break and basement. LFO... breakdown bass and LFO... *Hold until eternity*... rattling kick, snare hiss snare, in and out of the rhythm of the bass. Robots in distress, bubbling slap, cathedral chords, sound the alarm, the seagull cries – *ah ah ah-ah, ah ah ah-ah.*

Ah ah, Lee responded to the seagull. Ah ah, Lee asked it, how had it started? Where did you come from? When did it really begin? When did it change from being just a sense of something out there, something whispering in the trees, to full possession and running arms outstretched into the roaring wood; into the wild, untameable jungle welcome? The answer was there for him, dormant and dusty but intact; the story resided within. It was a story well told; chill-out areas and after-parties across East Anglia, Essex and East of London had heard the story of how he'd got into raving, where he'd started, where he'd been, what he was on. Unused and neglected for time, it lay there still, ready and waiting like ancient alien sci-fi technology, a thing of wonder, full of promise and, full too of unknown and frightening power. *How did it go now?* he thought to himself. What is the version he would tell himself now if he was out there in the chill-out, squatting on a crate or a bale, or a grimy ledge, sharing cigs with a stranger and feeling like this was a place that felt like home and that there was nowhere he would rather be? He would start during that year or so before Mangled at The Barn, from the long hot summer of '89 to the summer of '90. The music then was a siren song for him full of hints and intrigues; experimental, evolutionary lines which spun the '80s into the '90s, overlapping, looping, moving in parallel, buffeting into dead ends, merging and separating, until – when viewed with hindsight as Lee had often viewed it in the past, especially in his chats with Zoe and Rob – until, at Mangled, there was coalescence in the face of chaos and chance.

# SIX

LEE SENSED THE NEW THING THAT WAS HAPPENING out there and all around him throughout that final year of school. It was a presence as he applied for college, finished school, lucked a few mediocre GCSEs and began a hot summer smoking hash and working at the chicken factory. He gathered up hungrily, wherever he found them, pieces of evidence that spoke to him of the new phenomenon. It was mostly under the surface, mysterious and appealing, mycological. It showed itself tantalisingly in a different kind of music on *Top of the Pops* or John Peel's radio show; it was present in anonymous cassette tapes borrowed from older brothers, older cousins, listened to in a smoke-filled bedroom on a one-speaker tape recorder; it also appeared in news reports of massive and uncontrolled Acid House parties and whispered reports of events and happenings more local; mates of mates, brothers of mates and cousins of mates all brought intelligence. Piece by piece, Lee began to create a picture, and although he did not quite see it at the time, it was a picture he wanted to be in more than he wanted anything else. Why that was he could not have told you; it was an indefinable and irresistible draw; it was a calling. How to respond to it he had no idea but, subconsciously, he did respond. He heard the calling and he knew it was his destiny, and his destiny manifested in the shape of Baz.

'Mangled at The Barn, mate,' said Baz. Baz was Rob's brother. Rob was Lee's best mate from school. 'You're underage so front it a little – but don't overdo it. You're both big and ugly enough... should be fine... sweet... don't matter what you wear, just don't look like a fuckin' tramp and... yea... don't be a fuckin' dickhead... well, don't let it show anyhow.' Baz enjoyed the reflex dig; would never tire of it. 'You're not a fuckin' dickhead, are ya, Lee boy? Eh? Eh? I know Rob is but he can't fuckin' help 'imself and we've all just gotta live with that.' Baz enjoyed this even more and laughed loud as he ground a dirty roach into a crowded ashtray.

'Fuck off, Baz... there's only one dickhead in 'ere far as I can see,' Rob said, looking squarely at Baz and joining his laughter. Baz was quite a bit older and a definite, certifiable bad influence. Baz knew people and Baz was involved in stuff; he was into this and that. Baz got them sorted for draw, brought them tapes to listen to and spun tales of London, parties, warehouses, sound systems and fields full of dancing, nutted youth. Rob and Lee loved him for it.

'Right, forget all that now. Consider that fuckin' sorted. Now, you gotta listen to this. Fuck, just listen to this. *This* is why we're goin'.' It was Baz's latest enthusiasm. A night that happened at The Barn. He'd been a few times and now he was getting them in on it. Mangled at The Barn. Mangled was *not*... emphasised Baz, '...about beer, birds and fightin'... that is not... what it's about. If there was any o' that cobblers

48

I'd have nothing to do with it. No, chaps, this little escapade is gonna change your life. Listen. Fuckin' listen.' Baz opened the cassette player, inserted the tape, snapped the door shut and punched the play button with his index finger in one fluid movement; a spin of cassette, fingers, sovereign and signet. The small speaker struggled. There was virtually no bass on the machine and what there was created a pulsing distortion. It was like looking for something rare and shiny dropped in a muddy river.

'Fuckin' 'ell, Baz, it sounds shit. What d'ya do all night when this is on?' said Lee over the pounding surf noise coming out of the tape machine. 'Drink to forget?… It reminds me of one of them dodgy pirate videos Keith sometimes gets. You know, the ones that look like someone's had a fuckin' camera balanced on their knees under a raincoat to do it… and you know that that is how they actually did it.' Baz reached out and turned the music down, then turned to look at Lee and Rob. The loud laugh had gone and there was a look of sincerity and seriousness in Baz's face that neither had ever witnessed before. It had a powerful quietening effect on them and they sat expectant.

'Now listen, Lee, I'm bein' serious now and speaking in all honesty to ya. After you've done one of these nights you'll listen with new ears. To everything. Maybe we'll play it on some'ing better than this box of bollocks 'n' all,' he said, throwing a sneer at the Sharp music box. 'New ears, mate, I'm tellin' ya… new fuckin' ears.' There was a pause and the phlegmy hiss and knock of the music filled the space. Lee tugged at an ear in sympathy with Baz's words and Baz struck like a cobra. He caught hold of the lobe of Lee's other ear and began pulling at it, sincerity out the window. 'Look at my new ears… look at my fresh new ears…' he chanted in a mock US accent in time to the spluttering warehouse music. Lee pulled away, laughing.

'Fuck off, Baz,' he said, seeing Baz fully restored to his teasing, digging self. But something of Baz's soulful lapse hung residual in the air with the smoke and the spray of the white noise of the music.

'Yeah, well, we'll see. A little bit o' billy, 'alf an E and we'll see who really knows woss goin' on... yea, we'll see...' Baz knew he had them now. They had been up for it anyway – rave at The Barn, yes please – but now he knew he had them tight with the mention of E.

'E?' said Rob. 'Ecstasy?' like he was mouthing sacred sounds.

'E?' echoed Lee, the same wonder in his voice for the vowel. He and Rob and their mates smoked hash and they'd done mushrooms – at least they'd done the ones they'd found growing on the field behind the institute; wet, slimy and gag-worthy but still a laugh – and getting out of your nut was always a given for them these days – 'Braintree's better on drugs,' they always said. But they were ready and looking for new adventures. The impulse to alter reality went deep for him and was enmeshed in his love of music, and both he and the music were moving on. He could still remember the way the scales had fallen from his eyes when someone explained 'Lucy in the Sky with Diamonds' to him, and 'Purple Haze', and 'Itchycoo Park', and... and... and... the list went on. He had experienced then almost a grateful relief as he absorbed the implications of what he learned about the inspirational genesis of all this music, about all these bands and artists; moments of shift that fit together the world in a new way; a certain sense, absent before, now present; the scope of understanding extended over old horizons. It was like he had reached a place where he could stand and breathe and look back out over the territory he had covered and see it all in one sweep behind him. He sensed that he was reaching another of those points; he had had his back to the land for a time as he laboured on and up, but there was a ledge before him, another place where he could stand and invigorate a new reality. Ecstasy, he thought, that was proper. He felt its edge and tasted his nervousness, wariness and deep curiosity; a spirit from another dimension was moving amongst them. Lee was taut with excitement and looked at Rob to verify what he already understood; that Rob was as up for it as he was. Rob grinned uncontained at him and he returned the favour and they sat there, grinning at each other, he remembered, like a right couple of herberts.

'Yeah, I'll need fifteen notes each for the Es – and that's a fuckin' bargain,' said Baz, 'but the billy's on me. See ya later, round ours at seven for a smoke. I'll leave the tape but don't forget it when you come round, you fuckin' helmet.' Baz closed the door behind him, the backdraught tearing up the slow wreaths of smoke that hung in the room. Lee turned the music back up. The quality of the recording seemed improved or, maybe, he thought, it's my new ears come early.

## //

They sat in Baz's car in the lumpy, potholed car park of The Barn. 'Get there early to get your bearin's 'n' that,' said Baz.

'It's just one big room, innit? Not a fuckin' labyrinth?' said Lee as he looked over to the door of The Barn in the near distance. They had parked as far away as possible from the entrance, and as they gazed across the car park they could make out two bulky figures in long, dark coats at the door. A short, untidy queue shuffled and puffed smoke about itself, confirming Baz's assurances about the dress code. The haphazard line of punters surrendered itself steadily through the guarded door of The Barn, each admission celebrated by a sudden cut of coloured light and noise and motion as the door opened and closed. These sudden cuts, liberated, escaped away over the stones and gravel and made off into the cooling night. Lee and Rob had decided, even before Baz's advice, that it was too risky to take anything into the club – not so much because they might get caught but because they might lose the valuable drugs. Baz, with his prior experience of the Mangled world, confirmed their instincts; he was not about to countenance behaviour that could lead to the loss of their smileys; the loss of all the potential for the night that was bound up in their lattices of crystal and nano-scopic chemistry.

'Right, 'ere you go, lads, a smiley and a little bomblette I prepared earlier.' Baz put a scruffy white pill and a knotty twist of Rizla into each of their hands then, turning, threw his head back, moving his open hand up to his mouth. He followed this with two gulps from a bottle of water. "Ere,' he said, passing the bottle to Rob in the front seat beside him. Rob looked down at his open hand briefly before repeating Baz's actions and passing the bottle to Lee. Lee was still staring at the pill and the speed bomb, cupped in his hand where Baz had dropped them. The daylight had almost gone and the few streetlights and the lights of The Barn cast ragged shadows across the car. The headlights of vehicles passing on the main road beyond the car park swept them intermittently like searchlights. The pill and the bomb lay cradled in the creases of Lee's palm. The pill looked like an old mini-mint that you'd found loose in your pocket; a dirty mint, he thought to himself. A lovely, scary, dirty, little mint, and with that thought Lee repeated the hand-to-mouth-swig-from-the-bottle sequence of moves as if he'd done it so many times before, and smacked his lips.

'All done,' Lee said with careful innocence to hide a simmering trepidation; he added in a school teacher voice, 'I hope you know what you're doing, Barry Mitchell. I really do.'

Baz looked at Lee in the rear-view mirror, his mouth a line of wicked mischief.

'I wouldn't go that fuckin' far, mate… but let's just say you can thank me afterwards.'

'Come on,' said Rob, back through the open passenger door, 'let's be 'avin' ya, this show needs to get on the fuckin' road.'

'All right, Agnes, keep your fuckin' clogs on,' drawled Baz, and they spilled into the car park, a flurry of slamming doors and flapping jackets, to join the untidy, twitching, shuffling queue. Ten minutes later, a cursory up and down from the bouncer, a once round the inside leg, a pursing of the lips and a world-weary flick of the head, and a sudden cut of escaping light and motion took them inside.

## //

The music pulsed and squelched; it had liquid sinews and plotting bass patterns that worked their grinning way around your head. It spoke to you from the inside and filled the outside with tribal ghosts playing anxiety from the future. Lee was nervous but more than ready to explore the new planet. He could hear something of the tape that Baz had played earlier but it was transformed; there was punching clarity, air-moving volume and bass. The music held and insisted like no music Lee had ever heard and, probably no more than ten minutes after thinking that, Lee estimated later the next morning when trying to explain to Zoe how he felt at every point during the night, he began to soar upwards from the base of his spine, up through his stomach, his lungs, his heart, everything of who he was rushing, receding and rushing, until his whole body roared, moving at speeds hyper, impossibly fast to the point of stillness. He felt the movement like bright light streaming from every part of his body. His external senses gradually withdrew, first the DJ, then the crowd, then his friends, until he was totally alone, totally himself, taking breath in long, intense draws through his nose and releasing in broad exhalations through his mouth. His eyes were closed – and he thought about this but could not remember closing them – and behind his lids, patterns of green and red light, dots and lines and squares, and they turned and tracked and blinked. The intensity eventually subsided, plateaued, and he felt the music come back, strong and friendly. He opened his eyes and Rob was there and the two girls, the one with the orange hat he'd seen before, and another in dungarees, and there was that grinning bloke with the ginger hair and baggy white t-shirt with Daffy Duck on it, who seemed to be everywhere. And there was Baz, a face full of meaning, sheen of sweat, fists and head pumping, sparking grins with his show of effort, grins returned with interest. Lee bathed in it, floated, crested the summit, took the prize, bestowed the gifts and felt victorious.

*I'm aware and in control*, he thought, *and I can ride this rush anywhere and any way.* The music seemed to do just what he wanted and he marvelled at the mixing, the continuity of beats, the narrative the DJ made. He couldn't tell where one tune began and another ended; it was a flow, one tune, a soundscape for the night created by all of them. Every person Lee could see was open to the suggestion of the music. Their faces were in expressions of triumph, he noticed, and decided it was because here they were together doing this, to this music. He nodded to himself and caught the eye of the girl in the dungarees. She grinned and he returned it, nodding and turning his grin this way and that, sparking more and more smiles across the packed dance floor like flashes of light in the dark. I can read their thoughts, Lee told himself. No, not read their thoughts, read their feelings. Lee's sense of his own profundity was hugely satisfying. He smiled broadly and again caught the eyes of others doing the same.

I am the rhythm; I am the music, he declared to himself. He felt like Spartacus. *I'm the music.* He mouthed the words as he danced. Everything was fluid, silver and curved like the dream-wave of a surfer. He crouched, poised in a curl of roaring surf, serene in a huge rotation of tumbling water. He held the crouch and touched with fingertips the moving glass of the tube, held the rising rush of the music, the rush of the drug in his blood. Lee felt his reality shift to a new point determined by the way the universe spoke to the new chemical mix in his brain. My consciousness, Lee thought, is a path of smooth stone; is huge steps on a path of flat-coloured stone; I am a path of moving stone. It's like a dream, he thought; a dream where you are in control. A lucid dream. Seagull cries in a dream; seagulls in the music – ah ah ah-ah, ah ah ah-ah. You cannot, absolutely cannot, beat a bit of seagull in a tune, thought Lee; other birds are good too, but seagulls… he hoped he could remember this to talk about later.

Layering and building – repeat, repeat, reach a pitch then relent and… hold the groove. The place you want to be. This is it. Drops out to a synth break-down, gradually draws the drums back in. *Drop the Bass Now.* Slow, snorting bass complies, deep and subbed out. Low frequency oscillation. Deep echo twang of a plastic pipe, high-hats, high-hats, quickfire on the wood block. Snares. Bragging bassline, bowling, groovy, swinging, cheeky, swagging along and rolling with the marching snares. *Huh, huh, huh, huh,* pitched up.

I feel like I know every vocal sample off by heart and can sing along, thought Lee. I am joined with the music; I am joined with these people around me, the DJs, the bar staff, the bouncers, these two smiling girls, one with an orange hat with a flower on it. He felt indivisible from the music and the other dancers around him. They were part of the same spinning system, atoms round a nucleus, planets round a sun, bees round a flower. That was when the dungaree-girl asked him his name. Mystery bell-chimes and warning beeps. Arpeggios of synthetic strings and grinding guttural organ pipes. Video game and computer noises – clicks, whirrs and explosions of laser. The radio and TV are on together and someone's playing Atari tennis and outside someone else is swinging a whirly wind pipe and playing with clackers. In the street, marching bands and a steam fair; in the background, floodlit factories of steel and fire set rambling against the velvet emptiness of space, spinning with planets and studded with stars.

The rest of the night was, in the words of Rob, 'fuckin' mental… unbelievable…'

'Ya know what, Rob-a-dob-dob, for once in ya life, you're right. Is he right, Zoe, or is he right?'

'He's right.'

## //

'Ya know, I reckon I met the entire population in the place last night,' said Lee, looking along the line of Rob and Zoe and Kelly, who sat on a large old sofa in front of him. A chipped and scarred G Plan-style coffee table covered in ash trays, mugs and cans, crossed the space in front of the sofa; Lee sat in an over-stuffed, stained, lime green armchair on its other side. He had slung himself between the arms of the chair so his legs hung over one arm and his back rested on the other. Behind the sofa and across the dark low-ceilinged room – more of a big shed really, he thought – stood Baz and his mates; he supposed they were mates, they were at least people Baz already knew – Jamie, Timbo and Marcooze, Jo, Nicky and others whose names were space in his head. They had all been there last night. They were at Jamie's farm, well, Jamie's dad's farm, and they were in Jamie's den; more of a big shed, really, he thought again. Fuck, a place like this would be brilliant.

'...managed to say goodbye to most of 'em before we left 'n' all,' Lee added with pride, '... and... I made sure to check that they'd all had a mental night, a fuckin' outstandin' good time...' Everyone laughed. 'Mate, the music... I dunno... it was fuckin' extra.'

'I think,' said Rob, 'it has changed me as a person.'

Zoe laughed. 'You two are the best rave virgins there have ever been,' she said.

'Virgins?' said Lee, 'so how many times you been out there again, Zoe?'

'Twice before,' said Zoe with a hint of defiance.

'It's not the quantity, it's the quality,' chipped in Kelly, who had been struggling to build a spliff and had, at just that point, finally succeeded.

'Thank you, Kelly.'

'I agree,' said Lee, 'quality... and that was quality... I have, overnight, no word of a lie, completely re-assessed all my ideas about music... ya know, I now properly get it... now I know... now...' Lee had obviously charged his words with significance as three sets of eyes were now on him and three sets of ears waited for him to explain further. '...now I understand what I was missing. See, before I was listenin' to music that moved me, lots of bass, reggae and dub, funk-soul and hip-hop and Stone Roses, Happy Mondays maybe, older heavier stuff, Led Zep, Sabbath – lots of bass, weight, lots of smoke. The thing is, that stuff is meant to be listened to on its own. D'ya know what I mean? You listen to one track, then you listen to another one. Even if you listen to an album, it's one tune then another, even if it's a fuckin' concept album it's still like that. But that, last night, was different, yea… and it's not just the drugs… but that did help… you know… the stuff I've just mentioned is cool with a spliff and that, but last night was not like that; it was not a night for relaxing and laying back… so the drugs, yeah, a part to play… but the point is… what was the fuckin' point again?'

'Yea, c'mon, man, what was the point?' chipped in Rob. But Lee was not to be deflected and with clear and impressive determination he regained his thread.

'Yea… so this was music for a buzzed-up mind, the tracks all linked and worked together so it's like a single track, one piece of music.' Lee was actively processing his first experience of hearing music mixed. 'I mean, that's the DJ's work, but the tunes 'ave gotta be there for him to play. They've gotta be made like that. I mean, before, I liked that Detroit 'n' Chicago acid stuff but I didn't fully get it, and a few years ago – you know, *Blue Monday, Brutal House* – lost on me a bit really… but last night I got it. Tunes made for dancin'… DJs workin' those tunes to a single stream and playin' to a crowd of up-for-it, nutted people… the way they made the place rock, the groove extended, the way they get you amused but serious about what you're hearin' and how it made you feel, and how it made you want to move and groove and jack ya fuckin' body. Am I making sense here or what?'

They were staring at him, silenced by his passion and his articulacy about what they had just been doing. Zoe broke the silence.

'You're right,' she said. 'I know what ya mean. First time I came 'ere and did a pill, it was the same. It was like I'd been driving with the 'andbrake on 'til then. You should write it all down, Lee, keep a kind of ravin' diary – I mean, you're gonna do it again, yea? – yea, keep a kind of diary about it. I'd read it.' They all considered the idea for a few moments but did not comment.

'Well, it was wicked,' said Kelly eventually, 'tha's all I know.'

''N' all you need to know,' said Lee. 'Now what the fuck is Baz doin'?' They looked across the room at Baz. He was stooping over a table and touching at the records spinning on a couple of turntables in front of him. His head was crunched to one side to hold the cup of a headphone between his shoulder and his ear and his head nodded back and forth. Jamie leant round the table behind where Baz was standing and the room filled loud with kick-drum, snare, purred bass. Muscle and mind memories of last night returned and everyone began moving. Lee bounced up out of the lime green chair and moved towards Baz and the decks, and the dance returned to his eager body. Jamie removed a record from one of the decks and returned it to a sleeve sticking out at an angle from a crate by the table before turning back with another disc taken from a sleeve also poking out from the crate, which he placed on the spare turntable. The deck was still spinning and as Baz passed the headphones, the needle was gently dropped onto the edge of the revolving vinyl. With light touch of the fingers, the junction between sapphire tip and grooved plastic was moved to just where Jamie wanted it. Lee watched and took in the arrangement of equipment and the activity of those operating it. He had never seen this happening before. Wedding DJs used an all-in-one unit, like the ones he'd seen in his mum's *Littlewoods* catalogue; the night before at The Barn, the DJs were on a platform behind a console and you couldn't really see. But now he could. There were two decks; silver, square, snaking tone-arms and between them, a mixer, two vertical sliders, one horizontal and three columns of rotary knobs. He could see in the tangle of cables that the decks fed the mixer and that the mixer fed the amplifier, which must have been on one of the shelves on the wall behind.

'Wanna go?' said Baz. Lee started at the offer and looked around for support, advice, direction. The offer seemed immense and munificent. He wanted to more than anything and yet at the same time was awed by the idea.

'I'll 'ave a go.' It was Zoe. He hadn't heard her join him at the table, the music was so loud and he was so absorbed by what he saw. Great, he thought, I'll watch Zoe first and then have a go. Before he had finished the thought, Zoe had taken Baz's place behind the table and was touching the spinning platter and moving the pitch fader while Baz pulled a record from the crate.

'Done this before?' asked Baz.

'No,' replied Zoe, 'tell me everything.' Baz smiled and began to go through the basics of operating a turntable as part of a two-turntable system set up to enable the mixing of two records together so as to create a continuous stream of music that would provide an audience with a groove they could dance to without interruption.

'Pitch controller changes the speed of the platter, changes the tempo of the tune... match one to the other through the headphones... move the record around like this to find your cue point... and cue it up on the beat... go... use the fader to move the sound from one deck to the other... create the mix... use your hand to keep it in time... adjust the pitch... adjust the levels...' The record already playing finished before Zoe could get her mix in, but Jamie let her switch decks and the next one was not far out. Lee was no expert but within a short time, it looked to him like Zoe was handling the mixing as well as any of the others had been.

'She's a fuckin' natural,' said Marcooze, admiringly. Coming from him, that was probably saying a lot, thought Lee as he recalled how Marcooze and the other bloke – what was his name? Timbo – had both held forth when they first got to Jamie's den, about how they had all missed the best raving days; that it had all been better in '88 and that the scene was not what it was. Fuck that, thought Lee, I've just had the best night of my life and rediscovered music, and I'm about to have a go on proper decks. I don't see how it could be any better for me, right here, right now. Lee took his turn on the deck beside Zoe. He'd been following Baz's first tutorial carefully but he was no natural like Zoe. Still, the first time he took control of two tunes playing simultaneously, first in the headphones and then out through the speakers, he was smitten, taken in, rolled over and reborn. He could see the same glow of discovery and epiphany in Zoe's face, and as their eyes met, they each confirmed this for the other.

Fucking hell, thought Lee, I only met you a few hours ago and now we're having a spiritual experience together. In fact, as far as he was concerned, this was the second revelation in less than twelve hours that involved Zoe. The first had been "getting it" last night, he told himself. At the height of his feeling of indivisibility from the music and the people around him, he had found himself with Zoe and Kelly. Exchanging ideas and emotions in his moves. Calling and responding with them, having a laugh.

'Wass ya name mate?' Zoe had said.

'Lee, you?'

'Louis?'

'Na, Lee. Wass yours?' he said, more deliberately and closer to her ear.

'Oh, right. Zoe,' she said in his ear, 'and this is Kelly.' She gestured with her head back towards the other girl. 'Where you from, what you on?'

'From 'ere, you know, Braintree.' Lee wasn't sure how to address her second question. Was it normal to be so open about doing drugs in this situation?

'Yea, Dunmow. Done a pill and a little dab of whizz…' She stared up at him, challenging and dancing.

'Oh,' said Lee. 'Yea, yea, done a pill too. Nice.'

'I could tell,' she said knowingly.

'All right, nice one,' he said, laughing, his uncertainty replaced with the warmth of shared confidences. 'You 'avin' a good time?' he added.

'Surprised you need to ask...'

'... more of a statement really,' he shot back, and that seemed to cement the deal. The four of them spent the rest of Mangled together. They were still in a bubble at the end as the bouncer guided them with open arms towards the first white-gold smudges of a summer dawn. They'd meandered around the car park looking for the car and Baz, although none of them were really looking and two of them didn't know who Baz was, nor what car they were looking for. They'd eventually attached themselves to the right vehicle and Baz found them soon after. As was usual for Baz, his arrival prompted a hiatus of discussion and the rapid setting-up of a kitty to take advantage of Baz's car-park connections and supply themselves with a quarter of Moroccan split four ways. Baz returned with the goods and three mates.

'Jamie, Timbo and Marcooze,' he said. 'Real names obviously... this is Lee, Rob and...'

'Zoe and Kelly,' said Kelly. Jamie was a Braintree face, and Lee recognised him, probably from seeing him at Baz and Rob's. The other two... probably London mates of Baz's. They didn't look local and they had a big-city edge.

'Thought we'd go back to Jamie's and 'ave a little wind-down. It's early yet and I'm still fucked,' said Baz. 'Jamie's got decks and we can piss around there 'til the day gets goin.'

'Yep,' said Jamie. 'All welcome... a friend of Baz is a friend of mine.' Lee heard the posh accent and wondered how Baz knew Jamie. He considered that maybe that was where the hash came from. *Did it matter?* he asked himself. Not really, he answered, and he looked at Zoe and Kelly, effectively repeating Jamie's invitation by raising his eyebrows and shrugging.

'We ain't got a car,' said Zoe.

'There's room with us,' said Rob, 'if one of you goes with Jamie.' He looked at Marcooze and Timbo as he said this.

'Marcooze, you come with me then,' said Jamie. That left six of them to bundle themselves into Baz's Peugeot. Once the car was uncomfortably full of bodies, Baz manoeuvred out of the car park and followed Jamie's Jeep out into the deeper night that lay with a gathering mist in the folds of the fields and valleys around the western edge of Braintree. It briefly occurred to Lee that two girls whom they had only just met had agreed, seemingly without a thought, to get in the car and go with them to who knows where at three in the morning. He dismissed the concern by referring himself to the relationship they had established in the few hours they had spent together, a relationship which through ecstasy-accelerated bonding, was full of a deep, mutual trust. Soon after, once they'd arrived at the farm, he asked Zoe about this.

'I knew it was all right,' she had said. 'I mean, you can always tell yourself not to do stuff... sometimes, ya know, you can tell something's dodgy... sometimes you're not sure... so either way, there you back off... but other times you get an okay and you just gotta go with that... ya know, otherwise, you're always watching out and never going out.' Lee nodded at her words like teaching.

## //

Not long after Zoe and Lee had enjoyed a first taste of playing and mixing vinyl on two turntables, they were bundling themselves back into the caramel tan interior of Baz's car and heading back to Braintree. The sun was well up and blazed golden on blocks of ripening wheat, and filled to full the bubbling chlorophyll canopies of stands of woodland that sailed between the fields. The pouring light set off hedgerows to chase them down the narrow country lanes that fell away between high banks, rose around blind corners and turned up quietly at isolated junctions where black and white cast iron signposts stood guard. Baz knew these roads well, they all did. These were the roads of their world, and their travel along them seemed part of the natural order of the day, like the sun coming up when it did and the way the earth fell away just there to meet a stream at the bottom of the valley, or swelled, lifted and flattened to make a place where people had come to live. Baz drove the car at speed. The four passengers sat transfixed by the cinema of windscreen, soundtracked by squirming, chirruping, funky-acid hypnotism; the motion of the vehicle, the music, and the countryside rushing by the open windows became a single, composite sensation.

As the road grew wider and drew tighter to home, Baz threw the car into a left turn back onto a single-track lane that ran steeply down the side of a valley. He sped the car over a small fording-bridge, sharply round an old mill and up the other side. Just before the road crested the further side of the valley, it passed beneath the overhanging branches of several big oaks that grew from the banked verge; just where the shade from these trees was at its deepest and coolest, there was a lay-by. It was scooped into the bank and part covered in moss and ivy and rotting leaves. Baz pulled in smartly and turned off the engine. The music went too and the car filled with quiet, then with birdsong and then the smell of damp hedgerow; the breeze in the leaves and branches of the trees rippled them in bars of gold and green. A kushti 'atchin' tan, thought Lee; that's what his Grandad Swigler would have said about this place; a sweet spot to pull up a wagon for a few nights.

'Nice stop,' said Lee.

'C'mon,' said Baz, 'spliff break, ain' it?' Lee approved. He opened the door, and it felt like the combined pressure of being three in the back of a small car sent him springing up and out like a jack-in-the-box. He let the spring bounce him up to the high end of the lay-by, where a tubular metal gate stood across the upward sloping entrance to a field. He heard the commotion behind as the others pulled themselves from the car and joined him on the planet. Lee felt intrepid and every step was a discovery. He reached the gate and leant over the top bar; the field beyond swept gently upwards, bristling and rustling with crops. It blazed lime and made a curving horizon of ripening ears where it met the blue of the sky. Lee climbed the gate and made his way to sit on a hummock of stony soil topped with grass and wildflowers. The others joined him in a mini-chaos of cries and talk and appreciative swearing. Baz had one ready rolled and Rob added another to the party and there, together in the corner of that field, in the gold of the sun, they smoked and watched the air in the wheat and followed the cawing crows that were coming and going from a spinney of taller trees on the other side of the field.

Lee was inspired by the birds; they prompted his memory of seagulls in the music. He tried to explain his ideas about bird sounds in tunes but got lost as his words opened a cascade of everyone else's reconstructed moments from the night before. The talk rambled on and the spliff and the scene mellowed the world for them, and as it did, they all agreed, solemnly swore, they would do it all again and soon. At this, Lee stood and turned to the others sat on the hummock now looking up at him.

'Things,' he said, pointing his finger up in the air for emphasis, 'will never be the same again.' He might have said this at various points during the night and this day that followed – and he was to think it and say it still more times in the months to follow – but it was here in this sun-flooded field, edged with cool shadows, that he really stopped, re-evaluated, noted the adjusted set of his mind and began to sense the magnitude of what he felt had happened to him. 'It'll never be the same,' he said more quietly, palms open towards them, behind him the light and the wheat and the green trees topped with crows. The others laughed.

'Fuckin' 'ell, mate,' said Rob, 'you know this is it,' and he stood up sharply, moved to Lee and grabbed him in a hug. Kelly and Zoe felt compelled by this to do the same and the four of them stood wrapped together.

'Never be the same…' repeated Zoe. At this point, Baz, who had gone back to the car for some Rizla, jumped down from the gate.

'Woss goin' on 'ere?' he called. 'Fuckin' love-in or what?'

'It's a hug-in, Baz, a hug-in, c'mon,' said Kelly, lifting her arm for Baz. Laughing, he ducked into the hug and they became a weird ten-legged creature shifting slightly round one way and then the other, muttering 'never be the same again'. And they were right, it never was.

## //

Lee pulled into Rockingham Road and parked outside his house with seagull cries in his ears. You absolutely cannot beat a bit of seagull, thought Lee, allowing the bird sample to splice time, memory, thought and place. The Mangled mix was still playing and he sat there, on stake-out, to hear it through. He used to have a thing, he remembered, where he couldn't kill off a tune or a mix out of regard for the music and would often find himself sat in his parked car, sometimes left behind by the others who had been travelling with him, waiting for an acceptable point at which to stop it and leave. He released

66

the seatbelt but remained in the seat. The phrase repeated, repeated, repeated again, reached a pitch then relented and… yes… hold that groove. This is the place when your whole being is dancing, he thought. This is what you worked for. This is it. It dropped out to a synth break, drums drawn back in. *Drop the Bass Now*, and a slow, fuzzy bass complied, deep and subbed out. Low frequency oscillation. Plastic pipe echoes, high-hats, quickfire on the wood block, and marching snares. Now the bassline bragged, bowling along, groovy, swinging, impertinent, rolling with the snares. *Huh, huh, huh, huh.* Drop for the chimes of mystery, warning bleeps and arpeggios of synthetic strings… muffled knocks and clicks and the mix cut and the file finished.

*Wow*, thought Lee. That was quite a ride. The funeral, the talk with Zoe, the memory stick, the memory, that mix… his recall of it had been full and vivid. He remembered little of the journey home; the forgettable roads forgotten in the rewind. It was like the memory had sprung fully charged from a split in his skull and played itself out before him. He laughed a little to himself at what had happened and looked up at the roof of the car as if he expected to see Rob grinning down at him, a spliff in one hand and a bag of pills in the other. *What is it they say about the '60s?* he thought; if you can remember it, you weren't really there. He laughed again, quietly pushing the air out through his nose. Fucking hell, he thought, if you were there in the '90s, you can never forget. Never, ever forget. Maybe, he thought, you remain there forever.

# SEVEN

LEE CAME TO, SATURDAY MORNING, SAT AT THE KITCHEN
table staring at a picture of his Nanna and Grandad
Swigler that was stuck next to a hand-drawn picture of a
bird in a tree that was stuck amongst magnets, notes and
other pictures to the grey door of a fridge – his fridge. His
and Marianne's fridge. He reviewed his situation. There
had been a funeral; a powerful event that had reconnected
him with a time he thought he'd left well behind him.
Returning home from that funeral, he'd experienced a kind
of flashback in the car. The next day, and ever since really,
his head had been all over the place. He had not slept well
and he felt out of sorts, wobbly. Yes, that about sums it
up. Nothing to see really, he counselled, still staring at the
fridge. He sniffed. Another coffee will shift things along, he
recommended, and a good morning of sorting should help
settle the wobbly brain. Lee put the kettle on and sat facing

the other way, waiting for it to boil. There on top of a low pile of letters and magazines he could see the file Zoe had given him; a slim white binder with a label in the middle, written on it in black marker: *Zoe Marr, Zoe's Kitchen – Spin Junky Magazine*. He picked it up and took out several sheets of A4 clipped together at the corner. He looked at the top sheet. *Zoe's Kitchen*, it read over two columns of text. There was a small picture of Zoe inset between the columns, head turned to face the camera, looking away from a small crowd supposedly stood in a kitchen, intently focussed on each other; they were presumably meant to be chatting shit, thought Lee. He couldn't help but like the idea, and although his experience of the last few days cautioned him to leave this alone, there was a cord between him and the writing and it drew him in.

Hello, Spin Junkies, and welcome to Zoe's Kitchen, a new feature in which I will be exploring a whole range of issues past and present which have excited the minds and imaginations of Kitchen Crews over the years and excite them still today. Every month I will bring to you in these columns an idea, a thesis, a theory, a point of debate which has come up in a Kitchen Crew discussion I have been a part of post-rave, post-club, or during a house party. You are all, of course, invited to the kitchen to get involved and I will include some of your responses to these kitchen chats in future editions.

This month we are going to kick things off by looking at a chat I initially had a long time ago with a very good friend in a field in Norfolk. I never tire of discussing this and it is a firm favourite of mine; it is as interesting now as it ever was and no one involved in this scene can resist it. So, let's go:

**"What are the influences that led to the development of Rave Culture in the UK?"**

Lee affirmed what he had just read with a nod. I'll just read this one, he thought as he made himself a coffee, and then I'll get up in that fucking loft.

Timing was everything as it always is. Certain things came together musically. There had been Ibiza and acid and the illegal M25 rave thing and, although those big events had effectively been closed down, that scene continued to bubble. It did so informed by the house, garage and techno sound of Detroit and Chicago and New York, and also the hard dance and techno flavours of Holland and Belgium and Germany. Hardcore Rave was the UK adding their own flavour to these sounds and ideas. That flavour was a rich mix. It contained the hip-hop they'd been into since the late '80s; reggae and dub from West Indian immigration to the UK and now showing homegrown talent. It had foundations in ska – that first expression of multi-racial Britain, taut and exuberant; it brought elements of democracy, equality and DIY spirit from punk; it channelled in the defiant experimentation and insistent spiky energy of new wave synth; and, finally, it drew, without prejudice, oddments and nuggets from their mum and dads' record collections. Beyond the music there was a wider society shaken by recession, desensitised by terrorism, and made bleak by the anti-social drivers of 1980's greed and individualism. But it was a society which could still turn its gaze in hope towards the epic beacons of promise that were the fall of the Berlin Wall and the release of Nelson Mandela. These events transcended the usual divisions of class, race and nation and stood as emblematic for the youth movements of the time.

Coinciding with this, there were several other important developments. There were changes in technology which meant that people who would otherwise likely have found the means of music production off limits now had access to it. They could relatively easily acquire the equipment and tools to produce at a high quality, in a makeshift bedroom studio, music which was influenced by how they saw the society described above, and, above all, music they wanted to go out and dance to. There was a change in licensing laws in favour of later and all-night events. There was a willing, waiting, and fairly bored population of young people who had been brought up with colour TV, cartoons and the first video and electronic games and devices; crucially, this was the first youth generation for whom car ownership was widespread and unremarkable. And lastly but in no way least, there was a fast-developing service industry producing mood-enhancing psychedelic drugs of great potency in response to massive youth demand for them. This all came together in the years at the end of the 1980s and the start of the new decade to produce the extraordinary phenomenon of the early rave scene of the early 1990s. A creative outpouring of unprecedented scale and scope. Over to you, Kitchen Crew.

Zoe E Marr/DJ Zoem, The Spin Junky, December 2006

Yes, thought Lee, as he caught the background drift of his own words in the article. This had always been a favourite. The "nexus of factors", he had called it. The bundle of fibres. The nerve ganglion, in his head an illustration of the nervous system, red and vegetative morphing and realigning as a mischievous smiley face covered in arrows pointing in different directions; and now it was an encased bundle of densely packed filaments and fibres pouring light from one end. He shook his head clear of the images and re-oriented on the Swiglers and the bird and the tree on the fridge. *What about mobile phones and the internet?* he thought. They've changed everything. Raving would not have happened in the way it did if those things had come along a few years earlier. He pursed his lips and looked out from under a frown of concentration. It happened as only it could happen, at the time it happened. Maybe, he thought. *But that wasn't a very interesting theory. Time to get up in that loft, he told himself.*

## //

The energy saving bulb slurred its way to a weak orange eminence. It hung in frosted coils like the nest of a solitary wasp from the head beam of the roof. It revealed, dimly, the loft space in which Lee moved crabwise amongst a couple of decades worth of applied adult life. There was an odour of cold dust; the sounds of life on the street outside. An east wind carried on it the machine hum of the nearby A406 North Circular. Grey-white, fat-free light peered in under some of the tiles. A cool glow settled on everything and waited.

Lee was slightly fazed, as he often was when he stood looking at the boxes and crates piled in the loft. The garden shed with its tottering collections of decorating, DIY and gardening equipment, could work a similar hypnosis on him. He was also still occupied by Zoe's article and the lines of spluttering gunpowder it had set burning in his head. They'd moved on pretty quickly after that first Mangled, he thought, moved on in such a free-falling way, not the only way it might have been but one of the only ways. And the first speed wedding, he recalled now, that was key to the way it had gone.

## //

Tammy's wedding was the first in a series of what Lee came to think of as *The Speed Weddings*. There had been a whole series of them; people still got married then, he thought and, because of that, we were good at weddings. We knew what to do at a wedding, how the day would go; we were familiar with the timing, the forms and the etiquette. Yes, he thought, there always seemed to be a family wedding in the offing. But Tammy's was the first; the first in a series of matrimonial celebrations before which he and his close confederates took plenty of amphetamine sulphate to spice up proceedings. The timings were perfect; Tammy got married at the end of July and, because she and Baz were the same age, knew each other from school, both Baz and Rob got an invite.

'I'm telling you,' said Baz, 'it's the fuckin' biz.' Lee was sat in the back of Baz's Peugeot, low-profile alloys pinging starbursts in the late-afternoon sunshine, tinted windows shading the activities inside. The car was parked out of the way, just the other side of the substantial cover of a brown Sherpa van in the car park of The Foakes Hall, Great Dunmow.

'You can't go to a wedding in a dirty car, Danny-Lee. You just can't, it's disrespectful,' Lee's mum had said a few days before as she organised him to wash their car. She had very strongly held ideas about manners and behaviour and she invariably explained them with "just". She would have thrown a fit at the state of Baz's car, he thought, the interior at least, but it was well hidden behind the Sherpa. Lee thought that her stand on cars that were messy and neglected inside was going to be the same as cars that were dirty on the outside; she'd still think it disrespectful because you knew it was dirty and had chosen to do nothing. It would definitely confirm for her what she already thought she knew about Baz. Lee leant forward at this point in his thoughts as Baz held before him a small origami envelope made from what looked like the pages of a magazine. Lee briefly sucked his little finger and then stuck it into the envelope; he withdrew the finger, its tip loaded with white powder, and stuck it in his mouth, swigging, as he did so, from a can of Coke passed back to him by Rob.

'Weddin's on speed, mate… they're a right fuckin' laugh, trust me.' On certain things, having a right good laugh being one of them, Lee had learned to trust Baz. They did a round more each of the envelope and then it was time for them to make their uniquely energetic contribution to the wedding reception. They were itching for it.

As he stood in the loft, Lee could almost feel the push of the speed; he had, he thought, experienced some of the most fun and rewarding moments of his family life during those super-charged weddings. Really, he had. The energy he had to talk to seldom-seen relatives was endless; his genuine interest in them was revealed to him and he wholeheartedly wanted to know all about them and where they were in life. Not too much different to booze, he thought. But with booze you eventually fall over, or get in a fight, or start crying into the sandwiches. Also, thought Lee, the thing about all that when you're sixteen, seventeen, older even, in your twenties, is you can get away with being an excitable and an over-the-top nutjob. In fact, at a family wedding it was almost an expectation, a duty even. No one would have had a clue. To be honest, he thought, I forgot myself pretty quickly what was going on.

He pictured himself, making his way one by one round the scattered knots of relatives and family friends who stood and sat at tables arranged at the back of the hall furthest from the stage at the far end. They were an assorted collection of seldom-worn suits, clothes bought for the occasion being worn for the first time, blocks of colour and floral patterns, hats on heads that rarely held a hat these days, and old school shoes. There were best watches, heirloom jewellery, chunky chain link identity bracelets and any number of gold sovereign rings. The guests were nibbling and drinking and smoking – the air streaked with grey clouds of cigarette and cigar smoke – as they chatted and settled themselves into whatever was their wedding groove. They were in the hollow, the gentle lull between the service and the reception, and they passed the time as they waited for DJ Jez's Disco Machine and the cover and comfort of music, with formulaic but nonetheless meaningful catching-up on family.

This is what Lee threw himself into. He checked on health, hobbies and opinions. He countered responses with his own personal updates, sometimes drawing in other family members; he offered free-ranging considerations about hot topics of the day and absolute determinations about sporting issues, two things about which he knew close to nothing. He quickly developed a patter and a routine, and instead of reaching a place where he no longer believed what he was saying because he'd repeated the words too often and over too short a time, he began to extemporise and improvise, varying and shaping his performance with virtuoso style for each different and particular audience. He was on a roll, and only Rob's two-finger signalling for a smoke break could deflect him.

'C'mon, mate. You're talkin' the fuckin' ears off that lot. Time for a calm-down reefer before the music starts.'

'Don't mind if I do, Robert, don't mind if I do, old chap.'

'I've been chatting to your cousins from Bury,' said Rob as they joined Baz, Zoe and Kelly in the Foakes Hall foyer. 'I think we should go out with them sometime. Nights up their way sound wicked.'

'Yea,' said Lee, distracted by the sight of Zoe and Kelly and confusion about why they were there. Because you invited them, he reminded himself. He'd promised Zoe it would be a laugh and she only lived just up the road, near his dad, in the Newton Green Circle of Hell, as his mum called it. Zoe wanted to bring Kelly, and Lee generously told her that would be fine. You need to check with your Aunty June, his mum had said, although Aunty June hadn't really cared.

'Yea,' said Rob, bringing Lee back, 'we should go, get out in the sticks. See what's goin' on.'

'Yea,' said Lee. 'Let's do it. Sounds wicked.'

## //

Ten minutes later, they bundled and stumbled noisily back into the hall. DJ Jez's Disco Machine was flashing squares of coloured light at them, and oil gels swirled on the walls and slid across the floor.

'...ladies and gentlemen, boy and girls and... you lot at the back...' said DJ Jez as eyes swivelled to the back of the hall where Lee and the rest of the smoking party were re-orienting themselves back into the world of the wedding party. DJ Jez was a top-drawer wedding DJ and MC, unimpeachable style. Lee put his thumb up to Jez and gave him a grin as he imagined Jez in the DJ booth at Mangled. '...welcome to the wedding of Tammy and Chris... they would love for you to join them as they take to the floor for the first dance... their favourite and special song... well, I think you'll find the title says it all.' The hall filled with the opening bars of Sade, 'Your Love is King', and Tammy, struggling with impossible yards of wedding dress, began to dance with her new husband. What was his surname again? Lee concentrated thinking about Tammy's new identity. His ability to hold a subject in his head long enough to understand it was being severely challenged by the very strong weed that he had just added to the flickering jitter of the speed that was now well established in his system and activated to breakneck maximum by his recent extreme family interactivity; that and the discourse of the smoke break. *I'm not that close to her, am I?* he thought, excusing himself his lack of attention to Tammy's changed status as if he was being picked up on it by his mum. He turned to look at the others and saw his own state more or less reflected back at him. That was reassuring. Right, he said to himself, actually voicing the word in his resolve to focus. Right, he repeated in his head, just relax. Once they put on some dancy tunes, you can channel some of that jagged energy. While he waited, he reviewed the action of the smoke break.

Minutes before, seven of them, including Lee's cousins Scott and Jason, had been stood behind Foakes Hall. They looked out over the small park that made up the ground that fell away at the back of the hall and swept its way down to a large formal pond a few hundred yards away. A couple of spliffs were making a circuit round the group and Scott was delivering a strong pitch for the East Anglian rave and free-party scene, prompted, Lee guessed, by his chat with Rob about Mangled. He was selling it hard but the door was already wide and wedged open. They were more than ready for a new venture.

'Yep,' concluded Scott in a tone of professional assessment, 'you lot need to come out with us. Some fuckin' great parties round Thetford. In the forest, warehouses, all that, it's goin' off.' As he said this, his slight Suffolk burr still sounding, Scott looked out across the park which lay spread beneath them as if he could see Thetford out there, just beyond the Doctor's Pond.

'Yep,' said Jason, 'if you think it's wicked at The Barn, then just come up our way for a night... mind expansion guaranteed.' He rolled his head from side to side as he said this to emphasise the point.

'Well, let's get something sorted now? Organise something now?' Zoe was excited, and the others got behind her enthusiasm with murmurs of approval.

'Right, okay, let's look for a couple of weeks from now,' said Scott. 'Bound to be a forest or a warehouse night... waddaya reckon?' Scott scanned the Mangled posse.

'Yea, why the hell fuckin' not?' said Baz.

'Let's get in-volved,' added Rob.

'Right, sweet. I'll call you, Lee. Come up ours and we'll go from there.'

'Yea, yea, we're there, mate, we're right there with ya,' and for a moment, as Lee stood looking out towards the pond, staring out blankly at the boxes in the loft, he was there. He was right there and he felt again his sense of premonition at Scott's words, his clear view that he was headed for another time of revelation, another place to be transformed.

The wedding resumed for Lee in a swirl of information and fragments; his conversations with relatives, the spliff outside, the rave plans being hatched with Scott and Jason, being with Zoe and Kelly at a family wedding, DJ Jez having a pop at them and Sade's sultry dinner-party croon threatened to overwhelm him. He needed to dance it out and DJ Jez needed to deliver. Lee still remembered that next tune – Double Trouble and the Rebel MC. It was like a gift, a personal gift, and Lee expressed his gratitude with energetic demonition. From there the wedding proceeded in a frame-slipping spin of vintage dance favourites from the rock 'n' roll hall of fame, country and western standards, cuts from across the spectrum of the 1980s and a sprinkling of Top 40 hits from the first six months of the new decade. Lee took it all on, interspersed, of course, with several more smoke breaks and a handful of increasingly garbled and gibbered conversations with people very unlikely to remember any of it afterwards. It was a family wedding to represent all such events.

# EIGHT

LEE SHIVERED. THE LOFT WAS COLD AND HE FELT he had been standing still for a while. Okay, you are here for a purpose, he coached himself, and that is to sort unopened boxes and to find… to find what? There had been something specific. You are trying to find something, he told himself. What was it again? Fuck's sake. He reprimanded himself, told himself that this was why he no longer really puffed anymore, despite loving it. The next time Sami invited him to "Ere, 'ave a little go on this, mate,' he'd tell him to fuck off despite his strong feeling of need for it halfway through a difficult Friday at work. But he also felt that the spliffs at the back of Foakes Hall all those years ago had somehow got into his system and were playing with his perception. He sought focus. Ah, the old CD boxes, he noticed. They'd seemed chuckable at the time but he'd bunged them up in the loft all the same. Good move, good move, he congratulated himself;

sub-vocalised his self-appreciation. The CDs now looked like the treasure of a bygone age. He peered down at the plastic cases, pictured himself downstairs picking discs from the box and rediscovering sequences of tracks, mixes, playlists… Distractions. Bloody hell, loft missions and their endless distractions. Leave the CDs, move away from the CDs, take your mind back only five minutes and work out what the fuck you were trying to accomplish in the loft – and try to explain to your wandering self what success looks like.

Okay, okay. That was it. He was there to find a box of vases and ornaments. Vases? Or as Nanna Harker used to say, "vawses". Why did we need these things? Why? Because we want to use them, Marianne had explained as condescendingly as she could. He smiled. She was joking but she also meant him to know that she thought that sometimes he could be a bit stupid. Right. Focus. *Baby Clothes* said the marker pen scrawled on that one. *Keepsakes* on the next. The next one was unmarked. He shifted it towards him and freed the cardboard flaps that had been counter folded across each other to semi-seal the box. What have we here? He hummed as he looked down into the space of the box. If the CDs had shone to him like old treasure, then what was in this box blazed as if he'd opened up the lost ark. He felt his body jolt and what he saw made the skin across his skull ripple and tighten, as it had in the car on the way back from the funeral. He inhaled deeply. This box. He knew it was there. In theory. But here, in practice, with the living accumulation of stirred and relived memories of the last few days still fresh upon him, it was a different story. Recent movements had been tectonic; previously buried layers had pushed up and lay exposed. He saw them like strata on an exposed cliff, like the gilt pages of a book, like the rings through the trunks of trees.

He looked down at the box, looked at how it was formed by sandwiched corrugations of thick paper. The box had sat up here undisturbed since the last move and, even before then, it had sat undisturbed, a lost archive of papers and artefacts from a time in his life he considered over. But the box belied that idea; it was insistent and alive to his presence. Stupid, he thought. It's just a box; but it refused to sit and be just a box. It shifted in the continuum. It made immediate and irresistible demands of him. He thought of Zoe handing him the memory stick and the folder of magazine pieces. He thought of Baz's metal card, Kelly's photos. He thought of playing the Mangled Mix on the way home and the ragged edges of canvas that had come loose at the edges of his dreams and been flapping in the half-light since Thursday.

He opened the box and looked in. There was an old biscuit tin on the top, a picture of a royal guard on a horse on the lid. There were some magazines, old raving titles, *Ravescene, Destiny, Cloud 9*, early *Mixmags* and an old sketchbook. There was a black record bag stuffed in at one end with, by the looks of it, a handful of records in it and a shoebox full of tapes with another notebook on top. At the bottom of the box, holding all this up, was a hefty pile of flyers which themselves sat on top of a split cardboard folder which looked like it too was full of flyers. Lee squatted down, took out the biscuit tin and opened it: Two whistles, one with a rainbow lace through it; passes and tickets on lanyards; loose tickets and passes and a club membership card; a green plastic grinder, its grooves and teeth grubby with resins and use; lighters – throwaways and clippers – one in a smiley holder with a lace so you could wear it around your neck. Lee dug under this top loose layer and found a crumpled, blue, king-size Rizla packet with a few skins still inside, some photos and two keys on a little bongo drum keyring. He put the tin down and took out the box of tapes. Recordings of raves and nights he'd been at and ones he hadn't. Some pirate radio stuff too; he noticed mixes that he'd seen on Zoe's memory stick a few days before. They used to be in a proper tape box, he thought. I wonder what happened to that. He put the shoebox down and pulled out the record bag. World Class Records, red letters on a black bag. Probably no longer there, he thought, and paused, briefly, in reverence to something lost. That shop and others like it had been like a community centre for ravers in the area, a common room, a coffee house, a gentleman's club. He looked inside the well-used bag; the records, although few, were corkers by the looks of it, although Lee didn't remember buying or owning half of them. He'd never really followed up on the whole DJing thing early on – he'd been too busy enjoying the party to give it the time it demanded, and it was expensive. He thought he'd already given all the records he had to either Rob or Zoe before it all came to a crashing end. They could be someone else's, he suggested to himself. Plausible but who knew now?

He pulled out a disc in a black sleeve. Moving Shadow logo on a white label, Kaotic Chemistry, 'Five in One Night'. He pushed it back and slid out another; Jazzie Joint on Nervous, 'Pump, Pump', *play at 45* scrawled on the yellow label. He made it three with the Positive Feedback EP, black biro on a white label. Nice, he thought, and grinned. In his head, just quietly, there was a rhythm. Lee pulled the box to him now and reached in and managed to get his fingers to grip on the edges of about one third of the flyers – so fucking slippery, he thought. He pulled them out into the now less feeble light of the ecobulb. They were clearly in no particular order and many had scruffy paint-specked discs of old Blu Tac on them, cleared from his old bedroom wall at his nan's, Lee explained.

"In The Beginning", Lichtenstein explosion on the front; there was a Mangled link to that night, same production crew, that's why he'd gone. Saw Mr C there for the first time.

*...offering the new faces on the scene the chance to hear the best of the top-class tunes that got the scene started and kept it progressively moving on. We offer you no sideshows, gimmicks or fun fair, just pure rave in two rooms of madness our aim...*

Fucking hell, Lee thought, it's like Shakespeare, or maybe Yoda...

*...to bring the people together in unity once again. An opportunity for all the original ravers who were there In The Beginning to come forward and show the people how it's done. Peace.*

Can't say fairer than that, he thought. And they're already calling for the "original ravers" to come forward and represent in... when was that? '91? Lee began to sift the flyers: *Destiny All Nighters... Fantazia takes you into 1993... Equinox... Love of Life... Labrynth...* more *Destiny... Eclipse... Dance Paradise... World Dance... Proper Stuff... Seduction... Peace Fest... Bliss.* He noted and namechecked the events as he shuffled and rifled through the shiny stack of sheets balanced on his knees. He took in the basic, photocopied, postcard-sized bedroom productions, with little more than a meet point and the names of a few DJs on them, to those with full-colour artwork on A4 sheets, featuring intrepid fantasy figures, John Pitre-style, matrixed landscapes, visionary worlds and mythical creatures. There were logos and trademarks on some of the later ones. In such a short time, thought Lee, a whole self-started, self-managed and directed industry had created itself. Graphics and design was his business and he knew it well, was good at it and he marvelled now at the work and energy that lay behind the stack of material on his knees. He picked out a Proper Stuff flyer. A5 size. A 3D line drawing of a warehouse. *Meet*

*Tesco's Milton* in large black type, *Proper Stuff*, white outlined in black as if written on the grey side of the warehouse. *Saturday 1st February* across the top. Great fucking nights, thought Lee; car park meets, convoy to a warehouse, just the essentials but done properly. They knew they delivered, you knew they delivered, so nothing else was needed on the flyer. It was a masterclass in understatement.

He picked out a Rush-Reactivate collaboration. A complex gate-fold with a print of an oil-painted sunset over what looked like a recently harvested and burnt-off wheat field but which was actually, he assumed, meant to be the sea around Clacton Pier. It was full of copy and, as he recalled, it had done exactly what it said it would. *Rush Till Dawn* was the headline inside, supported by *Reactivate... Kickin' Serious Flavour... This spectacular event has been constructed by people who know what you want, so 100% enjoyment is Guaranteed. Our DJ list was chosen for listening perfection.* And there they were in white on black: Colin Dale, Ray Keith, Kenny Ken, Mickey Finn, Rocky and Stu Banks amongst others.

Underneath that a monster flyer, A3, folded to fit in the box. He opened out the shiny coloured sheet and stared at it for a while, trying to make sense of the artwork. There was a lot going on, a lot being suggested. How much of it related to the event it was advertising was debatable but Lee loved it. It was so suggestive of the time, its self-made spirit. The bottom half of the flyer featured eight naked male figures in different states, representing, he guessed, the different stages in the life of man — the imagery was far from clear. One of the figures was in the open mouth of a giant snake and another walked up some steps to a waterfall and river that flowed from a distant, magical landscape. These figures representing the life of man formed a circle around a much bigger figure of the god Pan, hairy goat legs and horns, who was dancing and playing pipes.

The naked men appeared to be dancing to Pan's pipes. The top half of the sheet featured another large circle to match the one below. This one was red and its circumference was covered in tongues of flame like a sun. In the sun a naked angel-like figure held a winged helmet, or maybe it was a complex ancient stringed instrument, and it too seemed to be dancing. Around this sun were naked male and female angels who pulled up the men from the circle below into the circle above as they finished the course of their lives.

Lee remembered the event, vaguely: *The Pirate Club presents Future Myth at Roller Express*. How the images on the flyer represented the experience of that rave was now definitely beyond him. In general, he thought, the sweaty, drug-hyped, laser-washed reality of hundreds of hardcore ravers rarely matched the fantasy futures served up on some of these flyers. But that wasn't the point. The rave was the crucible in which a co-creation of fleeting existence was brought to life by an act of communal will and desire – he'd had this discussion before. The flyer depicted a feeling, an emotion, an internal sense held by hundreds of people simultaneously, thrown like a hologram into the shared space of one night – that was what the image tried to capture. That is what it was selling. By the morning, only a residue of the idea would remain, but it was powerful stuff, and that was what you took away with you to keep for the next time, to keep you going until you could do it all again. It was an ember kept alive in a pot, blown to life to build the next campfire. That, thought Lee, is what these flyers are getting at… although, to be honest, he conceded, some are definitely more successful than others.

Some of the later ones were a bit more businesslike. He picked out a few of them but planet Earth still appeared in many, and aliens and alien landscapes, and serene, disembodied heads floating in the sky. Maybe the ideas are a bit clearer there, he thought, and these ones, the ones which depicted lip-glossed, soft-pouting computer-generated girls in poses of sexual come-on, were very clear, although, apart from stage dancers, he supposed, that was never really an aspect of raving that he had encountered. He was kneeling now and looking to one side at two Life Utopia flyers; one of a huge eyeball which held the cosmos in its pupil and floated over a bull elephant walking the African plains, and the other, the ghostly drawn features of Bob Marley, John Lennon and Michael Jackson rising from the flames of the sun as it dawned behind Stonehenge, all seen through an open doorway flanked by two spangly ravers. Fucking brilliant, he thought. That is fucking brilliant.

Lee became aware of his attention being dragged back from Stonehenge at dawn to the cold in the loft by a sound. A bell. Something was happening. There was a bell ringing. 'Shit,' he said out loud; the doorbell was ringing. He put the flyers down in a hurry and, a little faster than was safe, got himself out of the loft and downstairs to open the door, half expecting to see the head of John Lennon floating above pre-historic sarsens as the delivery guy was moving to fill out a *We missed you…* card.

'Yes, mate,' said Lee, 'I'm here.' He signed on the screen and took in the parcel. It was for Marianne. He went to put the box on the kitchen table, paused and placed it on a chair instead. Might be shoes, he explained to himself. No harm done with some superstitions, he thought, and shoes were a good example. There were plenty of good reasons for keeping shoes off the table, he reasoned. Who wants shoes on the table? He paused again as his eye fell on the folder of Zoe's magazine articles. His head was still full of the flyers and he felt hungry for more rave chat. He sat down next to the shoes and swept the folder towards him.

## Hardcore Rave – Evidence of an Underground Movement

The Hardcore Rave scene that flourished in the first half of the 1990s was one of rare musical creativity and collective cultural innovation. Central to the character of that scene was its anonymity, its democracy, and its authentic underground conception, production and performance. The scene was outside of mainstream society and culture and was produced, largely independently, by those who enjoyed it. While this is not in itself unusual, what was unusual was the length of time that it remained outside of the mainstream given the unparalleled scale and scope of the movement.

By the time wider society was beginning to pay attention, Hardcore was already, effectively, over. It had evolved and become the common ancestor of several different genres. Labels and brands and identities that swirled and morphed in the early years had become part of an establishment. For Hardcore, the main flowering was over and it therefore avoided taint by the machines of mainstream culture. One of the effects of this is that there is no clear record of the scene. The material evidence of it is patchy and haphazard. Even the music, which obviously provides the biggest store of evidence, can sometimes be obscure and difficult to pin down. Other evidence is even more tricky to manage – I am thinking here of mix tapes – including recordings of pirate radio, flyers, video recordings and, of course, individual memories. There are a few one-off TV programmes and documentaries from this early time which should also be recognised, but these are the exceptions which prove the rule.

Interestingly, it is not the music per se which provides evidence of the scale and the scope of the scene, it is the mixtapes and the flyers; through these we can appreciate the geographical reach of Hardcore Rave and the sheer volume of activity the scene sustained. An average raver's flyer collection will provide examples of events happening around their locale and more widely, on Friday and Saturday nights throughout the year, with some regularly involving thousands of people. Just look at the ticket distribution lists on some flyers and you get an idea of how huge this all was. The flyers also provide evidence of what a rave "offered". They describe the actuals, that is the line-up – very often stellar when looked at today – the technical production and the party extras and side-entertainments; and they also reveal, usually through the artwork on the front, the emotional or philosophical promise of the event – the "trip" that the event will send you on.

In some ways, it is the flyers and not the music that reveal most about the scene now because these are a way into the experience of the individual nights that ravers attended. That and the most important evidence store of all, the memories of those who were there. Personal memories really bring the other evidence to life and there is nothing like sorting through old flyers with a group of mates from the time with a few choice mix tapes on in the background to take you back. The old Hardcore Raver has all the evidence they need of the part they played; they have no need to go anywhere else for content, for review or for validation. They can consult their own personal archives and memories. But the very thing that gave Hardcore its cultural integrity – its development outside the mainstream – is the thing that could threaten its survival. The multitude of memory which brings the scene to life almost defies archiving and cataloguing; it is fractal and kaleidoscopic. Thankfully, some enterprising enthusiasts are building web-based resources of material, but even these tend to neglect the difficult-to-gather memories and personal stories. The Hardcore Ravers are a living testament of an extraordinary time that is in danger of being neglected and lost. More of the Hardcore need to record their stories because theirs is the story of the biggest youth movement ever to have been experienced in the UK. Over to you, Kitchen Crew.

Zoe E Marr/DJ Zoem, Spin Junky, January 2007

Lee was strongly moved to get back in the loft and look at the flyers again. He felt drawn there, like he was on a tether being wound back in. It made him nervous; a nervousness framed with excitement, bordering on unease, seamed with adrenaline. It was the edginess of a new venue on a big night; anxious to get in, anxious about getting in, held at a wincing pitch by ripples of infra-sound, just on the boundary of perceptible, which vibrate deep in the belly and tremor through the feet. He let the sensation subside and adjusted the pace of his imagination. He just wanted to check out one or two things on the back of what Zoe had said in her magazine piece. All perfectly reasonable, completely understandable. Shame she hadn't got on to the actual content of some of the artwork but that was probably another, and different, piece. All this and more circled its way around the net of Lee's mind as his body, almost of its own volition, moved up the ladder and disappeared into the loft through the square hole in the landing ceiling, the soles of his trainers the last thing to go.

# NINE

THE FLYERS WERE SPREAD ACROSS THE LOFT
boards where Lee had left them. The box of tapes, the biscuit
tin and the record bag were there too. The large cardboard box
they had been in and which once had contained forty-eight
packets of biscuits, was there too, waiting, patient, still. Lee
squatted by the open box and reached in for the main stack
of flyers. He quickly found what he was after and removed
a flyer for Helter Skelter, December 1993. He opened it out
and looked down to the lists of ticket distributors along the
bottom. *Just look at the ticket distribution lists on some flyers
and you get an idea of how huge this all was...*, Zoe had said in
her Disc Junky piece. He scanned through the list of agents.
Names of towns and contacts in small type were stacked in
columns across the base of the flyer: Bolton, Yeovil, Doncaster,
King's Lynn, Weymouth, Liverpool, Birmingham, Blackburn,
Sunderland, Swindon, Leeds, Bristol and Stevie in Scotland,

to name but a few. Phenomenal, he thought. The whole fucking country was covered by Helter Skelter's list of ticket sellers. He picked out a Dreamscape flyer – *Get Smashed 1994*. Similar story. No Stevie in Scotland but there was Colin in Gwynedd. Coaches too were advertised on that one. These were probably the high-water mark, he thought; there or thereabouts anyway. Nevertheless, still fucking amazing. He'd never paid those agent lists much attention at the time, but now the unity and community implicit in them made him feel like crying. He turned back to the Helter Skelter flyer and read the words printed in the middle, direct from the event management about their previous rave a few months earlier:

> …*The doors opened at 9 o'clock the warehouse filled to capacity and the party rocked for 10 hours over three thousand people dancing smiling communicating and most of all enjoying themselves. The chemistry was right we would like to point out DJ Sy did not turn up because he did not have a driver and Ellis-D informed us on the 17th that he couldn't remember being booked when he had been so could you please sort your lives out and not let us down boys! Our commiserations to Jack Frost who got nicked for speeding on his way to us…*

No punctuation, no PR filters, totally personal, totally honest, thought Lee. Phenomenal; quite simply, fucking phenomenal. And now his eyes did fill up and he clenched his jaw against the tears.

He moved his thumb through the corner of the stack like a flip book. His eyes were startled by the animation he caused. Logos and graphics, surreal figures and colour danced around his hand and, just faintly, he heard the mash and thump of music far away, rising and falling on the wind, giving a time and beat to the colour that danced around his hand. It was the noise of a party you've almost reached but can't quite find the road to, he thought. Let's park on the verge and walk across the fields. It seemed like a reasonable approach and he pictured himself and a small crowd, all MA2s, puffas and bucket hats, branded trainers and bum bags, abandoning two cars at the side of a dark, empty road. Apart from them and a broken fence, there are no other signs of humanity; rags of cloud flap overhead, passing stars and a thick, sickle moon, and they head out across a rough field of tussocks and fallen fence posts, towards the sound of a deep, pounding resonance and the green lines of lasers crossing and recrossing in a patch of grey charcoal sky just above a distant blotch of trees.

Lee recalled his attention and reasserted himself back to his place in real life, back to his loft, and the sound of distant music began to recede. Weird, he thought, and held himself very still as he turned and angled his head like a radio telescope to locate the sound. He thought he could hear something. He told himself it must have come from outside. A passing car. Maybe it was just the way the wind carried the sound of the 406. He flicked the flyers again. The sound began to swell. No, there it was again, he was sure of it. A mighty bass sound, near but so deeply contained and confined, he mainly heard it through the substance of his body, like a whale receiving vibrations through the ocean. The sound resonated and percussed, not clearly enough to identify but enough to reveal a rhythm. Again, his scalp prickled and sprung and set a wave that ran over and back across his whole skin. He shuddered and sharply exhaled, pulling himself quickly back up onto his feet. The movement was too quick and he struggled for balance; he pitched back and then forward, lurching towards the open mouth of the biscuit box. He thrust out the hand that held the flyers as a counter and as he did, he looked down the length of his outstretched arm at a pulsing mass of spinning colour where his hand should have been. He wobbled and put out his other hand to steady himself, placing it straight into the tin full of passes and membership cards. He grasped at a bundle of lanyards and lifted them out, held them in a clenched fist like proof of achievement, evidence of sacrifice, the laces and laminated cards dripping from his fingers. For a moment he felt stable and fixed, the two outstretched hands countering his inclination to pitch over, but even as he registered the moment of control he felt a charge surge in both his hands; light spun from his fingers and split the orange haze of the loft space while his head filled with the crump and skid of the gathering music. And now there were voices. Many voices sounding together to make a low, sustained roar. A roar like rushing water or wind. A roar that came through smoke and night air and chilled the sweat on his face and on his back where his shirt clung damply. It was before him, behind him, in his ears; it was calling him over and…

Lee shook his head and blew a soundless whistle to compose himself. There was no sweat on him. There were no voices. There was no music. There were no lights. He was in his badly lit loft, sounds of the street outside and a far hum of never-ceasing traffic on the North Circular. The weather, as usual, was paying no attention to the forecast and it was cold, and he, before a box of old stuff in his loft, some of it spread out on the bare, compressed woodchip boards, squatted, his outstretched hands grasping memorabilia from an energetic time. He dared to look up now and glanced from hand to hand, there the flyers, there the passes and the lanyards, and he moved his head slowly back and forth from one to the other. The rhythm of his movements seemed to enliven the air; it became neon on dark plush. It shimmered mathematically fine and fragile, marking out fine elevations from the infinite layers of dark space. The animations came on with fresh intensity and with them the noise of bass, this time seeping, squeezing and assembling itself through brick and concrete, and blocked and blanked windows. Waves of voices, chat and excitement, whistles and horns, to multiple powers of ten, roaring like tsunamic oceans in his ears... Lee dropped the flyers and the passes down onto the boards and the contact was broken. He braced himself with one hand on the floor and the other on the rafter in front of him. His head bowed, his eyes closed, he breathed and listened. It was still and the only sound a car door in the street. An engine starting, loud and full, then easing through the gears and away. He opened his eyes and looked up. The loft shone cold and pale as before, full of stacked boxes and crates, full of his archived past and exiled stuff. Before him on the boards the spilled stack of coloured flyers, just printed paper, a mini-display of the art of a bygone time. Alongside, where he'd dropped them, a messy twist of lanyards and old passes and membership cards from clubs and raves long over. The biscuit box they had come out of gaped like a spent jack-in-the-box. He relaxed a little at that thought.

He hadn't looked at this stuff for a while. Until the last few days he had kept thoughts and memories of those times a long way back. He had no need and no desire to go back there, why would he? Until the last few days he would have told himself that there was nothing there for him, that his business was in the present and his interest was in the future and not back over his shoulder. But the last few days had seen the past rush back up at him with frightening speed. So many things submerged had surfaced quickly, it had been seismic and, by all accounts, it had freaked him right out. *You've had a right bloody turmoil these last few days*, he counselled himself. History had surfaced too quickly in him and expanded in his blood like decompressing gases; gone to his head and made him see and hear things that were not really there. Well, he revised, they were there but they belonged to another time, one that he had boxed up years ago. It had been so many years, he told himself, that suddenly opening up the box had been... well... it had been quite overwhelming. And these words to himself, words that Marianne might have used, calmed him.

Lee reached into the box again for the folder of flyers that still lay there. Probably leave that for another time, he thought. Hang on, though; there was something else in the box; underneath the folder, right at the bottom. He pulled out the thick mass of a road map, and some of his recently restored composure ebbed away, replaced by vulnerable reminiscence. Lee had always loved maps and what they could enable, especially when combined with driving; driving and maps, two things that he loved. They were two sides of the same coin really, he thought, at least they used to be before the internet. With a car and a map you could go anywhere, find anything, reveal the world to yourself. Don't see many road maps about these days, he thought. I mean, who uses one? Someone had told him that satnav was now part of the driving test. Not even he had one in the car anymore. That was no fucking good, he thought. He would remedy that, pronto. A good up-to-date map was going to live in the pocket behind the driver's seat from now on, as it bloody well should. And Eva, yes, Eva was going to learn how to use it and how to love it; he would teach her how to read it, how to make sense of its lines and its marks and symbols. He smiled to himself, he'd have a go anyhow. He opened the map at random and it fell open to show the A120, the M11, Essex and Suffolk and bits of East London. There were crosses of biro here and there on the open pages which trained themselves on him like crosshairs.

He closed the map emphatically and held it before him like an empty plate. His right thumb rested on the corner of the inside cover from which a small rectangular piece had been untidily torn away. He opened the map and looked at the first page. The symbols and conventions of a road map spread in glyphic lines and shapes before him. Small orange-brown particles speckled the crease where the cover connected with the pages of the map. Old bits of tobacco, he thought. Probably some bits of hash in there too. *How would they smoke?* he wondered, squinting at the place where the pages intersected. He flicked at the map again; it fell open naturally at the same page as before.

His eye found the start of the M11 at Redbridge and followed the blue line of the motorway as it left London and made its way to Junction 8 and the A120. On this map there was no new road carving through woods and fields all the way to Dunmow, just the lumpy red line of the old road, sticky and congested, to Marks Tey. Lee followed the route back into London and picked up the North Circular back to where he now lived. As he did, the journey ran like a time-lapse across the screen of his memory; the North London Orbital, a grey rumble under and over, low-rise and neglect, semi and terrace, retail parks and industrial estate. He ran the journey back the other way, and the road sped like a game to pass Woodford and reach Redbridge. He picked up the M11 and swept into Essex; not the old historical Essex of Havering, and Barking, east of the East End, not the lands of the dirt chute A12 and A13, littered with dead cars and flayed tyres, like bodies in the ditch. No, this was open country, away from the industry of the river, still smeared at first with the greasy patina of London, but countryside nonetheless. The map showed how the towns here were surrounded by green and how, until the coming of the M11, they would have seemed very distant from the City. Lee saw how the motorway cut a careless path through this territory, bringing everything around closer to the gravity-pull of the urban centre.

Lee looked hard at the map, focussing on the section of the road just north of the M25. There was a point somewhere on this section where the motorway passed through a gap in the crest of a tree-covered ridge and you could really see the extent of the open country. The view here opened out before you, whichever direction you travelled. One way, it was a darkening grey and pink city skyline hovering over the field and the forest and the clay and the chalk beneath; heading back to Essex and away from the city, the land laid out like a quilt, a vale of farms and woodland pockets in a spread seamed by hedges and ditches, a cartoon-illustrated view of the countryside as seen from a hot air balloon. Next time he made the journey, Lee promised, he would find the point on the satnav and mark it on the map.

He continued to follow the route on the map, going north past the grey urban outpost of Harlow and the wedge of space across to Chelmsford to Junction 8, and the Birchanger interchange again. This junction was pivotal in his memory of the journey; it was the point where the City finally fell away and fully ceded to the old countryside of North Essex. While on the motorway, even though you could see the countryside all around, it was out of touch and London held you by a cord of concrete and tar and stone. But as soon as you were off that road and rose to meet the scrubby wood on the Birchanger Roundabout, more old-fashioned ways of travelling took over.

For Danny-Lee, this route was a journey immortalised and etched onto the soul. He wondered for how many others it was similar. How many others like him could, in the last decade of the twentieth century, trace the history of their young lives along familiar patterns of roads? The roads he had used in that time had taken on character; he knew them, they had life and they spoke to him. Lee thought again about the lists of ticket agents and how the roads everywhere had come to life to deliver on the promise at the bottom of the flyer; to deliver a communion of drugs and music and congregation that would change everybody's lives forever. The roads connected the places and carried the people between the places, the roads were the way in and their presence was the way back again. Being a part of this traffic and movement and flux and migration and import and export awakened a living spirit in the roads, reminded them of past glories and times before thoughtless mechanical to-ing and fro-ing. He realised then that he had already had a whiff of their energy on the way back from the funeral.

Lee turned the page of the map to show the roads into Suffolk and Norfolk and Cambridge and remembered how as well as taking him and his friends from Essex into East London, they had also pushed them out into the emptier spaces of East Anglia, again to lose their minds and surrender their bodies to the pulse of the music and the thrum of the drugs; to take up the magic that was being laid upon the land. *Was that what he was tapping into now?* he wondered. The music he kept hearing in the distance; the dance of lights and the flickering energy round his outstretched hands when he held the flyers and the passes? It was still there somewhere, wasn't it? It was still there; buried and latent but there waiting to be brought back to life, waiting for the time to be right.

Lee looked up from the map. But that time was over, he told himself. That party had ended. He had ended it himself. Knocked it on the head. Taken a priest to it. Roads had become roads again; some of them had even altered so completely that the character of the journeys made upon them was changed forever and the places they joined, changed too. Lee reminded himself that he had boxed up his flyers and his whistles and his old passes and memberships, the cheeky Day-Glo hash pipe and the little pill cutter – still dusty, he noticed – and the tapes and the records that had had no deck to be played on. He'd put the box in his mum's loft and then in a mate's garage, and when he and Marianne had moved to this house they went into the loft in which he had now rediscovered them. If he'd been asked, he would have remembered they were there, but he never was asked and they had remained out of his consciousness. But, he thought, I didn't get rid of it all. I ended it, I drew a line, but I kept a box and I took it with me. Did that mean something? Did some part of me know and trust in something that the rest of me did not? Was I always going to be in this place, this place where I am now, at some point? All this time, was there a thread that I was spooling out behind me, knowing that I would follow it back here? *Were there other ways it might have happened? he considered.* There were other ways, he concluded, but it happened this way.

Something flashed in his peripheral vision. The untidily gathered flyers fluttered. He picked up the bulk of them in his spare hand and the effect was instant. A sizzling charge and he rocked as it passed across his chest, down his other arm to the map and back again. The lines of the roads writhed and shunted in time to… He could hear the music again. Bass, big and resonant, nearby, yet confined and separated from him. His senses were becoming confused. He looked at the map and it writhed and turned on the end of his arm, to open before him in panorama. The roads looped and snaked across the land on the page. He watched them, mesmerised. He saw too how the estuary shape of the Thames was an elephant's head, its trunk pressing up between Essex and Kent to reach the headwaters of Middle England. London was balanced on the backs of an ox and a rat who sniffed and snorted, tails and whiskers twitching and trembling. Lee tried to bring his focus back to the drab stacks of boxes in the loft, but all he could see were the flyers, revolving now in a mad collage of colour and graphics and fantastic figures, the music louder, more insistent, more defined. The sound was coming from the box. The sound, the music, Lee realised, was coming up out of the mouth of the box. He could almost see it. He levelled his gaze as best he could at the dark square of the opening and saw it flex with music, saw the bass shudder the space like it was a speaker cone. Then, slabs of skidding synth sent the heads of Rob and Scott and Jason and Zoe and Kelly and Baz up out of the box and they spun around it, all talking at him, all with something to say. There were other faces too, unknown people from dark and smoky circus tents, sports halls, old cinemas and skate rinks; faces met once at random moments of intense significance and forever with him. Now he saw the faces of family as he systematically interviewed them at one speed wedding or another. Baz intervened now, saying this and that, and now Scott, and they were off, flying into the forest like bats, senses honed and faultless to move them impossibly fast between the trees; now skimming like skaters along the frozen channels and ditches of the Fens, reeds flashing by, with slower processions of ragged lines of Scots pine. Then to a braked stop-turn, a glittering fall of ice crystals and he was at Uncle Shane and Aunty Cynthia's house. Scott and Jason were laughing, clearly stoned, and he was stoned too and laughing with them. Aunty Cynthia was making tea. They'd been out all night and had just got back, and they shone with the collective energy of the party and it arced still between them.

Lee turned in laughter to suddenly face the road ahead. He was driving. No warning, just suddenly driving. There was a concentration around the skin of his eyes and a shard of sobriety lodged behind them that told him he was headed for home, although where exactly home was, was neither clear nor relevant. It was like driving in a video game; the movement was headlong and hovered around the very edge of control, often going over it and pulling back only with stomach-lurching effort. The road he careered down was a road on a map and it was paved with flyers. As he drove, the world unfolded around him and the road paved itself into existence in front of him. He could see it self-create in rapid sequences of programmed moves, and patterns spread out, branching and dividing, fractalizing, spreading in an intricate web, like nerves or blood vessels, nourishing and being nourished by the country travelled. The palpitating network connected all the words and symbols and colours of the map, strung together all its places and features like a mycorrhiza, like a living tangle of threads, linking life and knowledge in the earth underground. The network lived and was busy with talk and conversation and with whispered and hinted tales and secrets. Some of them came to him intact and coherent and he heard whole stories in an instant in the voice of Grandad Swigler. And Grandad Swigler, who smelt of tobacco and leather and shaving, sat next to him in the car and told him about the places he had been and the places he would go to, and he introduced him to every road, lane and path and showed him all their stopping places, the "atcha tan" and where the country was at its best. And he and Grandad Swigler, who always wore a hat and walked with a stick, were joined on the road by characters and their cars from the films and TV that he had loved as a kid – *The Dukes of Hazzard*, *The Blues Brothers*, *Knight Rider*, *Convoy*, *Cannonball Run*, *Back to the Future*, *The Gumball Rally*, *James Bond*. They drove together, and together they roared out of sight over the crest of a green-striped hill into the light falling from a brazen, falling, smiling orange sun.

Lee gasped with the intensity of the vision; it had come to him in a fraction of time – a micro-dream, he thought, and moved to steady himself. He dropped the map and the flyers into the box and they fell and continued to fall as if the box was bottomless. He watched them spin away, a strobe of light and colour, moving in and out of focus. He was leaning forward now, hands braced against his knees, breathing into the keening emotion. Sound from the blank space of the box drew him in. He reached out one arm as if to push back at the air and the noise and tilted forward with the effort, and then he was falling, the mouth of the box dark, open and compelling, defining the flashing colour of the map and the flyers turning over and over as they fell far, far down in the strobe-swept darkness. Lee shut his eyes and patches of retina-burn slewed on his eyelids; their shape an offer of descent and fall which he accepted in full and took the drop; the music moved on him nearer and nearer, clarifying, its sound broadening and then it washed over him.

# TEN

'O DANNY-LEE, YOU'RE TRIPPIN' LIKE A BAD-BOY. *O Danny-Lee, what can you fuckin' see? O Danny-Lee...*' Lee surfaced slowly from the wash of the dream-state he had been in to the sound of Rob singing a personalised version of 'Danny Boy' while slicing the air in front of his face with his hands. Rob wanted Lee involved in whatever was going on in the waking world and did not want him wasting valuable chill-out time asleep. Rob felt it was important to squeeze every last drop of juice from every weekend of raving. This was part of Rob's raving profile and Lee was familiar with it but, besides this sense of Rob's personality, Lee had no idea where he was in time or in space. Most of his sensation and his consciousness remained in the dream, falling without fear in a well of music. He watched Rob through one half-open eye as he searched his head for clues, for fixed points he could use to triangulate. He worked back through the madness of the dream; there were roads, maps, flyers and faces. Not unpleasant, but intense and loaded, and nothing stayed still or substantial for long enough to become sense. His entire self had been bound up in the dream and now, even though he was awake, it was as if he was still wired into that other world and disconnected from this one. Whatever happened next, he realised with amazement, would wire him back into reality, but it could do so at one of any number of points. The thought relaxed him and he opened both eyes and looked up at Rob, who still hummed his tune and made the odd dance move with his hand in Lee's direction.

Lee looked at the ceiling above him. A large fractal-patterned wall hanging was pinned above the bed on which he was lying. He turned to the wall against which the bed was positioned. About half the wall space alongside the bed and the area behind the headboard were covered with flyers. Cartoon faces, spirals, clouds, rainbows, moons, suns, dancing figures and trance-inducing vortexes. Scott's bedroom. They'd clearly been out the night before and were taking a breakfast stop and chill-out in Bury before heading back to Braintree. Lee put his hand in his pocket and felt the car key on its Skip-It Skip Hire key fob. He'd passed his test in September and his nan had given him Grandad's old car the following month. He was getting somewhere. It looked like spring outside the window. He looked back at the wall of flyers: Eclipse, Hhhouse Parteee, Bliss, Forbidden Planet, Richard's Parties, Protein, Kite High, Run Silent, Run Deep. The focus was tightening and he was close to touchdown. He drew back the curtains in the half-lit room of his mind with a decisive movement and the light flooded in.

'Rob, you fuckin' arsewipe,' he said, 'where'd we go last night?' Rob looked at him through narrowed eyes. He suspected a trick but a moment of scrutiny told him that Lee was genuine. Rob fully understood the possible need for such a question in the circumstances.

'Destruction...Thetford warehouse job. Finished early, didn't it... police, technical stuff, don't think anyone knew what was goin' on. We followed those lads we met to that thing in the forest. You know that old ruin... some geezer with decks in it... We stayed for ages. You were dancing with the Prodigy boys, you spangled fuckin' cunt.'

'Was I?' said Lee. He could remember the forest now and something of the warehouse, but dancing with the Prodigy had not stayed with him. He wouldn't recognise them anyway, he thought. Didn't really matter, did it? He shrugged. 'Don't really matter, does it?'

'It all matters, man, it all matters... so then when we'd agreed to go, you got talking to some other boys where we were parked and we stayed with them for ages. They gave us a pill, remember, a little black square. They had that Renault with the alloys and blacked-out windows... fuck-off Alpine system – independently powered, and a two K Sub – had the boot up and all the fuckin' doors open... we were dancin' round it. Fuckin' mint system that was... thought it was gonna shake the fuckin' car to bits.' As Rob said those final words, he shared with Lee a thought bubble; it showed a clearing in the forest, dark with shadows, the ground rough, tussocked grass carpeted with pine needles. In the space, several hatchbacks and a white van roughly encircled a yellow Renault which gleamed in the dew and half-light of approaching dawn. The boot and all the doors of the car were open; music exploded out, bass and drums thumping. Several figures in baggy jeans, in short dresses, in big sweatshirts with logos, in jackets – bombers and puffas – against the cold, heads in caps and woolly hats, long hair – girls and boys – in ponytails, dancing or just watching in attitudes of approval. The forest birds meanwhile persisted with the dawn chorus and dropped their song like samples into the spaces and breakdowns of the music. There was a beat between Rob and Lee as they recognised joint ownership of the thought.

The tetris of Lee's memory was assembling itself quickly now and he swung himself round on the bed and sat up. The drive back here with the sun coming up over the trees. Gold and green and crystal blue, and deep, dew-drenched shadows cast by bright slanting layers of lengthening light. How could he forget that? He'd nearly gone off the road looking at the sky through a gap in the trees. Yes, they'd been to that warehouse in Thetford before… bit like that place in Cambridge, the carpet warehouse with the big runway to a platform in the middle. That had been a good night, he remembered. Major comedown the following week, though. No proper flyer for that one, just a meet point, a number and a code word – "fishponds". Fiver on the door. Dodgy-looking security. Bit like last night really, he started to recall, as the earlier memory triggered the later one; dark, probably illegal, wicked lasers and a big rig. Shame it finished early, but then if it hadn't, they wouldn't have gone to the forest. Always options and opportunities, he concluded. 'Always options and opportunities,' he said, lecturing out loud. 'Where one door closes, another opens. There is always something going on somewhere, if you look fuckin' hard enough.'

'Yea, well, we didn't look too fuckin' hard, more like it found us.'

'Where are the others?' asked Lee as he finished building the spliff he'd started almost as soon as he'd woken up, putting the magazine he'd used as a rolling surface, together with associated spliff-building paraphernalia scattered on it, back on the small table next to the bed where he'd found it.

'In the shed, mate. Where d'ya think? Playin' tunes, makin' the most of the morning. You've got all next week to sleep and feel like shit.'

'All right, man. I'm up now. Chuck us the mirror.' Lee gestured towards a small mirror in a scratched wooden frame lying on the window sill. Rob passed it and Lee proceeded to tap a small amount of powder onto it from a small paper wrap. Lee chopped and crushed the powder with the card that was already lying on the mirror and deftly swept and arranged it into two lines and pulled a fiver from his pocket. He rolled the creased money into a tube as best he could and, with one hand holding one end of the tube in his right nostril, and the other hand holding closed his left nostril, he smartly sniffed one of the lines of crushed speed up into his nose. He savoured and managed the burn for a moment before passing the mirror to Rob, who repeated the action without question.

## //

The shed at Uncle Shane and Aunty Cynthia's was more than your average shed. The walls were precast concrete and it had a corrugated roof sealed with bitumen. It was insulated and lined inside and there was a small but powerful gas heater. It was big and divided into two "rooms". A large shelving unit and a curtain divided the space. The front half was a workshop and garage for Uncle Shane's Lambretta scooters; the back half was for Scott's decks and sound rig. As Lee pushed aside the curtain-door, Zoe looked up at him from behind the decks and grinned from under Kelly's orange bucket hat. She pointed a conspiratorial finger at him which she wagged in time to the music; 'Bitin' Back' mixing, big and self-aware, into 'Playing With Knives'. The others were arranged around the space on an old leather sofa and a couple of stools. The air was heavy with spliff and cigarette smoke. Uncle Shane and Aunty Cynthia were, Lee supposed, liberal parents. Uncle Shane was his mum's older brother.

He knew she officially didn't approve of "all that" – "all that" was how she referred to her brother's tolerant attitude to drugs and loud, *modern* music. Lee's mum tutted a lot and pursed her lips when "them and their ways" came up. But, deep down, he thought, he detected an admiration on her part for her brother and for the way he stuck to his principles and continued, into his later adult life, to enjoy the pleasures and adhere to the priorities he had had when he was young.

Aunt Cynthia was a kindred spirit – only a kindred spirit would have hooked up with Uncle Shane, he thought. They had been Mods. Correction. They were Mods. They had the scooters, the clothes, the music, the attitude and the fucking haircuts. And they understood that their kids were drawn by a similar power; the intoxifying power of youth combined with being part of a movement, an active movement and self-created lifestyle. It was them, through Scott and Jason, that put us on to *Quadrophenia* – such a wicked film on a comedown, thought Lee. For them, rave was another youth tribe – Punk, Teds, Two-Tone, Goths, Bikers, Mods, Hippies – and it was the one their sons had chosen and they got that. They didn't really get the music, they said, but they knew the appeal of self-organising to gather together in the presence of your music, played loud and powerful. Also, the drugs. They got that too. Education and trusted sources were their caution and guidance. They didn't do any of that anymore, but purple hearts and speed had been at the heart of their younger years. Sometimes they'd have a little stories-of-the-sixties session and try to best the younger generation with their tales of excess and scrapes with the law. They'd also talk about the violence, which was something Lee and his cousins didn't get. But they knew it was a big part of Mod culture; pitched battles with crude and improvised weapons as standard and not just for the beach on bank holidays. Lee could just about remember these still taking place when he was little. Lee's mum, too, who had been a half-hearted biker at the insistence of his dad, would tell them how she used to carry a hammer in her biker jacket to whack Mods on the back of the head as his dad overtook them on his bike. Lee had heard his mum and her brother talk and laugh about this on the rare occasions when they had had a family get-together.

'That's how it was, gel,' he'd say, taking a drag on his roll-up. 'No fucken 'ard feelin's…' at which he would smile wickedly, his mum laughing knowingly. About the only time she did laugh these days, he thought. As loved-up ravers, they were horrified and disbelieving but at the same time, knew only too well what "going-out" meant before rave; how "normal" going-out now could still be an activity where violence lurked at every corner.

Lee squeezed onto the sofa next to Kelly.

'All right, Kells?' he said, sparking his joint and adding to the smoke that already hung in the air. Kelly turned to him and blew him an affirmative kiss before turning back to whatever she was discussing with Baz. Zoe brought in some percussive piano, and the vocal implored him, had faith in his love, hit him with a sincerity that matched his own perfectly. The speed was kicking in and before the leather was even warm beneath him, Lee was on his feet and dancing. Hitting the breaks and the on-beats with his head, moving his hips to the shuffle-snare and piano-roll, fists in front, lifting up for the down-stroke.

'Heeey… Danny-Lee is in the house,' greeted Jason, dancing towards him like a crab from where he had been rummaging in the record crate at the side of the table on which the decks stood. They danced round each other for a few bars. 'Good sleep, mate?'

'Yea, s'pose. Didn't know I'd gone to sleep and didn't know where I was when I woke up. Mad dreams. All right now, though.'

'You was well on it last night, boy… top fuckin' banana. Good, wun it?… In the forest 'n' that… yeeer, boi.'

'Yea, man,' said Lee, and passed the spliff as Zoe came at him from behind the decks, her hard-fought-for deck time up.

'This, this, this…' said Zoe, a flyer held emphatically in her right hand. 'Let's go to this… next big night. It's in Cambridge, but not the Corn Exchange, the other one… that sports hall… Kedgeree Kedgeree, whatever it is. It was good last time. We always have a right laugh in Cambridge.' Zoe knew she could manage the itinerary as far as Lee was concerned. He deferred to her judgement on these things mostly and, she thought, encouraged it. Like he did when he helped her with getting on the decks and mixing. She could rely on Lee to make some "space" for her when the boys were buzzing and bent on world domination, as per fucking usual. She could fight her own corner, sure, she knew that, but back-up was always welcome. Lee took the flyer and looked at the kissing heads in a swirl of psychedelic hair.

He turned it over and read from the flyer: *Bliss… another night of ecstatic emotion… Kelsey Kerridge Sports Hall… Cambridge… From the branches of wisdom, stem the seed of truth, and from the seed of truth comes peace of mind… Bliss 1991.* Lee nodded. 'Bliss is good,' he said. 'Always bank on a Cambridge night. Let's go.' Zoe smiled.

'It'll be fuckin' wicked, you know it will.' She was perfectly convinced of her prediction and so was Lee. It was true, he thought, Cambridge had always delivered. Eclipses at the Corn Exchange, the warehouse parties with no name, meets at Milton Tesco's, Bar Hill, The Fountain, The Ship. Lee had no clear idea where these places were, even less how they managed to find them half the time, but the names were burned into his brain, and he had a flash-vision of the first one they went to… Rob bent over in the space between the front seats of the Polo – the sides of both seats already bearing the burn marks of previous, similar poses – trying to read the map with a lighter... Zoe peering through the windscreen trying to pick up clues as to which of the other cars on the road might also be heading for a deserted car park to meet up before going on to dance for ten hours in a carpet warehouse. Eclipse, though, was easy. Corn Exchange, centre of town, multi-storey car park. Wicked. That first Eclipse last year had been the first big licensed rave for all of them. Even for Scott and Jason, it was a new one. Lee could still feel the buzz in his bones from it nearly six months on, and he let it take him back, all the way back to that night and what followed...

# ELEVEN

LEE HAD BEEN STUNNED BY THE LIGHTING AND the décor of that first Eclipse. It had been amazing. That alone, he reckoned, would have brought him up and kept him there but, combined with a nameless white E, taken in two halves, he had had the most intense seven hours of his life. It was the first time he'd seen dancers and proper visuals at an event as well. And the giant inflatable balls. Fuck me, he thought as he remembered the way the balls had moved around the main arena like living things. The stimulation was at overload; the needle bounced against the instrument casing beyond the red. Pretty much everyone was on those same pills, he thought. They'd gone with their own supply, courtesy of Scott, but they were obviously from a bigger local batch and the whole place was on the same buzz. Shit, he said to himself, remembering that some people had clearly done a whole one, or more, including Kells and Baz. You could tell who they were, he laughed to himself, they were the ones hanging on to the walls or bent over in a corner rushing their fucking tits off. Even a half was almost overwhelming at first and he had been forced to find his own bit of wall to cling on to for a bit. He had then manoeuvred his way to the chill-out area in the foyer to work on basic coherence and orientation. That's when and where he'd met that bloke who'd spun his already fragmented brain round the fucking corner, talking about evolution and insects. Lee remembered how he had been largely incapable in the face of the bloke's hyper-drive stream of consciousness but had, eventually, locked on to the music in the main room to help pull himself up and back to the dance, his brain firing in all directions, tracking the arc of its own thoughts and dissolving them as it did so. Safe to say, he confirmed to himself, I was bolloxed.

Back in the main room, the music and the lights and the visuals took over from where insect-man had left off. But the effect was more mellow, soaring, rolling, smoothed out. He was more at his own disposal rather than being at that of another. He felt at ease and that the limits of his senses could now cope with the stimulation they were receiving. For a while he stood, swaying slightly with the vibrations of the music in the air, head tilted slightly up, looking out and around him from just under his eyelids. He took it all in, dwelt on details, focussed on individual elements of the whole. And he asked questions. How did they all know, all these people, what to do? Where did they learn it? All of them, every single person here, all these young, ordinary nothings from nowhere special, with nowhere to go and nothing to do at the weekends until they're old enough to drink and then that's all they'll do, how did they suddenly know how to do this? And, with that thought in the fore of his mind, shaping his whole perception, he surveyed 270 degrees around him, absorbed the defiance, the pure energy, the drive of imagination. The dancers, the DJs, the technicians, the promoters, the smokers, the chewers, the chatters and trippers; the smoke and the strobes and the bass and the lasers. Where did we get it? Who taught us?

And with these questions in fading echoes sounding in his head and his senses brim-full, he closed his eyes and purred away on what he had absorbed, like one of those toy cars you pull back again and again on its rear wheels until it has no more capacity and which, when you then let go, whizzes away across the floor. And Lee whizzed away, eyes closed, for a stretch of time he could not possibly account for; for time that moved backwards, that moved forwards, that tilted up and swooped down. The world of eyes-closed was astounding and bountiful. Astounding and bountiful, he repeated the words which he didn't even realise were in his vocabulary, and he regarded his new world. Before him, running and winding a way through the landscape of the world, a road; an illustration of a road but also a real road that moved beneath his striding feet at great speed, like a treadmill turning to the tempo of the music, the music that is everywhere and inhabits everything in the world behind his closed eyes. Illustrated trees and flowers blur in his vision as he passes them. Straight ahead, the regular rise and fall of his knees and the bouncy pad of his massive fat-white-fat-laced-fat-striped trainer-encased feet as they hit one side of the road and then the other. At the same time, his eyes are in the road like cat's eyes and he can see the soles of his trainers now and the shadows they cast, as they drop from maximum lift to bounce on the smooth stone flags of the road. Energy and balance are super-refined and he could just bowl along that road for as long as it takes. The world for Lee is yellow and green and blue and, in this world, he has become the moving white-lined figure projected onto the stage backdrop. He is incarnated as that figure, it has been brought to life as him, he is inhabited by it, he has taken possession of it; he has taken an avatar and in that form leads himself in daring expedition across the fantasy world of his own imagination.

Is that the music from *Space Odyssey?* He pitches and yaws with the unexpected classical break. *Crikey fucking O'Reilly, here we fucking go,* he says to himself, as the music reverberates in his nervous system and extends itself out through every fibre of tissue and bone. 'Here we fucking go,' he says to himself again, but this time, unknowingly, he says the words out loud, unknowingly draws grins and nods from those around him. And with that he just eases himself into the speed and leisure with which he travels down this curving undulation, this curving underlying undulation underneath. Another place, another time. Underlying, undulation, underground. Another place, another time. Underlying, undulation, underneath. He chants and sings to himself as he dances and watches the rise and fall of his piston legs planting big white trainers on the road. I'm my own MC, he thinks. Underlying, undulation, underground. To another place, another time. Underlying, underlying, underneath, underground. Another place, another time...

This went on for some time, or at least it seemed that way to Lee, who was so blissfully lost in the world he had created out of the smoke and the lasers and the music and the drugs and every interaction he had had that night and the evening leading up to it, that his sense of himself was almost completely lost. Like someone astral-projecting to another plane, he was tethered to his own reality by the most slender of cords. For him the substance of all those human exchanges of energy he had so far enjoyed that night and those that he anticipated were yet to come, became the fabric of the world in his mind. And he ran through that world in fat white trainers, and the rise and fall of the fat white trainers became the essence of the emotional completeness he was now experiencing; experiencing as a cartoon figure singing to itself as it is drawn into existence in lines of light dancing on a dark earth.

'Lee, Lee, Danny-Lee, oi, Lee...' Lee slowly became aware that someone was saying his name, prodding him with it relentlessly. At first, Lee had incorporated the noise into the music of the world behind his closed eyes, then the cartoon figure was saying it, but eventually the shape of the sound, his name, Lee, eventually asserted itself and brought him back to the reality of people with names. Lee opened his eyes in the direction of the noise and regarded Rob, who stood there; he regarded him with soft indulgence, as if he was a great guru patiently regarding a child. Lee felt full of giving and understanding. He could almost have reached out and put two fingers against Rob's head in a blessing. He could have done that to everyone around him. Lee felt all this in the moment it took his brain to process the information on Rob's presence that his eyes relayed to it through the action of electro-magnetism on the tiny fleshy rods and cones that made a micro-level giant's causeway of the surface of his retina. Then those ideas, clear and accurate for several instants, vanished with the world internal in which he had been running. His look of beatification slowly turned to inquiry.

'...mate. Fancy takin' a breather? Fag break in the chill-out?' Rob pursed his lips and made an exaggerated cigarette-to-lips smoking mime. Lee was feeling super compliant, and although he could have stayed all night in the world of his own making that existed behind his eyes and strived all night in effortless exertion, he knew immediately that there were other places and faces he wanted to see.

116

'Yes, mate. I'm there. These fuckin' pills, though... something else...' And they pushed back through the hot moving crowd towards the chill-out in the foyer of the building.

The foyer was echoes and hubbub. People, stood, sat, looked out from the balconies, and everyone was talking and chewing and smoking... yes, confirmed Lee, everyone was talking and chewing and smoking... he glanced round and a series of stills of people talking and chewing and smoking tracked his eyeline... only the clean-looking bar staff in white shirts were not doing these things. They were an exception proving a rule. He had never been able to understand that expression. He thought that maybe he did now, though. *Why were they dressed like that?* he thought. *They looked like they were about to give a class presentation*, thought Lee, as he watched them serve drinks, dead-pan, to people in various states of being E'd up, many of whom looked like they could barely remember their own names. Lee smiled broadly at it all and tuned back to Rob.

'Fuckin' hell, Rob, what is goin' on here? I think we're on a new planet.'

'I know, I know,' said Rob. 'It's fuckin' mental... here...' and he held an open packet of Embassy towards Lee, two or three of the cigarettes it contained poking out in invitation.

'Mate, mate...' Someone was calling out. Lee sensed it was for him and turned to see insect-man, eyes dark pools, arms moving like an Indian god, MaDMAn printed in black letters across the chest of his white t-shirt. Lee recognised, stopped and reached for the outstretched hand of the other, taking it, clasping high before embracing the shoulder of his counterpart as his counterpart did the same to him.

'How you doin', brother?' said insect-man.

'Safe, mate, safe. This is Rob.' More hands, embraces. 'Safe.'

'I'm Dave, by the way... Mike, Trish, Vikki...' He gestured behind him to three shiny, grinning, open faces. Lee and Rob moved towards them. More hands, embraces, some kisses. 'Safe.'

'Where you from then, mate?' exchanged both.

'Colchester,' said Dave. 'We're all from Colchester and Clacton.'

'Braintree. Well, Braintree and Dunmow,' said Lee.

'Yessah, Essex in the place,' celebrated Dave and they agreed to catch each other in a bit as Lee and Rob moved for the toilets.

'D'ya see his shirt?' asked Rob.

'Yea, man, 'cos I met him earlier, out here when I was comin' up and rushin' like a bastard. I got chattin' to him. Well, I don't think I was capable of speech at the time. *He* started talkin' to me. Gave me some of his water... billy in it, you know. Yea, so he starts talkin' about fuckin' insects... gets well involved and complex; you know, evolution, aliens, fuckin' DNA... Yea, top bloke.' At this Lee put his hands in the air in front of him and wiggled his fingers in what would probably be understood as an alien or insect-like way, while opening his eyes very wide and moving his head from side to side. 'Whuuuuhuhuhuh,' he warbled as he continued wiggling his fingers. 'Blew my fuckin' noodle... said I looked like a man that could handle a chat about the... *bizarre and extraordinary nature of life*... yea, so got well into the whole *what is life?* thing... well, he got well into it. I mean, I did as well but just in me own head, you know, from listenin' to him. I goes to him, "I'm not contributing to this much, am I...?" so he goes, "Mate, o fuckin' contraire, you are very much half of this discussion. You're listenin', and I can tell you're listenin', and listenin' is listenin' and that's all that's needed – listenin.'" No idea what he meant by that really. But you know... yea... well, fuckin' funny anyway... aaand... I learned loads... but... can't remember anything now. Didn't tell me his name, I don't think. What was it he said just then? Dave? Insect Dave I'll call him... Anyway, after that I went back in and tripped out my fuckin' nut and that's when you found me.' Lee opened his hands in supplication and gave a down-mouth shrug of acceptance to mark the end of the anecdote. Rob laughed at the story. Lee laughed too and loved the bloke in the white t-shirt for the vision they had shared, and he loved how he had taken the vision back with him into the arena and how there it had infused the character of his imagination as he tripped out to the lasers and the smoke and the insistence of the music.

As they returned to the foyer, they joined Dave and his mates where they squatted on the floor in a large group, and Lee recounted again the story of his earlier encounter with Insect Dave. This time, the story had new embellishments and some fresh content, including how he and Rob had just been staring at their massive dark eyes in the mirror and seeing how much like aliens they could look and how, if you stared at your reflection for long enough, it no longer looked like you. The story was even more effective than before; it slung lines between people, roped them together, sealed pacts and cemented bonds. Other people who were sitting on the floor by the stairs in this large, loose group also got involved in the story. Quickly it was, 'Donna, Danny, Clare, Tony... yea, we're all from Cambridge. We've all done them New Yorkers, white pill, like an aspirin...' And it turns out Cambridge Donna and Danny are nothing to do with Dave and his lot, they just happened to be sitting next to them on the same piece of floor. And across the foyer Lee can see Zoe and Kelly, chewing gum and smoking, engaged in intense discussion, including sustained periods of direct eye contact, with a small group of people they've just met who, freakily – if you are either Zoe or Kelly – also know Insect Dave.

## //

And that, thought Lee, as he looked at the writhing hair that embraced the kissers on the Bliss flyer, is how we all ended up at Donna and Danny's place, Insect Dave and associates included, doing a few more lines, sharing halves in quarters and getting smoked up. It was about 4.30 in the morning when Baz parked outside the red-brick and white-render, two-up two-down 1950s semi, located in a quiet, ordinary-looking cul-de-sac – full of birdsong and cheap cars – in Cherry Hinton. The bass in the car thumped like a caged space monster, and it bounded out down the street as they bundled from the car like a brawl in a cartoon. They went straight from pavement to sitting room, the room still night-dark with closed curtains, Danny already behind the decks. The place became busy as their eyes adjusted and it filled steadily with discernible noise as they worked out where they were, who was there and how they were.

They relayed in episodes and versions, to those already there, the story of the journey to get to the house they now stood within. They explained how they finally managed, with lots of difficulty and incident, to leave the car-door party in the multi-storey and make their way across Cambridge. They'd arrived like a bomb ready to explode; the internal post-rave pressure in the car, always likely to be intense, had been ratcheted up by extra passengers in the shape of a couple of Dave's mates. These mates had travelled by bus and needed transport to Danny and Donna's. Ian crushed in the wells between back and front seats, Steve in the boot space of the hatchback. The two of them had arrived that afternoon and whiled away the time smoking crafty reefers amongst the municipal flowers in a pretty park they later learned, to massive amusement, was called Christ's Pieces, and wandering through the trees on The Backs and along the river by Jesus Green. They looked round the colleges too, they said acting *clever* and pretending they were looking for some old university pals. Steve eventually felt so fucking clever he nearly broke his neck tripping on a wonky stair tread in a bookshop. The shop, he said, was literally just a big old house with everything taken out and all the rooms filled with books. Hundreds of fucking books on shelves and tables and loads of people looking at them. A small crowd gathered round him as he lay tangled on the bottom steps, checking he was all right; so stoned was he that he lay there for a bit looking up at them and thinking that all he wanted to do was get out of there as quickly as possible. But he was held by his paranoia and the thought that if he just jumped up and walked off like nothing had happened, it would look weird, and he lay unmoving, staring blankly up into the space created by the circle of onlookers. His sense of time distorted and experiencing mild panic, he more or less did get up straight away and, according to Ian, it did look weird, as predicted. Especially, Ian added, when he just stared up, unblinking, looked slowly round the gathered faces, before he then sprang up like it was a rehearsed move, and strode from the shop. Ian followed him into the street calling his name and from there, with an unspoken understanding, they broke into a run which reached a shoplifter's sprint by the time they'd gained the sanctuary of the flowers and the grass behind the bus station. 'Christ's Pieces,' Steve had repeated several times, 'ha ha ha.'

//

'The thing about last night…' said Lee later, while in the kitchen talking to Dave and Ian and Vikki and Zoe, the autumn light of early morning pouring through the window like pink diamond, '…was it set a standard and you kind of knew everyone felt the same. There was a buzz everywhere you went… like everyone meant it… like everyone knew everyone meant it. We met so many people. Unbelievable.' Lee listed some of them: 'You, Danny and the CHinton massive' (the last two words loud and with MC emphasis provoking raised fists and finger points), 'the Clacton Pier lot and… yea… yea… fuckin' tons of people. It was all about passion, people coming together, positivity, energy… creative collusion. That is what it's fuckin' all about…' Lee met unanimous strong agreement and he felt like a fucking leader.

No doubt about it, thought Lee, blocks had slid into place that night for all of them. New shapes formed, new configurations of communication and spirit. Everyone Lee had met had been interested in him and he in them. Yea, the drugs played a part, he maturely conceded, of course they fucking did, that was the whole fucking point, he said as he leant on the worktop, next to the sink, in Danny and Donna's kitchen, looking slightly back up over his shoulder to deliver the words to Danny, who stood leaning back against the worktop to Lee's right. The drugs had never made him do things he didn't want to, he explained but, sometimes, they did make him do things he didn't know he wanted to do, and tonight he saw that at work; he saw it in the connections he had made; meaningful connections, he told Danny, made with clear and conscious intent. And, he added, with emotion and no word of a lie, that he would carry this feeling with him forever. And as Lee recalled this in Uncle Shane's shed and many times thereafter, he could feel a charge, something deep set and glowing, an ember in an old and finely worked brass pot, a magic crystal there, a mineral stone of complex colour and character, ancient formation and deep vibration.

## //

Still later that morning, still feeling like a leader, still restless with the energy of the night, Lee experimentally suggested to Donna that they needed a walk in the outside world. Zoe had just finished a little work on the decks with Danny; the Clacton boys had wrested control of the mic from Kelly, which she had been using to put some avant-garde scat over the top of the music. Lee had thought it pretty good. Ian and Steve were entertaining too but Lee was enticed by the idea of escape; he wanted to smuggle himself out through the closed curtains of the living room and manifest in the world. Lee sensed Donna was a doer and an organiser and that she was a likely touch for leading an excursion. Armed with this intuition and knowing Zoe and Kelly would support him, he dropped the idea into conversation with Donna. His judgement was accurate.

'Yea, right, so who's up for a walk in the sunshine?' Donna canvassed to wide vocal support despite which the following twenty minutes were devoted to her chivvying and chiding distracted and fragmented ravers into a state, both individually and as a body, where they were fit to take on the great outdoors and the world of normal on a bright Sunday morning in September. She said she felt like Mary Poppins: 'Fuck's sake, I feel like Mary bleedin' Poppins with you lot. Fuckin' 'ell, can we please try to get out the fuckin' door before Christmas?'

A rag-tag platoon of survivors from the previous night eventually made it onto the street and the bright light of day. The purity of the light brought out a seedy and smoky unwashedness in their appearance which, coupled with the dressing-up box flavour of the borrowed jackets and hats and sunglasses they were wearing, gave them an air of pantomime or a decadent cabaret act. They formed a ragged wandering group which continually splintered and formed and re-formed in combinations of groups and sub-groups. The talk was of raves and pills, journeys and venues, DJs and tunes. The talk continued even during the one chaotic shop-stop which resulted in oversupply of blue Rizla and Lucozade and which Donna had worried might cause the shopkeeper to hit the panic button. But their good-natured politeness mollified him and compensated for the erratic, potentially alarming behaviour of Dave; Dave, oblivious, who swang to the beat of the DJ still playing inside his head, weaving up and down the aisles, picking items off the shelves to absently leave elsewhere, having decided he didn't want them. Vikki and Mike followed him, doing their best to pick up the pieces.

'Dave, pack it in, mate,' said Vikki as if she was his mum.

'Yea, Dave, you fuckin' dickhead,' added Mike with apparent venom, before turning to the shopkeeper and, in a markedly different and surprisingly apologetic tone, saying, '… really sorry about this, mate, we'll put 'em back.' Lee had opted to stand outside with Zoe and Danny, having a smoke, and they observed it all, quite dispassionately, through the window.

'No more stops,' said Danny, 'or we'll never get anywhere.'

'Where we going anyway?' asked Lee.

'I think Donna wants to go to the chalk pit.'

'Chalk pit?'

'Yea, just up the road… an old quarry… chalk quarry… chalk for building and cement and whatever… It's a nature reserve. We always go up there. It's well peaceful and…'

'All right,' said Lee. 'Sounds like a good place for a smoke in the sun.' Danny nodded meaningfully as he pictured them doing just that.

'Your favourite pastime, Danny-Lee... smoking in the sun, somewhere green and peaceful,' said Zoe, thinking of that first morning-after she had shared with Lee and Rob and Baz and Kelly, sat in the corner of a field staring at the sun on the wheat and sharing a spliff. Lee was thinking of the same and similar times. He truly did like to spliff up in the countryside. A fat reefer on a nice day, survey the scene, watch the clouds, listen to the birds. Must be from his mum's side... Grandad Swigler... always on the lookout for a stopping place... Grandad Swigler... always finding it was time for a smoke.

'True,' said Lee, 'but my other favourite is getting off my nut in a dark room with hundreds of other people and dancing my tits off.' Danny and Zoe laughed.

'I'm with you there, mate,' said Danny, 'but I would add, coming home after a night out and playing tunes on the decks for hours.'

'That,' said Zoe, 'is what I want. Lee, I wanna do that.'

'Well, you'll have to get some fuckin' decks then, won't you... and start buying records to feed 'em.' Zoe looked hard at Lee. He could see that at this point she found him unhelpful. He knew she had no money; he knew the cost of decks. She continued to stare and twisted her mouth with applied thought. Lee could see the determination forming in her head.

'Yea, thanks, mate. I've got one deck and I will sort it,' she said. Lee smiled at the thought of the old belt-drive in Zoe's room at home; so fucking light you could pick it up with one hand. He went twos with her on the fag he was smoking.

'I know you will,' he said, and meant it. The moment crystallised and lodged with both of them; they returned to it at times; pilgrimage to a moment of genesis. For Zoe, it was a defining moment. Nothing again was ever the same.

'Right, let's fuckin' go, kids,' said Donna, striding out of the shop like a deranged primary school teacher on a class outing. She glanced round once to make sure she wasn't on her own and continued to lead the Year Eclipse class outing to the chalk pit.

The way to the chalk pit was through a small gate right next to a busy road and junction. There was a pub opposite. Lee decided it was a shit pub and best avoided; their appearance, age and number made it difficult for them not to look at best incongruous, and at worst criminal. Lee dismissed the pub and surveyed unhopefully the urban noise, the traffic, the doughty screen of slightly exhaust-blown tall trees. On the face of it, it didn't look like the place he had hoped it was going to be, nor the kind of place that Zoe had had in mind when she'd teased him about his penchant for smoking in the countryside. Lee adjusted his expectations as they filed through the spring-loaded gate and the curtain of trees that grew all along this section of road. The old chalk quarry was quiet. There were walls rising up all around of stratified chalk in different colours, and grass and shrubs grew up out of cracks and fissures in the rock. Insects buzzed and flitted everywhere in the still air, and birdsong from the trees echoed on the stone. It was like time was suspended.

'This,' said Danny, 'I've always thought would be a great place to take acid. Don't know why I haven't done it yet, to be honest. Too many great places to take acid, I s'pose.' Lee looked at him, interested.

'I've not done it, mate.'

'What? Acid? No?' said Danny. 'Well, mate, we'll have to sort that out at some point. Definitely, mate.'

'I reckon,' said Lee, 'and I'll hold you to that. So, what's this place again?' And Danny told him all about the pit.

'Fuckin' 'ell, Danny. How do you know all that? You a warden or something?' asked Rob.

'School,' said Donna. 'Always did a GCSE project on the chalk pit, eh, Danny? Used to come here with school… fuck about… eh, eh, Danny, fuck about.' Danny signalled assent with a turn of his head.

'And,' said Insect Dave, more to himself than anything, 'all these lines in the chalk are different eras in the time that this was all the bed of the sea…'

'And how do you know that?' said Lee.

"Cos he's a fuckin' brainiac,' said Tony. 'Teacher's pet.'

'Yea, well, not really, was I?' said Dave. 'Whatever else I was, teacher's pet I fuckin' was not.'

They settled into a state of quiet, brief talk and slow investigation of the quarry and its bands of chalk. On the advice of Dave, they looked for fossils, found none but filled their pockets with interesting pieces of chalk and flint as the sun warmed the rock and the air and insects around them.

Lee clearly remembered the drive home from that milestone night and morning. Baz at the wheel made the car glide through the quiet and shadowy green that early autumn had brought to South Cambridgeshire and North Essex. Baz had judged this route a better option than the M11 – less likely to attract the Old Bill, he said, and gentler on the mind. His wisdom was approved, the experience from which it was born respected and there were no objections. The car was quickly filled with appreciation for Baz's decision as the air and the light and the colour of the day looked on them, cast rippled reflections into the car through the tree-lined, hedged banks of the road, and enervated their senses. They passed like a boat, an open canoe, moving with the flow of a fast river, mere twitches of paddle needed to maintain course, and Baz master steersman. As it first launched, there was noise in the car; there was music and post-rave analysis (something they came to understand was an unavoidable and necessary part of going out) was in torrent, and there were some minute-by-minute accounts of situations and incidents that might ordinarily not be considered worth such detailed scrutiny and consideration. Lee was conscious of this as he recounted again his Insect Dave encounter and how that led to meeting Danny. He decided it was a story of genuine merit and would bear a retelling, especially as at least one person in the car had not heard it before.

This standard was also met by Kelly's explanation of how she and Zoe had met Ian and Faye and the Clacton posse, who also happened to know Insect Dave and, independently, knew other mates of Kelly's who hadn't been there on the night. Lee also told them about tripping-out to the music. He explained how, before he had closed his eyes to bounce and stride through the landscape of his own rave-imagination, he had just stood and looked around him, taken it all in and, as he had looked, he had questioned what he saw. He told them that he had wondered how they all knew what to do; wondered how and where they'd learned it. The MC, the DJ, the dancers, the crowd, every single person there, all those people just like him – young, ordinary nothings from nowhere special with nowhere to go and nothing to do at the weekends until they could drink and fuck and then that's all they'd ever do. How did we, he'd asked them, asked himself, how did we suddenly know how to do all this? And Lee had swept the air with his hand as he said this, and it made him remember how he had turned and scanned the arena, absorbing its diverse energy and defiant variety, its spellbinding imagination, the sheer exuberance of what they were all doing, the lift that was felt just by being there, by being one of many striving to make together something far greater than the simple sum of its parts. Dancers, DJs, technicians, promoters, smokers, chewers, chatters and trippers. Who had shown them, who had shown us, who had taught us, where had we learned it all, what had revealed this to us?

There was deep silence when Lee finished and the breakbeats, kicks and snares and the high-hats and the bass coming from the speakers of Baz's car continued in rhythm and noise the thought and ideas his words had initiated; it was a full silence in which they all relived their own moments of similar revelation and wonder. The silence faded and in the up-draught of a piano break and stuttered vocal chopped into the beat as the bass and drum were reinstated, the noise of the car and smell of the autumn air returned. Zoe then mentioned a girl who, a bit freaked out by the intensity of it all, had been sick on a wall but then felt much better. The others waited for more on the sick girl but Zoe was finished and defiant; for her the anecdote was fully developed. Rob suggested that perhaps you had to be there. 'Also,' Zoe remembered, undeterred by Rob and ignoring his sarcasm, 'what about that fuckin' sweaty old bald bloke, the one with his eyes halfway round the back of his head who kept trying to touch girls? He was a fucking pervy creep.' She had got Ian to tell him to fuck off, she'd added. This information was more of a declaration and was well heard and understood. They registered something like this as an exceptional flaw in the overall shape and pattern of the night and responded with unanimous condemnation.

Baz had been silent throughout the anecdote exchange, head moving to the music, eyes flicking round his mirrors, right arm laid along the ledge where the top of the lower half of the door met the glass of the window. He held the steering wheel with his left hand, fingers and thumb gripping round the junction made between the outer ring of the wheel and one of the spokes.

'It was a fuckin' good night,' he said. 'This thing is really 'appenin' now, I reckon. It's kickin' off all over the place. You know what…? You know what…? Make sure you proper enjoy it. I mean, really fuckin' drink it in, lap it right up… been a long time coming but it's finally arrived.' The others in the car were not really sure what Baz was getting at; there was a far from typical mystery and portent in the way he spoke; but the feeling in his voice, the experience hinted at, demanded attention. 'We're doing things for ourselves, by ourselves and this… this is what it looks like… like nothing we've ever seen or heard before…'

Baz paused and let his brain rotate a few cycles. '…but the roots are there,' he continued, '…there is form, there is origin.' He paused again. 'A lot of things got us 'ere to where we are now. Seems like it came outta nowhere, don' it? Bet you lot think it's all just fuckin' appeared outta thin air… but it's no accident… plenty of fuckin' chance, mind, but no accident… no such thing. You know what…? I remember the first time I heard music, you know, loud, on a proper rig. It was Hip-Hop, Synth Funk, Jazz Funk, Soul-Boy-Disco. That was at The Barn 'n' all. Blew my fuckin' world up, threw it up in the air, rebuilt it as it landed… same thing with Two-Tone and Ska; I was younger then, obviously, only saw stuff on TV, but it was still a big deal, big impression. Powerful behaviour and I was hooked in straight off, big style. First time I'd ever seen black and white British people performing together. Not many black people in Braintree in them days… in fact, I can't remember there being any black kids in my school. Maybe a few Indians, Pakistanis, but that was it. Yea, really fuckin' switched me on to music, politics, protest and all that malarkey. I'm tellin' you, at the time it was a fuckin' statement; for someone like me – and I was sensitive to it – yea, for someone like me it was the biggest thing… the combination of playing instruments, dancing, fuckin' about, as well as the anger and the style… well, it fuckin' moved me.

130

I thought it was wicked. I can still remember now how it made me feel... gives me goosebumps.

'I got that feelin' last night too. I'll tell you something for nothing right now, you'll look back on this time and you will buzz with it... shit like that cannot be taken away.' Baz resurfaced the image of black and white youth, smart in a way that defied and challenged – like the Mods, he thought – off-beat rhythms and fat basslines, no-nonsense streetwise vocals and dancing with purpose. He savoured the vigour of Brit-Funk and New Wave that brought him kicking and jumping onto the battlefield, and then came the Acid. That wave has broken, he thought, but it has shown us open spaces and unguarded opportunities; that wave has broken but this one is just gathering.

'People need to let go, people need an outlet,' said Baz. 'There's been a lotta shit for a lot of people for too long. I remember the riots in the '80s... only on TV obviously, but when I saw those people fighting back... well, it felt like I was watching my own family. I remember looking hard at their faces in the paper and I saw looking back at me self-belief and righteous anger. Mum and Dad saw a violent mob but it weren't no mob to me... it was people screaming back at the bleak, at the mean, at the tap, tap, tap of unrelenting bullshit. I heard that scream in the music 'n' all. Two-Tone, Hip-Hop, New Wave Synth – it was all protest then. Just the way some of those blokes looked – particularly the blokes – it was fuckin' insurrection, sent a lot of people right off the deep end. You know, some people, at the time, would have outlawed it if they had the power.'

Baz inhaled and exhaled deliberately at the thought. 'Wankers,' he said. 'You know what, for some, just the idea that *a band* could just be a snidey-looking geezer poking a keyboard – well, for some, that was off the fuckin' scale –

still is… *"that's not real music… they're not even playing real instruments."* Baz put on a playground whine for these last words and everyone laughed. 'Yea, it's been a long time comin', all this, but I reckon we might just have reached the big one. Like I say, fuckin' enjoy it. Could be a golden time.' He nodded. 'It's always just after the start that the thrill is at its best… the time when no one realises that something is going on.' Baz mused on his own idea; the time when we realise we're doing something… that something's going on… when we think… *it can go like this or it could go like that; let's try this, now let's do it this way…* but we haven't become self-conscious yet. That's when the time is golden, when the groove just flows, the body moves and there, a moment of weightlessness, complete concentration with almost no effort. He felt a bit like that now with the driving; he could see and read the road far ahead, check behind in his mirrors, register the instruments and the state of the occupants of the car, seemingly simultaneously and with complete and broad understanding; patched directly into multiple sources, he was able to mix the flows to a single read-out projected to an awareness just behind and between the eyes. The bass wobbled and the sound of blocks of moving steel slid around amongst the distortions. The country sped by and home approached and silence settled in the car. Only the sound of the engine and the music.

# TWELVE

LEE REMEMBERED THE HOMEWARD SILENCE THAT
followed the sermon of Baz, and it intruded into the reserved
space of Scott and Jason's shed. He ushered it back into the
past but did not try to hide or ignore it. It was the pattern
set for most raving nights out; the creeping thought of going
home the next day. Home was not about the promise of
comfort and relief but was dominated by the looming threat
and scowling demeanour of work the next day, the next week,
and the guilty nag that anticipated suspicious interrogation
by his mum, goaded on by arsehole Malcolm. Lee was still
working at the chicken factory and the long shifts were brutal,
and the smell first thing in the morning was more brutal
still. You could never get used to that, he thought; steaming
hot water, disinfectant, blood, feathers and chicken shit. He
shuddered and put it from him. *Deal with it tomorrow... deal
with it tomorrow...* he repeated to himself as a mantra – a

chant to guide him through the difficult country that lay in the twilight between rave and the week, that lay between him and the next weekend. On that journey after the first Eclipse, no one else in the car was working; they were either at college or they were Baz, and who knew what he did? Rob kind of worked, but for his uncle, so it didn't count. Thinking this had made Lee feel sorry for himself, that life was unfair. But he'd turned his thoughts to Eclipse and the night they'd just had. That was the way to get through it, he told himself, and that when he was driving it would all be better. Why he had thought that would be the case was not clear to him. Driving made many things better but this it did not change.

In any case, that homecoming had not turned out so bad. The house had been empty when he got home and it smelt of Sunday roast and hot apple. The effect on his digestion was almost like coming up; the hunger was demanding like nothing else he had felt before. He found a plate of food, covered with another plate, in the still warm oven. He didn't even consider who it was for before starting to eat; half of it he ate still standing and the other half, as he lowered himself to sit. By the time he was properly at the table the food was gone. His whole skin radiated with the nourishment of it; he could feel his depleted blood and organs drawing from the food the vital energy and vitamins they needed; if he had been a computer game, the empty red life bar at the side of the screen would have surged upwards to nearly full. He turned to the half-eaten dish of crumble and took a couple of large spoonfuls straight from it. Then, upstairs, he ran a bath and lay in its steam, watching the condensation move and gather and make tracks on the frosted glass of the window. He lay in the protection of the warm water, his whole body submerged and his head back so that the level of the liquid came just to his ears and he could hear it lapping there through the music that still shushed and shrang in his ears. He looked along the plane of the water's surface and saw it shiver as he moved; he raised his eyes to the wall above the toilet and the particles of yellow paint vibrated independently and dissociated. Warm and trippy, he retreated to his bedroom wrapped in a towel and lay for a while as his body dealt with the suddenness of the food and the heat.

He tried sleep but it had no chance. The music still coursed and sang in his head and a stream of image and noise – dancing ravers, chill-out chatting, shop-stops, multi-storey car parks, chalk pits, lasers – told him he was not going to get away easily. He sprung off the bed, went to his jacket and pulled from a pocket the Eclipse flyer Danny had given him. He smoothed it out and rummaged in a drawer for an old cardboard folder he knew was there. He put the flyer into the folder, on top of several drawings of birds – mainly hawks – done in the Third Year. He then rummaged in an old cardboard box under the table, once used as a desk, and pulled out an exercise book. It had his name written on the front in 3D-graf wild style. He tore out the first few used pages and threw them into the tin bin under the window by the bed. He then armed himself with a biro and arranged his body on the bed, the book open on his knees, and began lettering the word "Eclipse". This is what he was doing when his mum and Malcolm and Angela came home. Feet, voices, plates and cutlery moving. Anxiety.

'Lee, you in?' He heard his mum's voice, more accusation than question.

'Yea… upstairs.' He infused the words with as much casual normality as he could. He thought maybe he'd overdone it. Silence.

'Okay,' came back to him. Clipped and perfunctory. He couldn't be sure if he was reading too much into the scant words that were coming to him up the stairs. He felt sure there were looks and mouthed words being exchanged between his mum and Malcolm, looks full of well-rehearsed complaints and concerns about him and words edged in anger and spite. He pretended hard that everything was totally normal about him, about his weekend, and about what he was doing now. Even though there was no one to see him, he adjusted his position and his expression to reflect the total normality he was trying to bring to the situation.

'Is everything all right Danny-Lee?' His mum again.

'Yea, mum, just drawing…' He winced. Drawing? That was not a normal thing to say or to say he was doing. It was fine, he told himself. Fine. New hobby. Rediscovering an old love.

'All right… nice to see you sometime this weekend.'

'Not for me…' said Malcolm so he would hear.

'Yea, in a bit…' he said, with no intention of going downstairs. He carried on with the lettering.

When he had finished he wrote in the corner of the page, *Eclipse Cambridge, 1 September 1990. Rob, Baz, Zoe and Kelly. Cherry Hinton chalk pit with Danny and Donna, Insect Dave and the Colchester Crew and Ian and Faye and the Clacton Crew.* He finally sunk slowly into sleep, drifting down away from the noise and the light like a fragment of shell, to rest as nothing on the silty bed of a warm prehistoric sea. Here buried in darkness under tons on accumulated tons of particles of plankton and pieces of sea creatures, he was compressed and folded into rock until, after countless millions of planetary rotations, he glimpsed the light once more, an exposed chalk outcrop, the side of a pit wall, dug for building stone.

## //

Work passed in a blur that week. The individual minutes felt long, but the bigger blocks of time sailed by for him and he watched them go as if he was a spectator to his own life. He felt precarious, high in the water, as if the slightest nudge could capsize him, but knew that if he held his nerve he would make it to the haven of the weekend to come. Also, he still had puff from the weekend, and he had Rob's as a sanctuary and a quiet place to smoke. The smell of the factory in the morning was a major assault, but he had anticipated this and was ready for it. He kept his head down at work, quite literally at times, and avoided discussing in anything but the vaguest terms what he had been up to over the weekend. He had no raving allies at the factory, and if the subject ever came up, as it sometimes did if a story made it to the pages of the *Sun* or a local paper, the attitude of the canteen and the locker room was fiercely anti the …*crazed, drug-fuelled hedonism*… that was depicted. To an extent, these reports were accurate – *crazed drug-fuelled hedonism* was not far short of the mark – but they had no balance or depth; they made it sound like going to one of these events and getting involved in some *crazed drug-fuelled hedonism*, was an experience dominated by fear, distress and confrontation. Lee could have attested that this was not the case, at least not for him and, anyway, if it was like that why did so many people want to go? But his ideas and arguments about it were not developed and he was not about to reveal that he was a participant and, still less, as a junior and recently arrived hand, to take on single-handedly the media-fed prejudices of the whole smoking room.

The temperature around all this was raised too that week by news that filtered into the factory about Jamie. Lee had not known Jamie, no one had really known him, no one really knew where he was from, who his family were or where he lived. He had no friends at the factory. It was widely accepted that he was off his head most of the time, his face split with a permanent grin, and his large eyes, made larger by his severely shaved head, seemed to stare through and beyond everything to somewhere distant. *Drugs* was what most people said. A few were more precise and said *Acid*; that he was on acid all the time. Lee considered this and often thought of it later, and he recoiled from the idea of being on acid and working in the chicken factory. But maybe it was true, maybe it helped Jamie manage the brutality of the place and, who knows, the shit of his life outside. Whatever it was with Jamie, the news was passed around that he had been found dead over the weekend. Cause of death was "drugs". That was it, "drugs". As far as Lee was aware, acid could not kill you. There was obviously much more to this story and he felt pain for Jamie, sharpened by a feeling of kinship, and Lee wondered how it might have turned out if he had got friendly with him, if he had invited him to Eclipse; if… if… if… But Jamie was hard to reach. Even if you said hello to him, the most you would get was a turn of the head and a moment or two in the full beam of his glazed gaze and grin. Still, thought Lee, still… as he blew smoke up towards the tiles of the suspended ceiling in the narrow locker room – the only place in the factory you could smoke – and narrowed his eyes in thought, the smoke rolling back on itself.

His mum heard about Jamie too; of course, she did. She had friends in the factory. That's how he had ended up working there. She always knew someone and she knew all the women who worked the guts-line at King Crown Chickens – the women who sat on high stools, yakking as they dragged the innards from the arses of the plucked and headless chickens that swung by, hanging by their scaly yellow feet.

'I heard about that boy who worked with you at the factory. Dead from drugs. Terrible. His poor mother.'

Lee kept his head down.

'Yea.'

'Why do they do it? Such a waste.'

Lee thought of the long shifts in the factory, the noise, the smell, the monotony, and pictured Jamie with his big senseless grin and swimming eyes.

'Yea.' He knew what was coming, but he was prepared. He had been prepared since Sunday night as he sat on his bed writing.

'You don't do drugs, do you, Danny-Lee? You know, when you go out. Rob and that brother of his, Baz, I bet they're into that?'

'No, Mum, I don't. Don't worry about it.'

'But I do worry about it.'

'Well, you don't need to.'

'What happened to you this last weekend then?'

'I told you, I was with Scott and Jason.' Lee deftly omitted that while he was *with* Scott and Jason, he was not *at* Scott and Jason's.

'How's Shane and Cynthia?'

'Oh, you know... I didn't really see 'em.' That was the truth, Lee congratulated himself, and the tone was a perfect balance of engagement and disinterest.

'D'you go out anywhere?'

'Yea, we went to this thing in Cambridge. It was all right.' A picture of lasers meshed in a grid of green precision flashed before Lee's eyes, and his ears filled with the noise of bass and whistles and a cranking MC.

'Cambridge? You went to Cambridge, did you?' Lee heard a change in his mum's voice. Her attention had been diverted. 'We used to stay in Cambridge. When I was a little girl. Trumpington. Grandad and the boys would get rabbits on the Gog Hills. Your nan and her mum sold pegs and heather on the High Street. That was when Grandad sold our big covered wagon. Sold it to a professor at one of the colleges. He wanted it for Borneo.'

'Borneo? Why?'

'I don't know... All I know is that me and Aunty June had to sleep in a tent after that.' She laughed. 'It was bloody cold in the winter.' She was thoughtful for a moment. 'Never got any prejudice in Cambridge,' she said wistfully. Lee looked at her and saw both warm nostalgia and nagging pain in the set of her mouth and the distance in her eyes. 'Lots of work around there then. I don't s'pose it's like that anymore.' Lee thought of the queue for Eclipse snaking its way round the Corn Exchange building and the gang of escaped lunatic circus artists who had made their haphazard way to the chalk pit.

'No, shouldn't think so,' said Lee. He knew about some of these old memories from Grandad Swigler. Grandad Swigler had always talked about that stuff to Lee. Lee remembered sitting in the passenger seat of Grandad's Sherpa, feet swinging miles from the floor, listening to the old man talk about his old life, words triggered by things and places passed as he drove. At the time, Lee did not understand it all but he absorbed the language and the emotion and often, now, things came back to him. It was funny, he thought, they especially came back when he was travelling, when he was in a car. Maybe that was the intention, his way of life had gone but Grandad Swigler wanted to pass it on somehow, to embed it in a younger generation. He was a deep thinker, thought Lee. He saw things early and acted on his insights. He had put aside a young lifetime of knowledge and honed instinct and moved himself and his family off the road and into a house. He must have known in his head it was for the best, even while in his heart he never settled and never stopped travelling. Lee knew from his mum the trauma of that time, but it must have been Nanna and Grandad who felt it the most. That's why, thought Lee, they had that

140

little caravan; that's why Nanna and Grandad Swigler had moved house more times than anyone Lee knew or was to know. Still, he hadn't heard the Borneo Caravan story from Grandad Swigler. That was a new one. Next time in Cambridge, maybe he could find the places his mum had mentioned.

# THIRTEEN

THAT NEXT TIME CAME AROUND QUICKLY; AND not only that, he was driving by then too. The event in a big carpet warehouse, somewhere in Cambridge. Lee couldn't remember there being a name for it. Started with a car park meet at The Ship. Not that one that got raided, the one where Kelly lost her job because she'd thrown a sickie on the Monday and her boss saw her in the footage on the local TV news. Nor was it the one that was supposed to be *near* Cambridge but which wasn't near at all; the one where everyone was so fucked up on the pills they'd taken that they all sat down in the main tent, too mangled to dance; they were meant to be E but must have been something else. Who knows…? Eventually, they did come up quite lively but they'd still left early for some reason, taken a wrong turn and got lost in the Fens with rain and mist coming in at them from all directions. The map didn't work and there was some freaking-out at the weather and the disorientation and he heard Grandad Swigler going on about the Fens. No, thought Lee, it was the one that started at The Ship. His first drive. His first trip.

The warehouse it was in wasn't far. It was a cavernous place; packed and dark and smelling strongly of new carpet and underlay. There was little décor just a few lights and lasers burning into the darkness momentarily revealing faces and bodies you had no idea were there. The lights also showed that at one end, the place was an unbroken wall of speakers, a foundation line of bass bins to vibrate your internal organs and force the air from your lungs. At the other end, built into the corners, were two small, low-ceilinged, single-storey rooms. One of them housed an actual toilet, inside a cubicle from which the door hung by two screws in the top hinge; the other was a blokes' urinal, cobbled together from guttering and steel cladding sheets, which exited the building through a rough-cut hole in the wall.

Cambridge Danny had put them on to this party and it was back to his for the chill-out afterwards. Like old times, they all agreed, laughing at their own joke, trying the new link, enjoying the process. This felt good. It felt like power and achievement and it felt like people at their best.

Back at Danny's, Lee found himself, as he often did at chill-outs, in the heart of the kitchen, going deep into the chat. The front room was too loud for decent talk, but in the kitchen, Lee maintained, you could take both from the music and from the gab. He was talking to Donna and her mate Clare, and to Rob and to Kelly. They'd swapped information about family and upbringing, in which Lee had included his own Cambridge connection, and they were now majored on the thesis that a chill-out is an essential part of any rave, especially one that finished before six. It's at the chill-out, or the after-party, that you can transform all those little contacts made during the night into something profounder. Plans can be made, ideas and dreams exchanged and new ones synthesised. There is mutual therapy and self-help, there is delusion and fantasy, and there is convolution and sheer entertainment at the spoken sound of your own thoughts. You can also smoke yourself to mongdom-come, said Donna, clocking a bloke just in her eyeline, slumped in the front room, deadweight in an armchair, eyes half open, one leg twitching occasionally at the music, a hand hung limply over the side of the chair, a fat, faintly smoking spliff between forefingers. She took a couple of paces, leant down and gently took the spliff from the unresisting hand. Donna returned triumphant and resurrected the reefer in a few puffs. They laughed at the scenario and Lee said the answer to mongdom-come was more drugs of the right kind and, with that as a cue, he offered round his reserve bag of speed for dabs. It was at just this opportune moment that Danny entered the kitchen with his own small bag of magic.

'Lee, Lee, Merry-Lee, Merry-Lee,' he sang to them, waving at eye level a little plastic bag. 'Guess what I've got... a little bag of sunrises,' and he proceeded to remind Lee of their discussion about acid the last time they had been together; he showed him the small squares of blotter in the bag; they were printed with burning orange suns, rays broad against a lilac sky. 'Let's do a trip and go out for a walk,' proposed Danny like a pantomime villain. Everyone looked to the weak, hazy light outside – it was becoming winter. Danny leant over the sink and peered out of the kitchen window and up at the sky. 'It's dry. There's even a bit of sunshine. It's not gonna rain, is it?' He made the final question a statement.

'I tell you what,' said Donna, 'I'm not gonna do one but if you like, once you've dropped, I'll take you up to the Gogs in the car. Lee wants to see 'em and the view of Cambridge.

Can't get better than that view from the down.' The plan was accepted.

It took longer than expected to get out of the house. The acid was potent and kicked in quickly, the laughs and the visuals and the disorientation taking them by surprise, and the innocuous challenges of getting ready to go outdoors began to appear insurmountable. But Donna was a capable group leader; she managed them skilfully, gauging appropriate dress and appearance, reassuring the doubters and reminding the forgetful. Lee had gaps in his memory of this phase but retained a short sequence of them as they bundled themselves into Donna's car; a mess of fabric, skin, hair and voices amongst stuttering shifts of red and green and woozing treetops. Donna's voice and instructions cried in the air like gulls and he saw Tony through the squirming glass of the back window lead another group of chaos to his car; and as Lee fell into the well in the back corner of the back seat of Donna's car, he put from his mind the challenge of driving, as Tony was, while tripping. Even though the speed Lee had liberally dabbed earlier had taken a little of the edge off the intensity of the acid, there was no fucking way, he thought, that he could drive.

Lee was still marvelling at this, having noticed none of the journey, as they pulled onto a small muddy lay-by, little more than a half-scoop into the verge at the side of a road at the foot of Magog Down. A gap in the hedge at one end of the scoop indicated a path went that way. Outside, the air was cool and still, warm in pockets where the low sun slipped through and hazed the middle distance that lay in a soft band across blank fields, swept and striated, and a fine-textured sky. Lee moved towards the gap in the hedge and stopped, brought to stationary by the whelm of the hemisphere above and around him and his cognisance and intuition of its overarching physical presence. He stood and drank the ambient colour and sound, took the slightest of breezes and heard them whisper in his ears. He turned where he stood in the open air and activated the nerves of his face to the slightest of acupunctures as individual droplets of water vapour, held microscopic in a still cushion of air, pressed to his skin. He heard in their touch readiness for evening and readiness for the temperature to fall; fall and condense them out into drops of sparkling, drenching dew.

Lee freshened and inhaled pure silver. He turned back to look at the others stood in tableaux around the two vehicles they had travelled in; two vehicles steaming and blowing, at rest, tethered muddily at the roadside. His companions moved like walkers on the moon, slow and weightless, and around them blinked the damp air's dew-dropping promise. A vow of silent devotion star-burst around the point of disembarkation, halo and aura about his companions of the road. Lee felt a wave of vitality, an intensity of consciousness, a supra-awareness and intimate connection to everything he saw. He let his eyes leave the site of first encounter and lifted his face to the pale orange sky and held his arms wide. He stood. He stood and his standing pushed the earth up through the top of his head where it met the sky, which poured down and streamed out through the soles of his feet.

'Danny-Lee, we coming for you...' floated Zoe's voice in the damp, breathy air.

'Acieeed... Acieeed...' Lee heard distinct and shaped over a bubble of voice-noise, like the call of a wetland bird. Maybe, he thought, it is actually a bird; a bird sounding like a person, sounding like a bird, calling 'Acieeed.' He listened for other birds singing 'Acieeed' but Zoe got to him first.

'Take us to the top, Danny-Lee... take us to the bridge.' Zoe grabbed his arm and Clare took the other, and so in knots and pairs and small chains with simple bonds, they made a way through the hedge and up the rough-cropped flank of chalk-down meadow towards the high point in the land. Seventy metres up above the modern sea was the top of the fold in the chalk that had been looped up by the compression which had made the Alps. Lee was unaware of the way the Alps figured in where he was and how those mountains linked to this gentle chalk down, but his feet sensed the age of the land on which they walked and read deep-bass vibrations, shaking still, from past epochs. He looked at his muddy trainers, at the dirty white mud on them.

'The mud's white,' he said. Zoe and Clare looked at the three pairs of moving feet, the flashing trainers, and watched them as they printed marks on the chalky mud and watched them as they licked up skids of muddy chalk and took it with them. The six feet tied tight in their six trainers became the six feet of a single creature; a rapid walking giant of Albion; a swift, svelte goddess of the moon; an ecstatic, multi-limbed sun.

'Look at our feet,' said Zoe. 'Our feet are like god-wheels and our legs are the spokes,' and they all looked down at their spinning feet, spinning them to the top of the slope. They stopped and releasing each other, turned together. The land dipped away in a gentle curve and stretched out in a hazy plain, tinted rose and orange by the sun. Spires of mist rose in thin columns like the smoke of campfires. Spires and chimneys and rooftops, indistinct, in an angular mass of grey and red. 'Is that where we were raving last night?' she asked no one in particular.

'That's Cambridge,' said Donna as she made the top with Rob and Kelly, the three of them sharing two spliffs between them as they climbed, Kelly's camera swinging from its strap around her neck. 'Flat as anything, eh? All over there behind it and out that way,' she gestured vaguely to the right, 'is the Fens.'

'Yeah, we got lost out there somewhere the other month. Well weird. Freaked us all out.'

'I've seen some of the pictures,' said Lee mainly to himself and, as he said it, the long-distance view dissolved and he looked at a covered wagon, and horses in a field. Kelly stood behind him looking at him looking at the view through the viewfinder of her camera.

'Lee...' Kelly called, and as he turned she pressed the shutter button and a slice of light at 125th of a second caught him against the tinted sky, huge in outline imposed over the city spread below him. The image imprinted on Kelly's retina and repeated in the air before her like a strobe. Lee stopped and looked as Kelly spiralled in duplicate upon duplicate of herself, her eyes opening and closing like the iris of a camera, cascading light. Lee smiled and turned back to the view and watched as it again turned into caravans and horses. It became a still shot of a woman stood holding one enormous horse, the beast's whole head, and most of its neck, fully above the woman; a flash of white, an elongated spear shape, down the length of its nose. The woman, his nan, Vancy Swigler, stood in command, the horse held by the bridle, and stared, defiant, into the lens. Two young girls, his mum and his Aunt Elvira, he guessed, stood by under the protective presence of an older boy, but not much older, hair wild and tousled, cloaked in a greatcoat slightly too large for him. He reminded Lee of the Artful Dodger in *Oliver*. He also reminded Lee of himself. The scene receded slightly in the smoky air and another appeared beside it; two older women, creased faces, sat, probably on little three-legged stools, rounded and padded with skirts and shawls, upside down mushrooms, on a pavement of flagged stone, drinking tea from bone china cups covered in hand-painted roses which they balanced lightly on the edge of gilt-edged saucers held fine between worn fingers banded with gold. A basket of heather and flowers lay on the ground between them. Lee didn't know who these two were.

'Your mum's gran and her sister,' said a voice to him, labelling the scene as if, at the same time, carefully inscribing it on the reverse of the photograph in already faded copperplate. That voice, thought Lee. That was a faded copperplate voice. A voice like Grandad Swigler's but more old-fashioned. A copperplate Grandad Swigler. 'They still lived in the wagons then. How old's your mum in that one? About ten, I reckon. Don't look too happy in that one, does she?' The voice laughed and lungs squealed with the wheezes of tobacco and nights slept outdoors.

Still living in wagons, thought Lee. And in just ten years from that photograph he would be born. In just ten years from that photograph. Ten years, he repeated to himself. And he felt both how close this life was to him and how far away. What could his mum have known then about it all? How much more did she know ten years later? Maybe that snapshot is when it started to unravel.

'Yus, still living on the road and in them old tents 'n' all. Leastways your mum 'n' her sister was, 'cos your grandad sold one of the wagons.'

'Sold it?'

'To a Cambridge don so he could live in it when he was in Borneo.'

'Borneo? Why the fuck did he want it in Borneo?'

'Who knows, Danny-Lee? Cambridge don. Studying them tribes out there maybe? Trying to work out what they was up to with their funny customs and carry-on. All that dancing about, beads and drums and shaking spears… You need a don for all them shenanigans.'

'Did he know him? The don?'

'Must have known him a bit, eh? They always stopped around there; I s'pose he took a fancy to the wagon. Maybe thought it would bring him closer to the natives he was studying.' Lee paused on this and tried to fathom it; to imagine what "living in a tent" must have meant. He tried to manage his own life – basic as he considered it to be – into the straitened implications of "living in a tent". He failed. "Living in a tent" was not something he could successfully wrap around his own circumstances. He could not conceptualise it at all. He thought of his mum then, just a bit younger than his little sister, lying in a damp tent, the canvas greening in places where the winter damp rarely left, thinking about… thinking about what? Where would her imagination have taken her? In her thoughts was she a woman wrapped in skirts and shawls drinking tea in the street from china cups and selling flowers? Was this the source of her bad mood in the photograph, or did her imagination take her to other places? Lee wondered where they had camped. Had they lived in the fields where he had stood before the speaker stacks and lasers of a big open-air party? At the very least they must have used some of the same roads.

Lee was looking now from the top of the small chalk hills just to the south of Cambridge, back across the city below in the plain. He thought of the thousands of ravers, himself included, who would be out there in the city, in the fields, dancing somewhere, dancing themselves to transcendence until the sun came up, and he mixed them up with the travelling people who used the same roads and the same fields. Now he looked again and the city, swimming in the haze of winter sun, reasserted itself, and behind him he could hear the others, and he could hear also his grandad and his nan busy with rabbits and firewood. And back down there, out on the river plain somewhere, his mum and her brothers and sisters, sitting with the wagon and the tents and the horses, and the iron and the kettle and the fire.

Lee tried to put himself in place of his son or daughter, if he ever had one; he imagined them in their youth, doing what he was doing now, thinking about his mum's family and how far her recent life was from the life he was living. What view would they hold? What would they know about all this, all this as it was for him? Lee turned, and the others were spread across the hilltop in silhouette patches, stuttering with tracking. What would they know? How would they know? He looked at himself as if he was the unborn person he imagined. He saw himself standing on the hill, late autumn trees and empty fields all around and just him, a figure on a hill. A figure on a hill is how he would appear in the photograph Kelly had taken; a giant, smirking figure planted on the hillside, astride the muzzy town beneath, where the topography swept level. He circled three-sixty about the figure, uncertain that this could really be the person it claimed. How both connected and disconnected they would feel; the person he was then, barely older than they were now. How might they speculate and reach to understand their own currents and seasons from once-him on a hill? It was strange to think. It felt like trespass; of going against a confidence of trust, but in all innocence.

'Lee, you fuckin' plonka, what you doin'?' Rob's voice carried to him in shreds on the wind with ricochets of crows and seagulls. The vision collapsed in on itself and blinked to a point of persistent light, like turning off an old TV. He turned to see Rob loping towards him with flapping arms. 'Are you gonna do the electric boogaloo…? Give us a fuckin' hug, man,' and first Lee, then Rob, followed quickly by the others, joined in a huddle of psychedelic warmth and colour. They held in the blue-white sky that jetted over the wintery grass of the limestone hill that overlooked the hazy town on the edge of the watery flats of East Anglia, and when Lee opened his eyes he found himself back in the smoke and the music of Jason and Scott's shed.

# FOURTEEN

LEE DROPPED LIKE A STONE DOWN A DEEP, DARK well in the week that followed the Thetford Warehouse, the Thetford afters at Jason and Scott's. They all did – Lee, Rob, Zoe and Kelly – to some degree. But for Lee and Rob the fall was harder. It was harder for two reasons: they both had full-time jobs – Zoe and Kelly were at college and worked only part-time – and, once Zoe and Kelly had been dropped off at home, the two boys made their way back to Rob's and finished off the drugs they had left. A pill between them and a little speed. Not much but the cumulative effects were enough to guarantee a long night of delirious eyelid gazing, brain switched on permanent short-circuit to replay and edit scenes from the weekend, accompanied by eight bars of something on permanent loop and just on the tip of his tongue. The fall was protracted; a series of long-wavelength ricochets, the echo of one still fading as the next occurred. Only the presence of each other, just about enough hash and a tree in a quiet lay-by to smoke it under, *Twin Peaks* recorded from the week before and a video of *Quadrophenia* made it endurable; that and the faintly visible, far and distant summits of next weekend.

Lee and Rob had not even discussed what they were going to do once back from Scott and Jason's. One moment they were in the car, just pulling in, and the next, they were sat in Rob's bedroom, music on loud, dividing the remaining chemicals; unspoken agreement clearly reached that the weekend had, after the warehouse, the forest, Jason and Scott's, the drive home, one more scene to play out. Even if they had been told at the time that this scene would be unexpectedly long and, at the end, quite distressing, they would still probably have proceeded. The immediate rewards on offer seemed to exceed any possible downside. For Lee and for Rob too, this was the way the equation always balanced.

Once the drugs kicked in, Rob's room was not enough; they badly needed to get out, to smoke. This involved going downstairs, negotiating the hallway, exiting the house, entering the garage, all without interaction with other humans, especially if they were Rob's mum and dad. Usually, thought Lee, Rob's mum and dad presented no issues, but on the comedown, freshly wired with the leftovers and feeling… well, well, jagged, best not.

## //

The Friday evening before, just a few days ago, had been quite different. Lee had chirpily pressed the white button of the doorbell and heard the electronic chimes in the hall behind the front door. 'Oranges and Lemons', he thought. Shapes like *Predator* moved in the bubbled glass set at head height in the door; it opened and presented a short, broad woman, wearing an apron. She had darting, interested eyes; cheeks ruddy with dog walking; her hair pulled back and contained by a shiny patterned scarf. Lee had always thought Mrs Murgan looked like a typical farmer's wife; she wasn't, she worked in a school or something. Rob's dad worked with the Electricity Board. The house was a semi on a sprawling estate in Braintree. Maybe she cultivated the farmer's wife look, thought Lee; or maybe it was down to them being on the corner and having the extra big garden. Who knows...? He would never ask and the subject would never come up. Still, every time he saw her, he thought it.

'Rob in, Mrs Murgan?'

'Robert, it's Lee for you,' she shouted back over her shoulder towards the stairs. 'Come in, Lee, dear, he'll be down. Tea... and have you come to play with the car again?' she asked conspiratorially.

'Er, yeah, I s'pose... and Rob's gonna check me tyres... bit bald I think, Mrs Murgan.'

'Like my Martin,' said Mrs Murgan dryly. Martin was Rob's dad. Lee smiled and raised his eyes; the way you do when uncertain as to the balance of truth and jest in a personal comment made by one half of a couple about another. Older adults often seemed to throw these at you and, as far as Lee could judge, they were largely intended to discomfort you about the realities of long-term adult relationships. Lee returned to his purpose:

'He said he'd be about.'

Lee was, ostensibly, there to get Rob to check his worn tyres, but the main reason was to give Rob his share of the speed Lee had picked up. Still, coming to Rob's to play with cars was a ritual he and Rob had been into for years, going back to primary school when they had both got their first bikes. Rob had been messing with bikes and cars since forever, thought Lee. He was a natural mechanic, born with carbon under his fingernails, Rob's dad would say. All Lee knew was that he used it to get away with all sorts at work. On cue Rob appeared in the kitchen door. He did look a lot like his mum, it had to be said, thought Lee. He would tell him that later. Rob was taller, though, had shaggy hair and dark, bristly stubble, nothing like a farmer's wife.

'All right, Danny-Lee bwoi,' said Rob, two right hands grasped, the left wrapping the shoulders of the other. 'Shall we?'

There was a large garage to the side of Rob's house. It was set back from the front of the house and extended at the back to make a large workshop. This was where Rob and Baz played with cars and this is where they were headed, time-honoured, to make plans and chuff. Lee knew little about cars beyond what was needed to get him from one place to another, but he played up his interest to Rob's mum and dad; it made his frequent visits more credible. Maybe not so necessary now they were older but they still did it, mainly for old times' sake.

'Just gonna work on the car for a bit,' Rob would say to whoever was around in the kitchen.

'You work on that car a lot, Robert, but it never looks any different. How's that?'

'Preparation, Mum, preparation. That's what takes the time… it's the stuff what don't show that makes all the difference.'

'Hmm, I'm sure you're right, dear,' she would say.

A lot of cars had been through this garage but there was one particular long-term project that was usually being referred to. It sat, full of presence, at the back of the space and it had been in there for as long as Lee could remember. A lemon-yellow BMW 2002. Originally, it belonged to a mate of Rob's dad, but he'd given up on it and given it to

Baz. Technically, it probably was still Baz's car, but only Rob did anything with it – and he did next to fuck all, thought Lee. The car was basically all there, but it was a wreck. It sat like a crashed spaceship, luminous in the back of the garage. Holed, rusted, trim missing or hanging off, one dark socket from a missing headlamp, dash uncoupled and laid across the front seats, steering wheel on top, wiring looms exposed and perished, bodywork and chrome dinked and pitted. But it was still bad and mean, like a wounded tiger, snarling and wary, its pedigree undeniable.

Rob's dad would come in sometimes, probably aware that nothing was happening in terms of progress on the BMW. He probably sensed too that Rob and Lee were really just sharing time and space and, who knows, he maybe even knew that a few joints were involved. He didn't know enough to put it like that, but he would wander in unannounced and sniff the air in inquiry, registering the tangy strangeness of the smell but not sure how to broach the subject, and anyway, if he was honest, he was more interested in getting a taste of the uncluttered friendship of youth he no longer had access to. He stood as an outsider, welcome and unchallenged but unable to go further than just inside the door. The trick for Lee and Rob was to register nothing as out of the ordinary, as the burning spliff wreathed grey-blue skeins of heady smoke and aroma around them, which lifted them, in slow turns, to touch the inside of the low roof of the garage. Rob's dad could not fully compute the situation. It looked simple enough but he could not break it down, analyse it sufficiently to give himself a legitimate place in the equation. Finally, he would give up and leave on the back of a little half-hearted small talk. Obviously, thought Lee, this view was likely highly distorted by the mightily stoned state of both himself and Rob; a state given a firm twist by the knowledge each had of the other. That knowledge was the icing, the spice, the very glaze on the cherry. These ideas occurred as a complete whole to Lee, appeared in an instant, and as they did, right to order, there was noise and movement at the door handle and the hefty garage door swung out, admitting a wedge of yellow daylight swimming with specks and dust like microscopic creatures in a splash of pond water.

'How's the car going then, lads?'

'Yer, slow and steady, Dad. You know. Parts are pricey but, you know, doing the prep.' Mr Murgan nodded.

'D'you take Winston out earlier then?'

'Yep, did what he should. All looked in order. I'll take him again later, if you like,' said Rob, which seemed to work, although was slightly overdoing it in Lee's opinion.

'Good boy. Good boy. Mince 'n' onions for tea,' he half whispered, like they'd just tortured him for the information. 'You staying, Lee?'

'Mrs Murgan already asked me, Mr Murgan. Looking forward to it. I'm Hank bleedin' Marvin.' Rob's dad frowned for a moment, then remembered what Lee's words meant.

'Plenty to go round when Joan's cooking. You hear that, Rob? I said there's plenty to go round when your mum's cooking.' Rob nodded a few times and his dad nodded back, then he turned smartly and left the garage. Rob turned to look at Lee, his eyebrows raised and a slight smile that said he could not really be sure how that had gone but he thought mostly okay.

'There goes the old man.'

'He's all right, your dad,' said Lee, and raised the spliff he'd held in abeyance by his side while Rob's dad was there. He sucked on it rapidly a few times until the end glowed, balls of smoke rolling from the corners of his mouth, before he offered it over. Rob rolled his head loosely and looked at Lee in neutral acceptance of Lee's judgement on his dad; he took the spliff from the fingers of the upturned hand held out to him and looked away.

Lee narrowed his eyes a little and allowed his memory to spread out across the soft roll of the THC and CBD now energetic in the blood of his brain; he could still see the five-year-old in Rob's face. The first face of Rob that he had known. The face that had lost its front teeth after they had been spying from the roofs of the estate garages near Lee's old house; spying on the golden pheasants and fancy birds kept by the farmer in pens on the other side. The sight of the plumed and jewelled birds they could see from the roofs inspired them to hatch a plan to find a way to see the birds even closer. They knew the track to the farm was on the way to school.

They knew that way but knew no one that had ever been down it. They reasoned that if they followed the track to the farm, it would lead them to the place where the pheasants lived. They jumped on their bikes and headed out. They quickly reached the place where the track met the path to school. In silent accord, they turned away from the school path and headed up the track with their bikes, their pace slow, towards the farm. They were near enough to touch the part-open white five-bar gate at the entrance to the farm when something spooked them. Maybe one of them heard or saw something or, more likely perhaps, they just got frightened by the gate and by the signals of property; for Lee the effect mingled in his head with images from Ladybird versions of *Hansel and Gretel*, *Sleeping Beauty*, *Rumpelstiltskin*, and the sense of peril was strong. Whatever it was – and they'd gone over the ground many times, each holding the other responsible for the panic that followed – their response was unanimous. Although they'd done nothing wrong, they both knew it was time to scarper, time to put distance between them and the magic trouble that might lay beyond the big white gate. They turned their bikes and fled. Lee was in front, Rob just behind, both with legs spinning as they pushed the bikes to the limit back across the stones and dirt of the track. In the whirl and whirr of their flight, Lee glanced back to see if Rob was still there. As he turned, time slowed and he watched in helpless shock as Rob's front wheel tilted down into a deep, rubble-filled pothole. The memory was still vividly there. The wheel jammed hard into the hole and suddenly Rob was flying; he went high and became horizontal in the air, Superman, but unlike Superman, his face wore an expression of pure surprise at the way things had unfolded – from spying on birds to being one.

Then time moved at double speed, making up for the slowdown. Rob pitched towards the ground; his face changed to a snarl of anticipated pain and the earth hit him with terrible force. He ploughed face-first into the stony, rutted ground like a meteor strike. His bike somersaulted over him and fell like shot game as Lee stopped in a long, arcing skid. When the last stone thrown up had hit the ground there was silence and birdsong and dust and the distant murmur of the main road. The air smelled of cow parsley and hawthorn. *He's died, he's died, what am I gonna tell his mum?* Lee thought. Bloody Nora. Then Rob moved and lifted his head towards Lee, who sat on his bike, looking back over his shoulder. Rob's face was a mask of blood, snot, dirt and small stones; a collage which was rapidly mingled with spilling tears. 'Shall I get your mum; shall I get your mum?' Lee was just relieved Rob wasn't dead and now wanted an adult to take over. They left the bikes and, as it turned out, Rob's teeth, where they were and slowly and painfully made their way home. Rob lost both front teeth but not his love of machines and not his love of mucking about with Lee. It was a shared combat experience, the first of many that would bind them to each other. Times of meaning; quality and meaning, thought Lee as he played with remembered images and sounds, jumping back and forth in time, cutting and splicing and assembling his own montage. Lee slowly refocussed and Rob's current face morphed back before him. Lee sniffed with a start.

'So, you gonna look at me tyres or what?'

'Yeah, yeah, keep your wig on, mate. Finish this first,' and with a cheeky half toke, Rob passed the spliff back to Lee.

## //

They spent the rest of the day in the garage smoking and listening to mix tapes. They talked about the rave just passed and others they'd attended; they balanced out the pluses and the minuses of illegals versus legals; relived the magic of dancing in the forest; got deep about how words were not adequate to explain, or to describe, the way a night out became an irresistible, all-encompassing wave of energy and unity and wicked vibes as the drugs and the music and the lights and the people uniquely combined. This pattern of discourse became a foundation for them both as the last of the weekend ticked away; then and thereafter, they set about the weekend's final phase, determined to squeeze from it every last drop, to celebrate the doings of the previous two days by doing more on top of more, until what was done, and why, was no longer clear. The characters cast in these final acts would vary, and the venue could be one of many – rarely was the same combination repeated. But the performance always included a post-mortem of the event; themes and ideas would be introduced and developed, images and jokes would manifest and become a bespoke reference, custom-made for that chill-out. The best of these might feature in future post-rave shenanigans and some were to survive many years. These snippets and pastings also led them into the intricacies of what they were doing when they went raving, what it meant to them, how it worked individually and collectively. They enjoyed the challenge such considerations presented, the challenge of finding the language and the analogies to represent, the challenge of retrieval of coherent memories and information from the sensory distortions that were part and parcel of every event they attended and the challenge of trying to maintain basic levels of concentration in the face of the residual stutterings of the drugs and the paranoiac hallucinations of sleep deprivation.

For Lee, it also delayed going home until a time when he could be fairly sure that his sisters would be in bed and his mum and Malcolm would either be watching TV downstairs or, in bed, watching TV upstairs. If the former, he would glide by the half-open door of the front room, plate of something grabbed from the kitchen in one hand, and casually say something as he passed. Usually, whatever he said was poorly prepared and immediately led to doubt and second thoughts, which would spur him on to take the stairs two at a time to reach his room quickly and to avoid potentially difficult comebacks on whatever he'd just uttered. In fact, any interaction at home at this juncture was fraught with issues; where'd he been for the last forty-eight hours, what had he been up to, what were his general life intentions in the short, medium and longer term? So, Lee always prayed for the latter situation; it gave him options – TV downstairs or his room – and it was his luck that this situation was the one he most commonly found.

That evening, after leaving Rob all but comatose in his garage, Lee had options. The front room was dark and he could hear the burble of the TV in the bedroom above him as he quietly picked his way round the kitchen, like a big roach, looking for food left over from Sunday lunch. He found plenty and piled cold roast dinner onto a plate, eating it as he did so.

Great, he thought, just take this and eat it while watching TV in the dark. What could possibly be better before bed? He shut the door of the front room carefully behind him with his foot and arranged himself in front of the TV. By the time he'd found something to watch, the food was gone and he was in a near-helpless trance brought on by his body's total survival-mode focus on the proteins, carbohydrates, fats, trace elements and minerals in the food he had just eaten. The music programme he'd found finished almost immediately and he drifted off on the tide of his fatigued, food-caressed blood; thin bubbles of sweat breaking out across his forehead, music of his own mind's making playing strong in his head. As he floated out, he looked up and it was as if he was underwater, looking out into the air and up at the dry land. He could see himself through the water's refraction and gentle movement, as a figure on a chalk hill. He was made of white stone and was living in a tent, and he understood the land and the sky and knew what to do about it. He knew that it had all been a long time coming; but he knew it was here now and that it was important for him to seize hold and to not let go. He looped around on these images and ideas and the fractal trains of thought they brought, until, slowly, he became aware of the sound of a voice. The voice came from the TV; the voice was the narrator of the programme that the TV in the corner was broadcasting into the dark room. The voice and the things it was saying had woven their way into the Mobius twist of his half-conscious thought and he lay for a while, focus split between his own thoughts and their internal soundtrack and the words and packets of information coming from the TV. The voice was calm and precise, clear in the presentation of complex information:

*...geology of Eastern England... Eocene... Cretaceous... sediments laid down over millions of years... lush tropical*

*forest and a warm shallow sea... fossil bearing deposits...inter-glacial warming and rising sea levels... diverted the course of the Thames... flint tools... early hominids...*

Occasionally, he opened an eye to look at an image of rocks in an old quarry, or an exposed cliff showing different layers of rock. He was theoretically interested. The programme was about East Anglia, Essex in particular; he knew lots of the places it mentioned but his waking awareness was closing down. He finally switched off the TV and made his way up the stairs to his room, his sense of dimension wavering so much that going up felt like going down. He lay on the bed and looked at the flyers that were steadily advancing across the wall and ceiling; inspired to one last effort of movement, he reached into his jacket pocket for the photocopied Destruction flyer that had meet point details for the warehouse rave just enjoyed. He put them together on top of the notebook he'd started after that first Eclipse. Something to do in the long, bleak stretch of the week ahead, he told himself. The thought and prospect of that week, already lying in wait for him, red-eyed, lank and sneering, jolted him with adrenaline and set off a cascade of chemical reactions. Lee stared hard at the ceiling. It was like the flyers were inflating and deflating, moving in and out, shifting back and forth between two and three dimensions. He closed his eyes; he needed to sleep, not to freak out about the week ahead. Easier said than done, easier said than done; he repeated the words until they became bullying, became the teasing words of the mean-eyed week that lay in wait. Lee needed to divert his attention somewhere else. He inhaled, closed his eyes and followed the lava lamp blobs of colour he could see on their lids and began to rewind and rerun what he had heard on the TV downstairs, things that had lain then so blissfully on his mind.

He'd missed the beginning, what was it? An Open University programme or something... presented by someone from the University of Essex, Cambridge University and somewhere in Germany... something Berg... one of a series, he thought he could remember. What was it that had grabbed him? The Clacton Spear... the fucking Clacton Spear. Yes, yes, show me the Clacton Spear... *about thirty centimetres long and probably 400,000 years old... found here on the seafront about eighty years ago... the oldest worked wood in the world... some of the earliest evidence of early human settlement in Britain.* Lee had opened an eye here and seen a long, thin, pointed, slightly curved piece of wood. You might have chucked it for your dog on the beach if it hadn't been so sharp. He pictured a hairy, half-naked ape-man, jabbing at a mammoth. The spear he used had a point like the Clacton Spear... *finds like this in the area suggest early Hominids coming north into Britain during the warmer interglacial periods.*

Lee adjusted his hunting scene to include the rhinoceros and hippopotamus mentioned in the programme... *at a time when the course of the Thames passed by what is now Harlow and Chelmsford and met the Medway at Clacton.* This was harder to visualise but the attempt was taking Lee away into the story he was making and away from the merciless interrogation of work the next day... *after a mega flood caused by warming and retreating glaciers broke through and destroyed the chalk ridge connecting Britain to Europe.* Chalk again, thought Lee, and he intuited that the chalk in Cambridge and the chalk in Essex and the chalk in the ridge that connected Britain to Europe were the same chalk. What had Insect Dave said? It was made from millions of years of the shells and shit of dead creatures falling to the seabed. All the chalk, then, must be the same seabed, he reasoned. ...*this short series of programmes will look back at the deep geological history of the earth. We will start at a time when all the landmass of the earth laid spread about the Southern pole – the region where, more or less, we now find Antarctica – and the rest of the surface of the planet was sea. We will explore the conditions and processes that led up to the discovery of the Clacton Spear on the beach around what is now Clacton seafront...*

Lee had memories of Clacton and its seafront from quiet, dusty family holidays at Rosebank Caravan Park. But the seafront and the pier were the beacon that steered him; the metal shout of amusement-arcade noise, shuddering street-van generators; the smell of chips and candy floss and beer and, entwined round all of that, the sound and smell of a dirty green sea sloshing straps and feathers of seaweed round the dark, barnacle-studded legs of the pier. Bet whoever dropped that spear could not have imagined what Clacton seafront would become, thought Lee, and he watched his hairy hominid with a spear lope down the pavement past the pub, the Gaiety Arcade, the Gameshow Arcade – *fun for all the family* – and on towards Jungle Safari. No one would bat an eyelid, Lee concluded.

*Palaeozoic... Silurian... Devonian... geology of this area really starts with chalk... the oldest rock that you can see at the surface in Essex... chalk provides the underlying structure for the London Basin, an enormous depression in the chalk layers which lie beneath London and Essex.* Fuck, I knew it, thought Lee. The next time I see Insect Dave or Cambridge Danny, they're gonna get the full chalk. *...chalk was formed in the Cretaceous... originally a horizontal layer... bed of a tropical sea... millions of years later, continental Africa crunched into Europe creating the Alps... crystal clear water... teeming with marine life... molluscs, sponges, corals, sea urchins and fish... mosasaurs... paddle-like limbs and big jaws lined with sharp, conical teeth... London Clay...* Lee was now adrift on a warm tropical sea teeming with life which swam around him and lived and died and floated down to the seabed. The chicken factory was on the seabed and it was half-buried… soon it would be encased in chalk like a nodule of flint. He drifted away from the chicken factory and saw his nan and grandad in the Polo he now had, and they were towing the little Sprite caravan they used to have. His mum and dad were in the back but he couldn't see their faces. The caravan was full of pies because it had become the pie factory. Outside the high windows of the factory was a sea teeming with life, and he saw marine creatures there waving down at him and he was a speck upon the water. Must be on their lunch break, he thought. *The pie machine, the pie machine, so much better than the chicken machine; the pie machine, the pie machine, so much better than the chicken machine* was repeating in his head and the noise of the words became music, became a tune, a wicked tune that he heard as the big cream-yellow pie machine stamped out pie cases from monster rolls of pastry; a wicked, wicked tune that he heard as he took a group of eager students to look at the Clacton Raver Outcrop. *The Clacton Raver Outcrop is an ancient sedimentary layer brought to the surface by geological folding caused by a distant continental collision. The layer is made up of flyers, baggies, Rizla, old trainers and water bottles which sank to the bottom of a cool green sea and, over millions of years, formed Ravercite Rock. If we look at the rock closely, ghostly fossil imprints of some of those things of which the rock is made can be seen.* The students looked baffled but polite.

*The pie machine, the pie machine, so much easier on the brain machine…* the noise of the words still produced music and the music rocked him as the sky went dark. A fanned deck of red light swept on and off in the velvet sky. Dark ink surrounded it and blobs of green after-image wobbled in its path. There was a nagging in the ink. Something prodding and something grey and unattractive, squatting behind him, just quivering in his blind spot. Lee moved his head slowly from side to side, testing the air as if he had whiskers like a cat. *My head is in a speaker*, Lee told himself, and he smelt dark paper and hot solder. The lights behind him were intense; he could feel their heat and they created a fanned deck of colour on the back of his eyelids and there was nagging and prodding.

Lee opened his eyes at the exact moment the hands on his alarm clock triggered the fat spring inside the clock to rapidly vibrate a tiny hammer against the surface of a small brass bell. He looked at the angry clock propped up inside its red case and a G-force lurch of acceleration took him, in less than the time it takes for an eyelid to open and fully retract beneath the brow, from less-than-zero-lucid-dream-trip to sixty-miles-a-second-Monday-morning-at-the-pie-factory. Above him the flyers on the wall and ceiling flitted like shoals of fish and made space-bending volumes in the deep abyss behind his eyes; heliograph codes fed down the funnel of his optic nerve. Lee closed his eyes in a hope that had no hope because he knew it was real. *Pies better than chickens*, he said to himself. Pie machine, brain machine. Keep it positive. Probably still be buzzing today once I'm up. Focus on that, get through this day… then get ready for the monsters on Tuesday and Wednesday. Deal with that when it happens, he instructed himself; it is enough for now to know there are options. *So many options*, he echoed to himself and closed his eyes again.

A banner streamed across the screen of his eyelids, a banner of names: Desire, Destiny, Fascination, Milwaukees, then to Rush, Labrynth, Bagley's, up to Roller Express, Eclipse, Dreamscape, Seduction, Kite High and now Utopia, Climax, Kryptonite, Helter Skelter, to the ones like Proper Stuff, Elevation, World Dance, Oscar's, Too-Toos. The banner circled him, slowly at first but gaining speed with each turn, and with each turn a bass reverberation. Six turns, seven turns, eight… The individual words on the banner split for an instant, then rejoined, more bass, more drum, they divided and re-formed, sheared and layered synth in mass precision plant a rhythm to match the drum and the bass, all synchs with the flash of lights in the gloss of the banner, the words there separating and relocking, separating and relocking; so fast and so loud; all individuality gone, and Lee, in a sea of resonance, was submerged. His entire physical and spiritual essence disintegrated; he became a mass of flicking, flacking, slippery flyers twisted into a tight-packed frenzy of manic activity, corralled like a bait ball, spinning and spinning and spinning. As the revolutions reached obliteration, the bait-ball mass was popped out through the sea's surface, taken clear by the lift of its own buoyancy to scatter in surf and wind, a tang of ozone and salt, a surge of blue, green and white...

## //

...Lee put out a steadying hand as if managing his balance on a boat at sea. His eyes were still closed and he was not sure where he was. Did he have to get up for work now or not? Something, someone, told him he didn't; it was the weekend. He trusted that voice. He took a breath, lifted his head, extended his chin out and opened his eyes to look straight up above him. Trusses and beams ran in neat patterns under roofing felt; roofing felt lay under roof tiles. There was a weak orange glow of an energy saving bulb somewhere just out of sight. Lee blinked and looked down. The boards of the loft around him were a scattering of flyers and notebooks and cards on lanyards. Tapes spilled from an upended shoe box over an open road map next to a half-full record bag. Lee drew himself together with a deep inhalation through flared nostrils, fixed each joint of his being into its socket, shook his head on his neck and began gathering up the scattered archive.

# FIFTEEN

LEE SAT IN THE CAR GENTLY SHAKING HIS HEAD. FUCKING
mad, he thought. Still seems fucking mad. I seem fucking
mad. There's been a lot going on, he consoled, but even
so... Despite these conclusions about his mental state, Lee
felt remarkably composed, and the feeling of clarity and
commitment to some unknown purpose remained. He
shrugged and relaxed himself, then turned to the things on
the passenger seat and reached for the road map, allowing
it to open according to custom to show the edge of East
London and Essex. The trunk of the Thames glistened
silver and the M11 was a blue vein into the heart. This
time the impact of the map was less confusing; there was
more sense to be found in its communication of coloured
lines and strange neuro-shapes; he was oriented, manner
relaxed, better able to manage the twists, the turns and
stretches of journey.

Lee now pulled the box of tapes his way. He wanted a set from those early times. He guided himself quietly with the years, '91, '92, '91, '92, his fingertips resting on the tape-cases. The air beneath his fingertips juddered subtly; he touched the tapes and as with the map, there was interaction. Talismanic. He could feel it; it was like the objects were part of a preparation, a ceremony. He looked round him then and the car was full of people, faces replacing and rotating like an interchange of slides on a carousel, slotting and spinning, turning on a huge gear. Everyone was in his car. His grandad, Baz, Zoe, his mum and dad, Rob, Kelly, Insect Dave, Donna, Cambridge Danny, that bloke from Labrynth, other nameless faces from countless rides from and to parties, some who rode in the boot, some who lay across the laps of those in the back, some to whom he gave a lift to the station. He saw himself there too, sitting on the passenger side, a different vehicle, his grandad's Sherpa, going to auctions, visiting Tilbury, his dad's old Cortina looking for unmarked battlefields, his mum's Fiesta going to Bury, going to Dunmow. Rob was there shagging someone on the back seat he had met that night, and there was Kelly sleeping in the driver's seat, Zoe sleeping in the passenger seat, the windows fogged from the inside, covered in condensing dew from the out. It was a kaleidoscope of faces and places and states of mind, a flic-flacking rotation of memory and it was preparing him, conditioning him, building the anticipation, providing an overture, gearing for the last leg of a multi-stage race. It all felt exactly the way he expected he should have felt right now; exactly the way. The positivity of the thought reconnected him with his purpose and his walk out to the car moments before. He had felt the potential in himself as if he was the point of deep control in a tune of otherwise unhinged Hardcore madness, full of menace and scintillating danger.

It was Labrynth that had been in his head as he had walked to the car; Labrynth and the Lab connection made after Bliss. That's when it opened up; they had taken the road into London and all then to another dimension. That first glimpse from Bliss, that feeling that it had all been leading up to this… that this was always going to happen. That feeling that it had been written. That that was just how it bloody well went. But Labrynth… Labrynth. The Four Aces Club, Dalston Lane (and on occasion other London venues for the ravers' delight), what a fucking place. Yes, something from that time was what he needed. But also something that made that Bliss connection. Lee tapped his fingers across the tapes, shifted some out, slotted others in their place. Far fewer tapes from those early years, he noted, but there *would* be something there for this journey. There *was* something there, ready and waiting to start this trip. And there it was; *Top Buzz Clacton 1991*, the words written in faded black letraset transfer on the cardboard insert behind the plastic spine. He held the tape box, the words pointed sharply at him. Obviously, he thought, nodding at the tape. Top mix, top night, all-time fave; the mix Zoe had put on for the journey back from Double Dipped. Double Dipped, The Secret Garden, his last rave; the end of the longest party, the last time he made the journey of journeys, the journey home from a night of fucked-up wonder. He scrolled through Zoe's memory stick. She must have it; he knew she would have it; it was an all-time special. *Top Buzz Clacton 1991*, orange on black in the little display window. Naturally… if Mangled was there then he was always going to find Top Buzz at Oscar's.

Been a while since he'd heard these tunes, he thought, then corrected himself; the hours of tunes he had already lived through this morning should have primed him up for this nicely. No, no time at all, he corrected, no time at all; it had been happening since he'd woken up, before then, since Thursday; but today it had really come alive. Yes, come alive and brought him here; sat him ready to drive back to Braintree, ready to just get fucking ready. Yes, he knew this morning was just the start and my God, he had forgotten just how fucking fine it had been. They thought they could see it at the time but no one really did. Not truly, you were too close and it was too electric. That's how it always is, he figured. Could it happen now? The question floated before him. Could what happened to them then, happen to anyone now? Zoe had touched on this one; she said it couldn't and he wouldn't argue with that.

Lee selected play... *all the way from London Town...* he mouthed the words of Mad P and The Tingler and as he started the engine and pulled away into the viscera of lines and ways and tunnels and bridges that connect us all to each other on the flat pages of a road map. And as Lee drove himself out onto the streets of North East London, his car filled once again with people and faces and voices. Outside, the space collapsed into many realities; it was a dark night on an unlit country road, then daytime in the fumy suburbs of North East London – the sun bright over terraces and slanted through the side windows; it was grey with rain falling in ropes down the windscreen, obscuring fields and woods; it was a roadside verge just down from the bend where two country lanes meet in a shady, hollow way, the car hot-boxed; now it was the M11, late evening summer half-light, the car surging south full of hardcore business and righteous breakbeat headed for a party; and now it was dawn in a cold world on the A120 between Dunmow and Braintree, the last stage of a long homeward stretch full of quiet, full of smoke, fogged with breath and damp bodies. Lee turned up the music... *In the place to be...* *Top, Top-Top-Top-Top, Top Buzz...* and he was taken back, on his way to Labrynth for the first time.

# SIXTEEN

THE FIRST VISIT TO LABRYNTH QUICKLY FOLLOWED
the party at the old farm. It was a first night in London for
them all except for Baz, who was there that night too. They
were full of tension for it days before, and by the time Friday
came around they could barely speak. Lee's plan was to leave
straight from his late shift at the factory. He'd put his raving
trainers and jacket in the locker at work, with other stuff he
needed, and would go live and direct from there. Zoe would
do the same and come with him from Bready Brothers; from
there to Rob's house, pick up Kelly and Rob, then Rob's to
Labrynth, London Town... wicked... get in the car, let's go. Baz
was meeting them there and others, Cambridge, Colchester
and Dunmow, were down to go as well... *Danny and Donna
said they're coming... heard from Mike and Dave in the week,
they're bringing a crew... Ian said he's on it...* There were
rumours about who was and who wasn't going and rumours

about rumours around every other aspect of the night; but, beyond his own carload and plan – an A-Z, the address, a firm intention to be there and the gathered promises that they would have nothing less than a fucking wicked time – Lee could not think.

The plan went well enough. The car was full of firm intent, rising to spitting energy as they left the garage forecourt at Birchanger and hit the M11 with the final fall of darkness and the last light dipping away below the Hertfordshire horizon. They tore down the motorway, concrete patched and frayed, past the ghosts of the Charlie Brown roundabout and on to Redbridge, historic Essex. Lee had a torch in the glove box and with Zoe going full spectrum on the A-Z, they managed the Redbridge roundabout and headed across the bottom end of Waltham Forest and into Hackney. They had no idea where they were. Road signs in London mostly failed to exist and the streets were chaotic with Friday; the light, noise and commotion of late night, early summer, spilled everywhere. The stimulation was immersive and the crafty line of speed they'd done before leaving, plus sips from the bottle of water earlier fortified with a fat wrap, ramped up the anticipation. They made it to Dalston and a side street east of Kingsland Road and parked up, erratic with excitement. The Four Aces Club was nearby, easily found and advertised with a queue that snaked off up the Lane towards the station; a queuing, chewing, shuffling, smoking monster with hundreds of feet. A good sign, a good sign, they all agreed, still dismayed by the prospect of handling their state while standing in line. But good raves started with fuck-off queues, and queuing with enjoyment was the first art of the night; the best approach.

By the time they were through the door of the Four Aces, they were familiar with other queuers several deep around them and with the fabric of that part of Dalston Lane. Most of it looked condemned, thought Lee, and especially the Four Aces itself. But the buzz in the queue... this was going to change things... he had a good feeling about it and managed some saunter in his stride as he passed through the door; this was his mission; he was briefed, primed and charged; he was ready to deploy, he was live; he was a ground-to-air system, hardcore driven, operating on hair triggers.

Lee would never forget that first one at the Four Aces Club. First London night, first Labrynth night. Things could never be the same again. The door of 12 Dalston Lane was a portal into another world in a way none of his raving had prepared him for, although, he sometimes thought, maybe it had always been about this. It was as if someone had put together, perfectly, everything needed to recreate the scene of a hovering-beyond-control, wild and energetic, dirty London rave club and had then decided, just for a laugh and for emphasis, to really overdo it. That was what it was like and that was what it was always like, no matter how many times you went, it hit you like that; that was why the people who went there came back week after week; that was why it stayed in their hearts and minds forever after. It was everything it should have been and more, taking the essence of the scene and compressing it to a singularity. Packed into an infinitely small warren of rooms and tunnels, an infinitely dense mass of grimy frontline London, righteous hardcore, railing youth, defiant sweat and volatile phenethylamines, super stimulating hallucinogenic entactogens, exploded each and every Friday and Saturday night, exploded with the energy of a new universe, rushing at unimaginable speed into space and time and light. That was how it felt, thought Lee – in a nutshell.

If asked to describe that night, Lee would have resisted, knowing that words could not convey what it was necessary to feel in order to understand. But if pressed, he would have said it was dark, full of noise, swept with light and beamed with lasers, that the fabric of the building flexed and vibrated with the music. He would have said that at times it was so full of moving people that sense of floor, of walls and of ceilings, disappeared; there were just bodies, heads, limbs moving in the scanned dark to the booming pulse of the music, the arms of anemones and sea-plant fronds, moving in the wash of the tide over a reef. As you entered, you could see some kind of platform or stage, at the far end; you could tell because the sweaty, shiny bodies were elevated here. Other elevated bodies were on top of the main speaker stacks either side of the stage. Further into the venue, there were tunnels and stairs and rooms and an impossible outside area, cupped up in the heart of the old building. Lee might have added how on that first night he lost everyone in the early morning crush that always seemed to develop at Labrynth, so many people, so crammed, it became near impossible to move – finding a somewhere and occupying it before this time, was wise strategy.

But Lee would also have said that losing everyone meant he met everyone else. He would have explained how he struggled through the pressing bodies and found a space at the back of the stage on some stairs that went nowhere and just sat and listened and looked and took pleasure in the state of grateful amazement he found himself experiencing. I could do little else, he would have said, and in this state everyone came to him: 'Wassyourname, whereyoufrom, whatyouon…?' 'Wassyourname, whereyoufrom, whatyouon…?' And every now and then, 'Youallrightmate?' to which he replied, 'Yea, safe, takin' a breaver…' which triggered… 'Wassyourname, whereyoufrom, whatyouon?' One of these encounters involved a young bloke, younger than me, thought Lee, a lot younger, probably, more a boy. He nodded as the boy approached, pursing his lips and screwing up his eyes in a complex gesture of greeting and affirmation. The boy sat down; he was bare-chested and wet with sweat, it sheened on his skin under the lights; his hair was plastered to his head and neck; dark patches spread from the waist of his jeans. His eyes, sunk back in their sockets, were deep, dark wells.

'Avin' a good one, mate?' Lee lifted his head and positively raised his eyebrows at the boy, smiling. 'What you done?' Lee mumbled something about pills and speed, but the motive was not finding out about Lee's consumption, it was to proudly reveal his own.

'Two pills and a gram,' he said, patting his chest like these achievements were medals. 'Double dropped, innit... mashed for a while but you know... there's another gram in me water.' He shook a bottle in front of him as he said this. The boy was free, released and loose with dancing and drugs, and in Lee he'd found an audience for the drama of his own adventures.

''Ere, listen to this.' The lad leaned to Lee's ear and began to chat rapidly, rhythmically, cupping his hand round his mouth to channel the flow. Lee was helpless against the manoeuvre; the words came, an unchecked torrent. Lee struggled to focus on the MCing but it was too much and most of it passed unmanaged and unheard around the mechanics of his inner ear. Lee felt the rhythm in the movement of the boy's head and the marking inflection on words that hit key beats, but that was as much as he could fix.

'Yea, yea,' Lee said, 'nice.' He had no idea if it was good or not. It didn't really matter.

The boy offered his hand at this point and said: 'Terry.'

'Lee,' replied Lee as he grasped the hand. The boy stood up in a reflex and, like a security detail, scanned the mashed and the sprawled and the shell-shocked. Chewing at one side of his face, he turned to stare at the first ranks of the mass of dancers in the main room; he began to beat time against his chest with a silver whistle that hung from his neck.

'Later, mate...' he said, turning and pointing at Lee, meeting one bottomless eye-well with another.

'Yes, mate,' said Lee, and the boy headed into the writhe of bodies that held the front of the stage.

As the night progressed, Lee would have said, pockets of space appeared and he found himself on the stage, dancing, inspired, physical, emotional, looking back out over the main room, his eyes tuned to the lasers searing the dry ice. He would have mentioned how he felt he knew everyone, how he felt tuned to the music, the whistles, the shouts and the horns, how he felt he had lived his whole life to the full during that one night, how he felt proud of the achievement that the night represented for every single person involved, and that every single person there had made a personal contribution, unique and particular, to the transcendent accomplishment that was finally, perfectly, exquisitely reached at the point the last tune played and the house lights came on. And as this happened, Lee looked about him with the gift of new senses; his receptors, nerves and cells enhanced and optimised; he was portal, conduit, sender and receiver, and the hardcore energy flowed into and from him; it radiated, it broadcast, acknowledged all in the place. Lee felt still and impossibly energetic, he knew high peace, raw emotion and the mad effort of human spirit. He looked at the other Hardcore ravers in the new light of morning and he understood that their journey had been the same as his; and he understood that they knew that about him too. Words had no need; lock hands, embrace, nod, smile. What he had heard that night, who had played, who had MC'd, what else had happened, he could not, at that point, have told you. It just was, it had just been. And in this rapture, he saw Zoe and Rob and Kelly, and Baz and his mates, on the main floor just below the stage where he stood, tall, yet humble, a model for a study in devotion. Those he looked on below were shiny and wide-eyed, newborn like he was, an attitude of new vision about and behind the eyes. Lee sensed too their concern to find him and was touched by it; he watched, entertained by the search; entertained by the way they bathed in slow sound, the sound of soft voices no longer raised to match the Ks of the Eskimo Noise, the quiet sounds of moving coats and shifting feet, the tidal wash of no-music that still played in his ears.

'Zoe, Rob, oi, Kelly...' They looked round and lit up both at the sight of him and at the sight of him on the stage, bright and gleaming, a mirror of themselves. He got down and they hugged and clasped and kissed like they had made it through something life-defining.

'Fuck me...' said Rob, 'what a fuckin' night, what a fuckin' place...' and they stood and looked at each other and milled around on the spot where they stood, just below the stage where Lee had been moments before.

Rob surfaced first. 'Where were you, mate?' Didn't see you all fuckin' night.'

'Did my second half at about half one... danced in the middle for a bit then got stuck in the fuckin' crowd and couldn't move... found some stairs at the back for a sit-down and some bloke MC'd in my ear.'

'Yea? We found them stairs 'n' all... stairs to fuckin' nowhere... but we were down in the tunnel most of the time. So who was the MC?'

'I don't think he was an actual MC... more of an enthusiast... yea... he was going so fast, I couldn't follow to be honest. It was too much, man. Fuckin' 'ell, my head was all over the gaff... it could have been good, it might have been shit. I told him it was wicked...'

'Naturally,' said Zoe.

'I don't think he really cared what I thought, he just loved the chance. Yea, so then I danced like a nutter at the front of the stage for who knows how long, tripped out big time, and before I knew what was happening, the lights come on, the music stops, and we're all in an underwater dream and there you are floating about looking for me. Where d'you lot get to?'

'Well, we went on a fuckin' world tour, mate. All over. Met loads of safe people. Had a few massages. Come up big time, danced on the stage for a bit, looked after some girl on the stairs – what was her name? Kerry? – anyway, rescued her from a downer, then danced our arses off in the tunnel with her and her mates. Fuckin' brilliant night.'

'All right, all right, c'mon, boys and girls. Ain't you got homes to go to? Movin' out now, make your way towards the doors, please.' The bouncers were moving amongst them, fanning and shepherding the beached and bewildered, the triumphant and the ecstatic, out towards the door and the cool, bright light of an early summer's morning; out towards the definite colour and shape of the city outside.

'Is that it?' said a bloke, jigging about in the melee just in front of them as they left. 'Is that it? For a tenner?' And he jigged off down the Lane towards a group of three or four hunched figures, waiting, but still heading slowly towards Kingsland Road.

# SEVENTEEN

LEE RE-EXPERIENCED ALL THIS AS IF IT WAS
happening for the first time. He was aware of his present self,
driving out towards the North Circular, following a compulsion
to drive back to Essex; he was aware that the space which filled
the car swung from being just empty air to being full of the life
that peopled countless similar drives made in different times;
and he was most especially aware of the countless, countless
possible scenes, scenarios and situations that knitted him to
the fabric of these roads. It was like he existed forever and
everywhere, like all the realities of location and history and
of thought and of time were simultaneous and never-ending.
It was like he inhabited the consciousness of many slightly
different people who all lived and breathed together across the
same span of years. And the music – the music of Top Buzz,
Oscar's, Clacton 1991, the music came strong to him – and
that too was woven in; that also connected him from space

to space, from point of origin through each and every new incarnation of every play. He marvelled at how the sequence of a mix could do that; could shift perception, create a unit, a new apprehension, a distinct and separate entity. Mind-blowing, he thought; the sheer multiplicity of variables, the thousands of woven strands of information and sensation to cause the air and the emotions to vibrate with that music.

The power of the insight opened Lee's mind to all the places in which that music had existed and how its existence in his car, right then, was, in turn, shaping the character of those parts of the world with which it was coming into contact. Like shuffles, riffles and running cuts performed over and over on a deck of thousands and thousands of cards, each one a nexus of time and space and people and movement. The music in the car, right then, was an aspect of this system. Yes… the music… and the music filled the car. The MC called… *and it happens to be Top Buzz all the way from London Town… actually from Tottenham… big up your chess… we happen to be the guv'nors in the place…* Lee heard the inflexions of the boxing ring in the tones of the MC, and he heard the whistles of the crowd at Oscar's, coming over the mic. His skin was in ridges of goosebumps and his stomach swooped; tribal, jungle-trance, the perfect soundtrack to bowling along the gum-pocked pavement of Dalston Lane; the ideal backbeat to leaning into the wind on an age-scoured street amongst the tangle of yards and bridges behind King's Cross; the rhythm of choice, spilling out, Holloway Road, pre-dawn and fresh; the king-step to greet the early sun blazing in long bands down the brick canyons of Charing Cross Road; the vital skank to prevail against the fun-resistant ducts and prefab cladding, Lea Valley Trading Estate. For Lee, now, every London street and season rang with the music; it sounded and purred in clear summer daylight and dark, winter dawns; colour and tones flexed in every stone and particle with the tunes of the night before. All those pavements bounced under his trainers, shirt still damp and sunglasses slewed off-centre on a slippery nose. A fire-resistant spliff, badly but heroically made from sweat-damped Rizla salvaged from wet, torn cardboard, pinched between thumb and forefinger, held in towards the palm.

It was a pattern, thought Lee. A pattern set as we came out onto the street after that first Labrynth; unknowingly, he thought, we set a pattern to be repeated over and over as we came and went to rave after rave; and not just Labrynth – other raves in the city, other cities, the country and all the bits in between. The exit from Labrynth itself, made so many times, after the most blinding night on so many occasions, was overlaid upon itself, multi-plyed to become archetypal, a mode. Even nights that happened pre-Labrynth were overlaid with it, captured by this rite. To a degree, *the leaving* became Lee's favourite part of going out; to him it mattered more than arriving; arrivals were too edgy, he thought, too much nervous tension at the prospect of six, seven, eight hours or longer of dancing and of buzzing hard. No, it was the leaving with the night still high inside you that really counted. Lee could access the memory of it through countless occasions intermingled. Always it started in jittery tension, always it ended in the undersea dream of the house lights, exit to the Labrynth standard, *hardcore generals in the place.* The world outside was fresh and they cut through the mayhem of confusion and fuckedness, flyer agents and minicabs, span from the tangle and rolled down the street, easy, everything in stride, springing to people only met the night before, bouncing with those already known, the dial on the frequency. The path to the car was a marked line on a map inside your head, featuring distractions of a stranger, a fellow raver in the street, a fleeting contact made to talk on about something about nothing, to the point of all forgetting why you're stood there in the first place.

Lee shook his head free of the reverie and reminded himself why he was where he was in the first place; he'd had a hunch in a train of consecutive tripping flashbacks that he should head back to Essex. It was a mission and a mystery; a hunch, hallucinations, a cache of artefacts and a haunted car. Yep, a haunted mission is about right, thought Lee, and even as he thought it the sense of the words spun his stomach and again landed him, a gymnast, on the pocked pavement outside the Four Aces. Another night of Labrynth and here he stood again, with Kelly this time, after the exit, outside on the street; the two of them contained and calm in the mayhem. Dawn was arriving but is always delayed by London and the light was only half there. Flyers were being pushed into hands as people blinked from the doorway of the club, mini-cabbers were milling and muttering, hustling for fares, and people in their same state, all about, milling too and waiting for friends. Some chatted, most just wondering what to do; so sudden for them the challenge of dealing with the almighty world in the absence of sub-bass. Cars were parked up on the pavement all down the road. Others moved slowly past, thumping, side windows scanning the crowd, door opening to a stop, picking up, diving in, sliding away. The other side of the street, early risers, shoppers, cleaners, church-goers, considered in their disinterest at the untidy congregations of sweaty, ebullient youth across the street.

Lee spotted a quietish eddy, with a good view of the door, and guided Kelly there. He felt it was important not to become separated at this point; any number of distractions could intervene. It was as true for Lee as it was for Kelly, and Lee told himself to stay focussed while they waited for Zoe and, hopefully, Rob. There was real effort involved in bringing this all together and the reward would be collapsing into the car, job done, have a smoke. Lee was relishing that moment already. He turned his eyes and attention to the door. The humanity continued to trickle out; it gathered, boys, girls, men, women, black, white, sharp dressers and scruffy bastards; hi-vis jackets, MA2s, fluffy coats, puffy coats and baggy t-shirts.

Shaved heads, bleach, rave-ponytails, fringes, dreads, bunches and top knots; Adidas, Nike, Fila, Reebok, chunky heels, yeti boots and Wallabees, grimed with the liquor of cigarettes, sweat and condensation. The bouncer at the door was saying goodbye to everyone, a big smile, and those leaving showed the man appreciation, shook his hand. Lee had seen it, had been it so many times but it still pleased.

There was Zoe, Rob right behind but unaware that he was. Rob held his mouth slightly open as if he was about to shiver from cold but, instead of juddering up and down, his jaws moved smoothly over each other, side to side; his eyes were half-closed.

'Oi,' Lee shouted, waving his hand in the air. Heads turned everywhere, instinctively interested in what the shout could mean. 'Here,' Lee barked. Rob and Zoe both registered and together altered course for Lee and Kelly. Painless, thought Lee, by any standard. He thought of the times when they'd been forced to send out search and retrieval parties, recover soldiers from nearby cars, arrest them walking meaninglessly in the wrong direction, find them drinking tea in a cabbie's café with a group of on-the-night friends, performing anecdotes to an enthusiastic reception. No, they were an intact group of four; and they relaxed. There was energetic exchange about the night, about the music, the crowd, the drugs, the dramas, and it might have long continued had Kelly not intervened: 'Come on, let's go. You can chat shit in the car. C'mon,' and she physically pushed at the other three to set them in motion down the road towards where the car was parked. 'Which street was it?' said Kelly, glancing down the first side street they passed. It always looked so different the next morning.

'Nah, nah, one more on,' said Lee. He added quickly, 'But just keep walking, keep walking, keep walking for a bit... yep... yep... no problem here... Old Bill... Old Bill up the road. Act normal...' and he laughed. A slow-moving squad car passed them and slowed as it clocked the hubbub and commotion outside Labrynth. It flashed Lee back to the night before. He had been in the main room, spacing out in the dry ice and lasers, eyes closed mostly; he'd opened them after taking a particularly extended journey through the rhythmic, psychedelic abstractions that seemed conjured on the inside of his eyelids. As a fog of dry ice cleared, he thought he could make out four or five identically dressed ravers in a line at the back; dark gear with hi-viz jackets, looked quite wicked actually. He stared some more, forcing tighter focus. Lee snapped back suddenly; the lack of movement was not bizarre, nor was the coordinated dress... Fuck me, thought Lee, it's a delegation from Dalston nick. Lee used an exaggerated sidelong glance to check his understanding; no question, even if the effect of the lights on the combined and, it has to be said, very high-quality hi-viz, together with the remnants of the dry ice, gave the police line an impermanent and ghostly reality.

'Here, mate,' he said to someone nearby, top off, dancing, pouring with sweat, lolly stuffed into one cheek. 'Is that the Old Bill at the back of the club?'

Without breaking rhythm, the bloke glanced back.

'Yeah, man. Why do you think they're dropping these tunes?' Lee tuned to the Hardcore, the headstrong breakbeat pounding from the speaker stacks. 'Show 'em how it goes, mate, know what I mean?' On his full stop, the music broke, horns and whistles in the place, the MC inciting insurrection; then the tune dropped, pandemonium, human-crescendo, and the bloke, renewed, picked the bassline and shouldered arms.

'D'ya see 'em last night in the club?' said Zoe.

'I was just gonna say that,' said Rob. 'All stood at the back… you could see 'em from the stage. Oh, mate, they dropped the baddest tunes for the Old Bill. Fuckin' mental.' Rob relived the moment and the squad car stopped at the lights; Lee glanced back and watched as it disappeared around the corner.

'Right, let's go back. Should be fine now.' They about-turned and started back for the side street they'd passed earlier. Other ravers meandered past them absently, clutching sheaves of flyers like flowers for church; one or two, hands thrust into pockets, marched, head forward, on their own mission.

Lee's car was there, a few cars down from the main road. A little beyond it a low brick wall, topped with casual loops of rusty barbed wire, made a dead end of the street. Lee gave the car a once-over as he approached; tyres and windows the main focus. It looked okay. A few cars down, just that bit further from the main road, the side window of another, smarter-looking, car had been done. Icy-looking squares of glass lay in the road, shining in the pre-dawn. The driver's door was bent part open.

'Some fuckin' low-life after the stereo…' Lee nodded at the damaged car. The others looked, disinterested, Labrynth standard. The attractions of the shinier other car and its more isolated location had probably saved his own, thought Lee. The others saw that too but it was of no real consequence to them. Like lions and zebras, thought Lee, only, in this case, it's looking good that attracts the predator. Lee shrugged inwardly; that kind of thing could ruin a whole night, toxify the day ahead. At least the downer came after and not before the party; they had got to enjoy it first, and, briefly full of commiseration for the unknown owner, he unlocked his own car.

The four of them bundled themselves into the Polo. It welcomed them with overnight cold, the smell of fags and hash and the slight octane of damp and oily engines. There was a commotion of seatbelts and coats and water bottles and sunglasses. Lee started the engine and added the roar of blowers and heater to the turmoil, slowly subsiding as they waited for the windows to clear. Frames of *déjà vu* cross cut across Lee's vision and he was looking down on himself in the car from the outside – his doughy upturned face, slow with sleep. He was alone and the rest of them outside clamouring to get in. Then, rapidly, a rich cast of characters, versions of him, switching places and locations, doors, windows, belts and blowers. The flickering stabilised and Lee inhaled through his nose deeply and quietly, a slow motion. He reached to steady himself by pushing home the tape sticking from the home-fitted stereo. The effect was instant and he settled, noting to himself that the speakers alone were probably worth more than the car. Repurposed, he critically adjusted the EQ to maximise the bass punch without losing the soar of the top end; stabs of spooked-up seaside organ bounced around the car and the insistent bass pulsed through the floor and into the tarmac below. The music picked up and flexed and the break ricocheted into the wide spaces of a reggae breakdown, bright off-beat guitar and rim-shots. The tape played and the car and its occupants sang. It's the music, thought Lee, it's the music.

The sound rebounded in the small space of the two-door Polo, and the motions and dynamics of the night just spent reasserted themselves in the faces and function of all in the car; the chemicals that still thronged their blood were resurgent and buzzed between helpless synapses. They sat. No one would have complained, or even really noticed anything was up, if they'd continued to sit and let the mix run its course.

Lee grabbed the wheel and, peering through the windscreen, geed himself up with a 'yep, yep,' and eased the car out onto the awakening streets of North East London. It was gliding time, the car on magnetised super-power, speaker-driven, and Lee collapsed himself into the task; driver, crew and machine in perfect synch.

# EIGHTEEN

'LABRYNTH, LABRYNTH,' LEE FOUND HIMSELF repeating under his breath as he negotiated his way further and further out of North East London, testing for a way back to the further side of Essex. The world he saw beyond the glass of the car was finely altered in a way he could not have explained; subtly shaped by the pitch and roll of so many shifts in memory and sentience. He checked the rear-view mirror just to be 100% that the car was empty – no passengers of any kind; he looked to the stereo display – *Top Buzz Oscar's 91 – ...now Oscar's, do you believe in the Hardcore? It had to be the fantastic Top Buzz. Two blacks and a bubble...* The words diverted him immediately and he knew without checking that the car was no longer empty; he noticed and accepted the further fine alterations; he noticed that the Top Buzz groove was techno and there was charge in the voice of the MC. But Lee was not swooped to moments of near panic; this time he met techno with techno, charge with charge; he rode the buzz and, guided by the music and by the map of his whereabouts, Lee dropped himself, body and soul, onto another London pavement.

From where he was, Lee could see the grubby white paintwork of his car a few hundred yards away. I only just cleaned that, he thought. He noticed too that the car was just there, like it had been abandoned at the side of the road. No other cars around. Lee looked for restrictions, wardens, police. A fizz of anxiety. He reassured himself but still had to admit that it did stick out a bit. As he got nearer, his anxiety deepened – the windows were steamed up. Why? And as he began to invent explanations, he found fragments of the night before. Rob, the fuckin' girl's blouse that he was, had left early and gone back to the motor.

'Hey, Zoe, is Rob in there?' Lee was feeling for his keys which he couldn't find.

'...reckon so,' she replied. Zoe reached the car and tapped jauntily on the window.

Tap, tap, tap.

'Rob, Rob, you fuckhead... what you fuckin' doin'?'

They could make out the dark shape of Rob through the mist of the window as he was beginning to surface. Tap, tap again. 'Robadee, Robadee, come on ruuuude-boiii.' Rob looked up at them through the fugged-up window. Zoe stood there hunched inside a Dreamscape MA2, woolly hat pulled down around her ears, hair streaming out down to her shoulders. She was bouncing on the balls of her feet, an index finger on the window. A crowd of some size was gathered behind her, made up of Lee and the others as well as a fair collection of interested on-the-night friends and quite a few others they had never seen before. This was what Rob could now see: Zoe's face behind an accusing index finger looming large at him through the window, surrounded in the background by a sea of other faces, some of whom he recognised but most of whom he did not. Once it was understood that it was just a bloke asleep in a car, the wider group lost interest but remained around the car nevertheless. They'd stopped here and no one had started to move again; it was an opportunity for a break and a breather, and they'd probably put on some tunes in a minute. The small crowd hung about, circulated, went twos, chatted and leaned back against the front wing to gaze with a look of deep and satisfied content at the wider scene. Beyond them, other figures and groups of figures passed, hands clutching water bottles, wads of flyers, out and away into the pale blue summer morning. Rob wound down the window and the wide stare of Zoe's eyes swam into the car along with a rush of early morning chill. Zoe's gaze roamed around the interior then settled on Rob.

'What's up, Robadee do daa? You been in 'ere all night?' Rob stared back, not sure what answer was needed here. He felt he was in several places at once, but the other places were receding fast, evaporating like a dream you felt sure you would remember as you woke but which in a filtering of shadows evades capture.

'Yea, yea... no, not all night, just about an hour ago, maybe two... needed to chill.' In truth, Rob had no idea of timings, and the reason he was in the car was, he remembered, because he had freaked himself out in an incident involving poppers and the stage curtain and had subsequently convinced himself he needed to leave the venue. He decided that he would probably keep that story to himself for a time. Zoe had, anyway, lost interest at the first hesitation in Rob's response and before he'd even finished his explanation she had skipped round to the other side of the car and, in a complex combination of fall, dive and jump, had collapsed herself into the passenger seat, the fabric of her coat sighing and rasping and blowing whorls of cold round the car. She left the door open so her left leg could remain on the ground outside, as if reluctant to lose contact with the earth that had supported her for the last seven hours. Turning to Rob, she said with a look of mischief, 'You're losing your touch, my friend.' She looked back out the door into the gathering day and the drifting knots of people outside. 'Hey, Kelly, he was out here the whole time, fuckin' girl's blouse.' Kelly looked towards the car, pushed out a plume of smoke from her mouth and grinned. Lee took over at this point, deliberately poking at the vulnerability that comes with waking up in public.

'O Robby boy, the pipes, the pipes are callin'.' Rob smiled at Lee, feeling the tease.

'You missed a blinder at the end, mate,' said Zoe.

'Fuckin' unbelievable,' added Lee. 'A spiritual experience, man, I'm tellin' ya, seriously, mate... never known nothin' like it... still, you didn't leave that early... fuckin' rocked non-stop start to finish... and, you know, I thought that was it... I mean, that's enough, rockin' start to finish... but at the end, right at the end, when everyone was on the stage in the main room, Ellis Dee dropped this tune and the whole place erupted... I mean, it went fuckin' mental, mate, off the scale. From the stage, where I was, it looked like the room was boiling with people; a rolling boil of bodies and arms and heads... and the whistles and the horns, slabs of noise... then the music stopped; the lights came on... but it just kept on fuckin' goin' ... the crowd surged forward and back, like in waves, making a roaring noise... and that was us, just opening our mouths and making noise, going back and forward, back and forward...' and Lee took up the rhythm of the words and applied it to his torso, which he moved, in time, back and towards Rob. As he did this, he made a pantomime imitation of the *whoaaaaoowhoaaa* noise that had happened in the main room. 'I'm tellin' you, mate,' Lee said with eyes wide, 'I've never seen anything like it. I am forever changed.'

Rob smiled and absorbed the excess energy Lee was giving off, enjoying the last act of the night vicariously before turfing himself out of the car, onto the pavement, to be taken in by the community of MA2s, hunched and hopping in a flock around the car. Lee poured himself into the vacated warm seat and, foot still on the road outside in imitation of Zoe, he checked his inside pocket. He was looking for the set list, written in marker pen on a torn half-sheet of coloured paper he'd found taped to the wall in the main room. One for the flyer scrapbook, he thought.

'All aboard,' he said and turned the key in the ignition.

'And we're off,' said Zoe, and pushed home the tape sticking expectantly from the slot of the car stereo. '...and it happens to be Top Buzz all the way from London Town... actually from Tottenham... big up your chess... and we happen to be the guv'nors in the place...' The MC vocal filled a spooky breakdown and kicked off a stomping breakbeat with flat, dry snares; whistles in the house. The sound swamped the car and rose, rapidly out through the open doors into the morning air. Lee loved the MC on this one. He loved the sound of all those early MCs; they were pioneers of the unexplored. The art was new and there was no one to tell, nothing to read or watch. The MCs started where everybody starts, from where they were, and Lee could hear where that was, hear it all in their words, the selection, the tone, the delivery. Lee loved it; the outsize and the epic of the boxing ring, the predator rhetoric of the man on the market flogging sealed boxes off the back of a lorry; the fruit and veg man shouting collies at Mum, the rhythmic clip of livestock auctions, the sneering fun-fair PA blaring at the waltzers; there were bingo callers and dancehall toasters; Punch and Judy, Hanna-Barbera, MTV and dub poets; there was hip-hop, there was carnival and even the strains of the rag and bone man. It reminded Lee of Grandad Swigler, of Nanna Swigler too; it was his mum and his dad, his aunts and uncles and all their friends; it was his friends and their families and everyone down the pub and on the street. Maybe that's why Hardcore spoke to him – it was the voice of his life and where he was from; it was instinctive, it signalled to bones and blood and it made him smile; made him smile, made him dance, made him come up on his drugs, made him wonder what the fuck the bloke was saying, made him stay up all night and still want more by morning. It was new art but in a voice as old as England.

Lee sailed on this happy raft of thoughts, buoyed on a ragga sample and a slow mystery of pipes and woozy synth, echoes on the brick wall along the road. The bass jumped on the tarmac and the unguided movements of the small crowd around the car were instantly coordinated. Lee saw it happen and laughed to himself as he reconsidered his parking strategy. Last night, he had reasoned, it seemed close enough to be convenient but far away enough not to attract attention when leaving. But here we are, he thought, doors open, music on and a crowd of spangled ravers dancing on the pavement outside as other ravers streamed by on every side. The music picked up, bass arched, breaks ricocheted like crows.

'Right. C'mon,' Lee decided but voiced too quietly as he pulled the door shut. Zoe took up the challenge on his behalf, put the whole top half of her body out through the open side window, twisted and projected from the bottom of her lungs.

'Oi, you lot, we're goin'… get a fuckin' shift on.' Her voice rolled out with the breakbeats and drew them until, finally, in the spaces of a reggae breakdown, rim-shots and off-beat guitar, the car turned up its collar and headed off into the early morning of the city. The tape played and the car and its occupants sang and they were broader than broad.

'Yes, we fuckin' well are,' said Lee over the music, in the mix, and the others joined their own vocals.

The car chorus was in the past and the journey settling when Zoe opened the next phase.

'You know, It's all about syncopation,' she said thoughtfully. 'I was talking to this bloke last night about it… it all comes down to syncopation… you know, the way the rhythm and the way the beats are expressed, the way they're voiced – or not.' There was an attitude of restfulness in the others – in this phase sometimes you wanted conversation but were, yourself, far from capable of being able to take an active part. Sometimes this attitude prevailed amongst all in a party, bar one. Sometimes this situation applied in Lee's car on the way home, sometimes at after-parties and, sometimes, in the chill-out area on the night; whichever the scenario, the *bar one* was, invariably, Zoe. Zoe was a champion fucked-talker; although, to be fair, thought Lee, she was a champion talker full stop. As she had already indicated she was, right then, about to deliver on something she had covered at some point with someone during the course of the night; this was a pattern. Listening to Zoe and her involved theories about music and raving had become part of the going-home ritual. She was often super-lucid and spoke with eloquence and passion; the modulation of her voice textured her words to lead in clarity a twisted mind; these were winning qualities for comfort on a drive. It often happened later in the drive, on the meditative second stretch of the M11, but this morning there was no waiting.

'Our music… It's all about heavy syncopation,' Zoe went on, drumming the last syllables. 'Ideas and feelings expressed through syncopation; and not just the drums, the bass and melody too, I mean… yea, obviously… and that's why, if it's done right, the whole thing rocks… yea… that's what we mean when we say *it rocks*; it's that total syncopation in tune with our consciousness. It alters and enhances our consciousness; it's not alone, of course… yea, yea… there's other substances in the mix, empathy and sense of engagement with the world are in hyper mode, but the music and the syncopation of the music are also mind-altering.' Lee thought about how altered Zoe's mind must be and marvelled at how she managed the detail and the argument in the last sentence. Sure, he could see the train of thought she was on but he was following, following intently and, even so, everything he heard and understood faded from his brain within seconds of him hearing it; *probably the only way I can follow Zoe*, he thought. Lee pictured her sat in the chill-out area deep into an intense discussion about the things she was talking about now. Zoe's voice came back into Lee's frontal awareness.

'So, syncopation helps alter our consciousness – and this frees us, frees our minds, man, and you know when you free your mind, your arse ain't far behind. The other thing is that we share our alteredness with others; it's communal. We share the substances, the music, the venue, the vibe and, finally, if the ingredients are right, if the DJ delivers, then the total syncopation of the music is in step with the rhythm of our enhanced perception; the feeling and the energy of the moment becomes its own thing, a new entity.' Lee agreed with a slight nodding of the head but said nothing; the overwhelm of information and ideas had taken all his concentration and he could not articulate any of his own. Makes sense, though, he told himself. Makes sense.

'Makes sense,' he eventually managed, 'defo makes sense. In fact, I would say I am persuaded, most fuckin' powerfully, by your ideas.' And Lee thought about how he had been self-medicating with this phenomenon for a while now. It was for him a powerful concoction and it moved mountains. In fact, he thought, I really don't know where I'd be without it. He thought better of saying anything and provoking Zoe into more words, and used the pause to seek refuge in the tune. A techno wind took the groove and the MC called ...*now, Oscar's, do you believe in the Hardcore? It had to be the fantastic Top Buzz. Two blacks and a bubble...* Everyone in the car got it; shoulders and heads bounced and the music that played, the focus of all minds. The reel of the city turned and Lee kept the car headed east.

# NINETEEN

Lee felt himself adrift on the years of his life; he felt he was travelling more than one timeline back to Essex; he felt he was present in more than one temporal space, and almost any idea, sound or sight could switch him between them. He felt anchored to the journey he was making back to Essex, his old home, inspired by the vivid reliving of old times, but he also realised that these flashbacks were not going to stop just because he was in the car. The road, the music, his own memory were more than sufficient to swoop him out and back through the years to other journeys, to other places, to other times. That last one, just now, had been the start of the journey home from Double Dipped, The Secret Garden; his last journey back from Bagley's; his very last rave. How had he got there? A memory of Labrynth? A random pick from his catalogue of famous raving exits as they fanned across his mind? Maybe it was the music? They had put on Top Buzz,

Oscar's '91 on that journey too. The mix was a string along which hung all the parallel scenarios that were now beginning to play interchangeably in the forefront of his awareness. Lee stared ahead, believed in everything and opted to let the music save him; the music was the only constant, music the only change; it brought reality... brought stuttered vocal echoes over twanging pipes, ancestral bass... *and we happen to be doing things on the pier...* more stuttered vocal and the sample haunts begging not to be left alone, over and over... and the old cinema organ glitches onto steel pans and break...

And Lee drove the tune, shifting down the grey of the North Circular towards Woodford and the M11. Lee loved this section of road; he muttered to himself, *where the North Circ meets the M11,* as it arrived. As a kid, the flyovers and slip roads of this junction seemed futuristic but also brutal and crude – dystopian he would say now. The roads were arranged in a complicated formation, the kind of difficult roads he tried to build with his Matchbox track as a kid; but Matchbox wasn't up to the task, he thought. The roads here rose on columns like those of a pier or an oil rig, strode like Pink Floyd hammers over what was below. Lee thought again of the legs and struts of a pier, seen from underneath – repeating iron work and columns green with weed and winking with barnacles – and thought of Top Buzz playing at Oscar's above.

Oscar's on Clacton's pier, or Clacton Spear even. Lee repeated the word trick a few times, still pleased with his old invention; he never failed to think of it whenever Clacton-related things came up. Oscar's, though, what a place was Oscar's on the pier. Kind of Labrynth-on-Sea. So many good nights, Ray Keith in residence, proper. They used to open up the whole pier, multiple arenas. Total mayhem and a bouncy dance floor. He'd seen the Prodigy there – blinding night – so good his memory of it was like an explosion in his head. He'd seen them already, a few times; they were fucking everywhere for a couple of years; never failed to deliver. Zoe and Rob always said that it was the Prodigy who showed what was possible, showed that you could go somewhere with this music and this culture – and still be from Braintree, Lee liked to add. Clacton's pier, Clacton Spear, who'd have thought it, he mused and coasted back into the mix, the one like Top Buzz coming at him over the speakers in the car, taking him back to the pier as it had been, Essex Hardcore in full effect, his head a drama of comfortable confusion.

## //

The music took on life and substance. It was breath with an echo, breath with an echo... and then on the run from the breakbeat peril, searing cyber-spite. But Hardcore justice was coming on through. '...*One way, one way, one way ticket to a high...*' chanted the MC. Yelp, yelp, yelp, electro-alarms, stomping bass rock, then breakdown, the groove, and reed instruments over hissing high-hats. Yes, yes. Lee was fully engaged with the sound now. He had been with Kelly and Zoe, out in the cold, on the pier by the dodgems. They'd mostly been going twos, shivering and pacing backwards and forwards, but now they were back inside. The sudden exposure to heat and noise brought him up again; he launched and joined the build and roll of the tune, the call of the MC. He felt himself finely engaged with the music; there was an edge in performance and he was just in control of a cornering speeding car. Total complicity and awareness enhance the ride, the thrill... the soft-edged soar coming off the corner. He felt parts of him break away to float on tethers; he became multi-limbed and dispersed; elements of his presence gathering with the presence of those others around him making the same journey. What was it Kelly had been saying outside...?

'Do you think this will change us?' she'd asked out of the blue as they watched a pair of dropped sunglasses get run over by a dodgem.

'What's that, Kells?' said Zoe.

'D'ya think this will change us? You know, will we be different to how we would've been... you know... how we would've been if we hadn't done this?'

'...Course, no question,' said Zoe. 'It's fuckin' changed me already,' and she leered at Kelly like a monster. Kelly returned the gesture. 'Seriously, though,' Zoe went on, 'you can't be a raver and not be altered by it... I mean, fuckin' hell, look at it.' Zoe waved vaguely around her, in a way which was clearly meant to refer to the whole pier of people, rides and raving arenas.

'Yea, I knew it really... that's why I asked... I mean, look at us... once you've raved together there's a bond between you which you can't explain. You remember after Mangled that time, when we first met and Lee said that things would never be the same again? I was thinking of that... it's the connections... you don't get it from nothing else... But, you know, is it real? Is it just the drugs?' There was laughter and cries of *who cares* and *yea, just the drugs, please*.

'What it is...' said Lee, when the commotion faded, '... is that the drugs allow you to reach in minutes what would normally take months or years, if ever. You know, you can meet someone when you're out and by the end of the night you're best fuckin' mates. I mean, you really are. Think of all our mates we met through it; good mates.' They all thought and nodded wisely.

'Yea, but could we have got the same thing from being into something else? You know, like God or bird watching?' said Kelly. There was a thought.

'Well, not fuckin' bird watchin', obviously,' said Rob. 'You can't compare raving and bird watching. No one's ever expected to get from bird watching what they get from a party... there probably are some other things that do it though... but this has gotta be the best.'

'Yea,' said Kelly. 'I can't imagine what it would be like without it, without those connections, the family of it. It's like, you know, when you meet someone new and find out you were at some of the same raves together. The buzz when you find out you must have been dancing virtually next to each other. The bond is instant... and it goes beyond that 'cos it's like you've known them since them raves, since before you met.' It made sense and they all nodded, the phenomenon recognised. They felt a bit enlightened about it all; justified that by taking Class A drugs while dancing in the dark to impossibly loud and energetic music on a small platform built out into the North Sea, they were definitely increasing the sum of positive human interactions around the world and generally spreading goodwill to their fellow human beings.

'Great, that's agreed then,' said Rob. 'I for one am now gonna neck another half, get back in there on these lively little pills and rush my tits right off the fuckin' pier.' It was a Pied Piper kind of comment and everyone followed Rob back in. As they entered, they were chemically lifted by the effect of heat after cold and by the turmoil of the main arena, and by the generosity of the conclusions they had reached about what they were doing. Lee looked round at them all and felt supremely glad. There was nowhere he would rather be. There was techno jungle and there was the MC... *coming fresh off the press. Rockamatic buzz...* and the tune spread soulful in the vocal, uplifting in the piano, disco house over a driving rhythm... it told him he was needed, his love desired. .

Lee overflowed with empathy. He wanted to meet everyone and know everyone. He broadcast what he felt as, with a big grin on his face, he caught eye after eye across the dance floor.

He could tell that the others were enthused by the same spirit coming back into the arena. The place was alight. ...*and takin' you to the limits*... and the church bell tolled. ...*Tik tok, tik tok, tik tok*... *and we happen to be on the seafront tonight*... and the charge is neutral, sine-still. Time to blow, reassemble, take in the slack and regroup, eyes bright with anticipation for the drop, the compulsion of the bass, the drum breaking cover, check, check, make ready, another sweep, fan out, take stock, onward, an ever-repeating sequence of territory, frames repeating to vanishing point.

## //

Five hours later, the uproar of the last tune and the reality shift of house lights coming up saw them emerge, blinking, onto the bright, slowly warming seafront, Clacton, Tendring, Essex. They had a high-level plan for this morning that now spread about them in daylight. Good weather was forecast and they were taking a drive up the coast with Ian and Faye and the Clacton Crew to Walton's Naze. Once there, the plan was to find a nice, quiet spot under the cliffs, do some acid and see what came next. They gathered in a loose mass, forming and reforming on the pavement outside the pier, and slowly moved to lap around the nearest newsagent's. There they stocked up on life-giving essentials before packing themselves into the car with the micro dots following a small convoy of other cars up the coast. Like most of those other cars they had an extra passenger, in many cases someone picked up in the talking outside the shop – it had been a wicked night and, for many, following it with psychedelics on a sunny beach was a venture they wanted to be involved in.

In less than an hour they pulled into the Naze car park. They unpacked themselves from the vehicles and after a brief hiatus during which they reminded each other that they weren't there to dance in the car park, they wandered along the beach. They set up camp on a patch of stony sand a few hundred yards up on a beach consisting entirely of patches of stony sand, just beneath a low, crumbly cliff of clay and sandstone. Lee could see layers in the cliff, raw and revealed by erosion, and he thought about the Clacton Spear and how he had unsuccessfully, and incoherently, tried to tell everyone in the car about it on the way up. And then, it seemed like the next moment to Lee, he could recall nothing else, he was in the enigmatic embrace of the LSD. The micro dots were strong. At least that was the consensus; after being up all night on a mix of stimulants and psychedelics, gauging the potency of anything was tricky. But, later, and in the cold and unforgiving light of the following week, they all agreed that they had been strong trips. Lee, in particular, felt the power of the lysergic acid diethylamide as it worked deep in the chemistry of his brain. After everyone had spent twenty minutes laughing at everything anyone did or said, or at anything anyone could see or hear, the acid really kicked in. The receptors in Lee's brain became so over-excited and sensitised that he panicked a little and channelled an anxiety about those people around him that he didn't really know; a growing sense for him that he had upset them and their families. He whispered to Zoe, who was sitting next to him looking out at the sea. 'Zoe, oi, Zoe... are they talkin' about me over there?'

'What? Who? No, mate, it's fine, it's all fine. Everyone loves you. No one's talking about you.'

'Zoe, Zoe... they are...I think they are. And Rob and Kelly... and Ian... Ian and Faye too... I've upset them all. Zoe, we've got to go. We've got to leave.' Inwardly, Zoe smiled at Lee's paranoia – she'd tell him about it later. But right now she knew that his anxiety was the realest, sharpest, most intense thing in the world. He needed comfort and distraction. She took one of his hands in both of hers and made him look at her.

'Lee, look at me, just look at me,' she said as she held his hand in hers. 'You've just come up weird on the acid... probably because you haven't slept all fuckin' night and maybe, as well, 'cos you helped plan this little trip you feel responsible or something for how it goes.'

'Yea?' said Lee, sounding completely unconvinced.

'Yea,' said Zoe firmly.'Come on, I've heard you talk like this when someone's having a bit of a freak. Relax into it, accept what's happening in your head, welcome its presence. Don't fight. What's the point of that? You've taken the acid so it can mess with your head. Don't get in its way now... mixed signals, man. Avoid that shit. Ride it. Balance. Look around. Smile. Breathe...' She inhaled deeply.'Come on then...' Zoe did the actions with him, inhaling, hand on chest, smiling, looking around.'Great,' she said.'Right, let's go over there for a bit and look at some stuff,' and she led him a short distance from the group and they sat on the sand looking out at the twin bands of the sky and the sea.'Okay, stop,' she said.'Look at that. That is the fuckin' great sky and below is the sea. Breathe it in and look right along the line where the two bands meet. Amazing, you can see the curve of the earth, almost like you could look over it.' And they both looked as into their sky came a flock of pigeons, over their heads from the park behind, fifteen or twenty birds, soft, grey and iridescent green and purple on the neck.

'Doves, doves!' shouted someone behind them as the pigeons soared over the breaking waves in a diamond.

'They're fuckin' pigeons, you spanner... wicked, though... look at that...' The birds banked and turned in the salt air, catching the sun on the underside of their wings, moving with each other, faultless, catching gold on their backs, then silhouette, bank and sheer, back and gone, over the cliffs and green striations of spiny marram grass against a blue-white sky.

'Wow,' said Lee. 'That was for us. It felt like that was for us.' He laughed. 'It was like the Southend Airshow.' Zoe laughed.

'Pigeon power,' she said, turning her gaze to the handful of stones and sand she had picked up while watching the birds. 'Look at this,' she said, holding her hand out and letting the stones and the sand spill between her fingers. The sand moved like a living thing, taking the light like the birds, precious stones in the sun. The sand returned to the beach and Lee saw that the beach had life and the sand was part of that life; a life of shells and flints, and pebbles and rusted metal, timber smoothed to felt, and pieces of old bricks made of coloured sugar. Lee saw the life and he greeted it.

'Shall I tell you a story about last night?' asked Zoe, poking at the sand with her finger. 'It's really funny... I don't know why I thought of it... probably because it makes me feel good...'

Lee nodded. 'Yea, tell me,' he said, his brain receptive now, recalibrated by the birds and the sky and the living sand.

'Well,' said Zoe, 'after we went back into the main room... you know, when we were out by the dodgems?'

'Yea, yea.'

'Yea, well, I started rushing big time. I thought for a minute I was gonna be sick... you know, sometimes I get that.' Lee nodded and had a flashback; a memory from the night he didn't know he had. He was beaming at everyone he could see as he danced, styling and scanning the crowd with a grin. He caught sight of Zoe, at the edge of his field of view, propped against a wall, bent forward, hands on her knees. He would have made his way to her but he saw someone else was already there; a shirtless bloke – cap, round sunglasses – put his hand on Zoe's shoulder and offered her some water. She'll be fine, he thought and never missed a beat.

'So that bloke,' said Zoe, 'helped me find a quiet spot to sit down, gave me some more water and then I never saw him again.'

'Is that it?' asked Lee.

'No, you fuckin' plonka, that's how it started. Listen…' and she paused as she gathered herself for the story…

Zoe and the bloke with the cap found a quiet corner, one end of a low platform which ran along the wall, away from the sea of bodies, the pound of the sound system, the flaring whistles. The platform was fully occupied, ravers blowing hard, ravers staring straight ahead, ravers fully engaged in interestingly focussed discussion. Zoe needed to sit down. The crowd pulsed in front of her, heads and shoulders, action poses in the strobe, UV glimmer on necks and shoulders, splintering in the laser. She badly needed to sit down. She scanned up and down and, as if at her thought, a big bloke who'd been sitting on the corner of the platform, head down between his knees, stood carefully, flared his nostrils at the night, patted himself down and moved off with purpose to the next place he needed to be. Zoe moved at once on the vacant space and put herself down next to someone skinny in a sweat-marked Hypercolor with his head between his knees on one side and, on the other, a shirtless raver; stocky, tattooed upper arms, who was turned in animated conversation towards an audience of two who were sitting on his other side. She accepted the relief the platform gave and allowed her legs to luxuriate in weightlessness; she let the upward push of the platform ease her lower back; she straightened the muscles there and breathed down to the pit of her stomach, quivering. The stocky bloke turned at the movement she made and she met his eyes in greeting. The face was full of potential, a look of communication and her look, in turn, seemed to spark him.

'All right, darlin'?' he said, "avin a good one?' She nodded. She was not ready to talk. Her already shaky equilibrium had found the act of sitting difficult, the changes to balance and perspective challenging. It was something that had to be dealt with.

"Ere, guess what I do then.'

'What?' returned Zoe, still recalibrating.

'Guess what I do...for a livin."

'Er...' Zoe's mind went blank as she looked at the broad-eyed stare and tried to match his excited face with a job. 'Erm... delivery driver... builder?' He watched her with the air of someone who knew that the person they had challenged to a "guess what?" was never going to get it right. Zoe gave up quickly, partly because the effort of trying was too much for her careering mind but also because she did not want to risk the bloke's disappointment by guessing correctly by some inspired fluke.

'Close,' he said, with real praise for her feeble effort. 'Close... I'm a fabricator.' He emphasised the final word as if driving home the final fixing on a complicated job of fabrication. Zoe, though, had no idea what he meant; the job title was not one she had ever heard of. Was it, she wondered, something to do with clothes or fabric?

'A fabricator,' he said again as if repetition would explain it, 'a welder, ductin' and metalwork, you know...'

'Oh right,' said Zoe. 'Yea, wicked,' although, really, she still clutched at shadows.

'Yea, you see out there... just off the front, by the little park...? Yea, well, I put up them new railings.' Zoe furrowed her brow, as if she really was, in her mind, scanning through images of the roads outside, until she found the one that showed the bloke's work.

'Nice,' she said, approving the craftsmanship but with no idea what she was approving.

'Yea, good job that… that's how I found out about this place.' He sniffed and nodded as he explored and confirmed the memory for himself. Once done, he turned again to Zoe. 'Guess what I used to be.'

'Er…' The guessing challenges were all too much for Zoe and, put on the spot, she floundered. 'Er… a milkman.' The bloke laughed uproariously at the suggestion and Zoe joined in too, trying to make it seem that she had intended the ridiculous answer.

'Nah, I mean before I started ravin' 'n' that.' Zoe shook her head with a look of helplessness in the face of superior knowledge. 'Football 'ooligan.' The bloke punched the words out with genuine pride.

'A football hooligan?' said Zoe, with real surprise, not just that the bloke had been a football hooligan but that anybody in the same place as her, raving, could be, or could ever have been, a football hooligan. Pictures came to her of men invading pitches, throwing seats and fighting in the streets. Once when she was little, seven or eight maybe, gangs of rival fans had come spinning and fighting through the Red Lion Yard shopping arcade in Colchester. She had been there with her mum, buying new shoes. Tall, long-limbed young men with shaved heads, bleached jeans and seventeen-hole Doc Martens – white laces – had flown through the air in slow motion, feet kicking and arms spinning, like a fight in a cartoon. She had cowered with her mum in a doorway, terrified but fascinated, peeking out at the violence from behind her mum's legs. Windows got broken and some of the men punched each other as they flew by and then, in a swirl of litter and dust, they were gone. She remembered the quick beat of silent, suspended reality that followed, then everyone had got on with their shopping and their lives. She looked at the bloke and wondered if maybe he'd been one of them. He didn't look like he'd been to Colchester; mind you, he didn't look like a football hooligan either. As if to answer the questions that were now building, he said:

'With the Arsenal.'

'Oh right,' said Zoe. She knew enough about football to know that if he was with the Arsenal then he almost definitely wouldn't have been in Colchester. She was relieved about that. She would not have wanted to have had that connection with him. He seemed all right.

'Yea, I was an 'ooligan all over the place. We used to travel, know what I mean,' he added with a panto wink.

'Yea,' said Zoe, now quite interested, warming to the topic and the task. 'So which enemy fans did you like fighting the most?' In her head she was now a TV interviewer. The bloke nodded at the question and savoured it, chuckling and muttering *enemy fans* under his breath, as he did so.

'Liverpool, Man U... any of them northern monkeys,' he said with a tone of menacing but genuine affection. It made Zoe think of war veterans from different sides fondly reminiscing about how they had nearly blown each other's heads off. Funny old world, she thought to herself, very conscious of the fact that she never used that expression.

'Funny old world,' she said.

'Fuckin' right.'

'Would you fight them now?' asked Zoe. The bloke put on a look of exaggerated horror that was intended to show his actual horror at the possible implications of the question.

'Fight 'em?' he said, 'fight 'em? I'd kiss 'em with tongues.' They both laughed. 'Kev,' said the bloke, putting out his hand. Zoe took it and said:

'Zoe, nice to meet you, Kev.'

'And what about him?' said Zoe, looking across Kev to the younger bloke sitting next to him, the one Kev had been talking to when she had first sat down.

'What, Dave? He's a farrier; from Basildon.' Dave tuned to the data-set and turned.

'A what?' said Zoe.

'Farrier, makes 'orseshoes.'

'Nice,' said Zoe. 'A fabricator and a farrier. Farrier and Fabricator; you and your mate could be a business.' Everyone laughed.

'He's not my mate, though,' said Kev. 'I mean, he's a mate now but I only just met him. He came over to talk about bare-knuckle boxing 'cos he thought I looked like a geezer who might be into it... charmin'... don't get me wrong or nuffin', I can 'andle meself... but I'm not into all that malarkey. Anyway, says he runs a fing...'

'Oh right' said Zoe. She didn't know what the "fing" might be but suspected some sort of illegal fight; the conversation, she decided, was taking one unexpected turn after another.

'The bloke sat next to *him*,' continued Kev, 'the one with the beard. Now that is his actual mate. Yea, he's havin' a bad one... he's just started being a muslim. Changed his name to Haydar – means lion. He's not done nothin' tonight... if you know what I mean. On a natural, innit?' Zoe nodded. She tried to do so in a way that she hoped would show she thought all of this totally cool. She looked discretely across to Haydar; he sat, looking quite serious, staring out at the commotion.

'So what d'you do?'

'Student and work in a pie factory.' Kev laughed.

'Pies, eh?... can't beat a lovely Isle o' Skye...' Kev drifted for a moment. 'So what d'ya study then?'

'Music, mainly,' said Zoe, 'and Art.'

'Yea, sweet,' said Kev. 'I might become an artist one day...
if I can be fuckin' arsed.' And they both laughed to silence.
Zoe saw Dave now; he was struggling intently, trying to build
a spliff in his hand. Kev saw too and offered his open palm;
Dave, gratefully, switched locations. Sensing movement, Zoe
turned the other way, towards the skinny bloke on her other
side. He had begun to unfold; his head came up from between
the knees and he slowly raised himself upright. He looked at
Zoe in an unfocussed way and smiled in greeting.

'All right, mate, havin' a good one?' she said. The bloke
nodded and stuck out his hand.

'Josh,' he said, as if he was checking with Zoe whether that
was his name or not.

'Zoe,' said Zoe. 'And what d'you do, Josh?' she asked,
inspired by the conversation with Kev.

'Medical student,' said Josh, grinning. 'I'm gonna be a
fuckin' doctor in the house yo... Here, d'ya want half a pill?'
And, as he finished speaking, he raised his hand to his mouth,
bit down, and passed Zoe half a Cali.

'Yea, thanks, Josh,' said Zoe as Josh stood up, put his hand
on Zoe's shoulder, gave it a gentle squeeze and walked away
back towards the main arena.

'So what the fuck d'ya think of that then?' Zoe asked
Lee. He looked at her. He had been right there; part of the
camaraderie, part of the humour; she had shared it fully.

'Fuckin' brilliant,' he said.

'Shall we go back with the others?' and they got up to join
the untidy pattern of bomber jackets and jeans and bottles
of water just behind them. Lee stood for a while looking at
his comrades lounged on the beach, looking like they had just
made the transition from sea to land. He looked too at the
crystal lattice of the cliff behind them; it swirled and circulated
with slow, slow, living energy. He turned back towards the sea

213

and took in the curve of the earth, the waves, the wind and the seabirds. He felt the sand and the stones beneath his feet stretching back in time and the clouds forming and reforming above, in patterns of air and wind and water that were almost as old as the earth. And he remembered then the TV programme; fossils – spearheads, sharks' teeth and all that – on this bit of coast; the Clacton Spear too, that he had tried to talk about in the car. It was all coming back, like he could hear and see the TV in his head. He listened... *if you think of the life of the earth as twenty-four hours, twenty-four little hours, then, on that scale, we lived at the same time as the people who left the spears and the arrowheads behind that you can sometimes find on this beach. We're not the same vintage as the sharks' teeth, though; they are much, much older. We are, however, in the same passing sweep of the second hand as the first hominids ever to tramp across this land, to raise monuments, to gather together in ceremony at significant times as directed by the sun and the moon and the seasons...* Lee radiated with thought and squatted before the others, bright-eyed with his enthusiasm for what he had remembered.

'Hey', he said. 'I've remembered about the Clacton Spear and the other stuff I tried to tell you in the car.' Half the people he spoke to hadn't been in the car and the others couldn't remember what he was talking about, but his rapture was clear and they were taken with it. They listened as Lee explained what he could remember about chalk and about London Clay, about fossils and flint and glaciers and stone-age man. Lee also listened to his own words as he spoke; he was amazed by what he said; spellbound like his audience. Rob was especially inspired; he felt pride in Lee's achievement, summoned by it, and as he turned on Lee's word to look at the cliff behind him, he was seized by a compulsion, a spirit, that drew him on to examine the feature more closely.

'I'm gonna check out the cliff, man… make a fuckin' discovery…' On the last beat of his final word, Rob spun to his feet and sprang away towards the orange-grey of the low cliff. The others turned and watched; it was a continuation of Lee's story. Rob poked about in the crumbly dirt where the cliff met the beach; mesmerised and lysergic, he saw the clay dense with individual particles; saw the sand grains and flints writhing in facets. Everything was interesting. He picked at a few stones, looked at them closely, put some in his pocket. Intrepid now, he looked skyward, tested the lower part of the cliff with his feet, reached up with his hands and tested the cliff above him. Satisfied, he climbed a little way up, face and body pressed close to the dirt. The others watched his conviction and encouraged him.

'Go on, Rob… What you found, mate…? Don't look down…' Rob heard but didn't register. He continued to scrutinise the earth and moved slowly on the cliff like a basking crab, unhurried and unworried. The audience grew fickle at his slow pace and the lack of feedback and turned back to the sea and to the sky and each other. It seemed like a long time then, at least it did to Lee, before Rob made any communication. Lee was looking at a tiny, far red ship, moving quietly across the slick band of grey-blue sea, right to left, when he thought he could hear his name being called.

'Lee, Lee… Lee…' The voice was quiet and untroubled and the calling rhythmic. At first, Lee thought it was a bird, a distant seagull, 'Lee, Lee… Leeee…' No, someone was calling his name. Rob. It was Rob's voice. Lee turned and saw Rob, late twentieth century slapped on the ancient dirt of the cliff. 'Lee, I need some help, mate… I can't get down.' Lee fully understood Rob's predicament; his actual height off the ground – no more than two foot – was irrelevant. Like Lee earlier, he had over-focussed and now everything was out of balance.

Lee made it to the cliff and clambered his way the short distance up to join Rob, and both of them were now starred against the cliff, faces to the dirt and stones, briefly part of the fossil record of the Naze; they had taken a time machine out of Oscar's and travelled past the Mods and the Rockers on Clacton beach, jinked through stray bombs and V2 rockets, over the new pilings of a Victorian pier, Napoleonic wrecks, medieval towns and villages lost to the sea, Roman villas, Celtic farmsteads, Neolithic flint mines and then to when it was before people. The dirt and the rock told Lee this as it drifted down to him, pressed against the floor of a warm tropical sea.

'All right, mate,' Lee said, 'wass goin' on?'

'Yea, I'm a bit stuck, mate... think I got some fossils, though... can't tell really... they're in my pocket.'

'Well, let's get down and check 'em out,' said Lee and, acting as guide, Lee eased them both back down onto the beach, Rob's predicament already vanishing.

Back with the others, Rob spread what he had found on a newspaper; mostly unremarkable stones and flints.

'They look different now I'm down here,' said Rob, laughing. But he did have one that looked like it could be something. It was a long, thin, roughly cylindrical piece of dark stone. It was ragged at both ends where there were small cavities and a couple of rounded protrusions and the whole thing was faintly grooved. It looked like a small piece of tree-branch but it was hard like stone.

'I reckon that's a fossil twig,' said Lee. Everyone laughed. The idea of a fossil twig was, in itself, an anti-climax but, after Lee's epics about the Clacton Spear and the formation of the earth, it was especially so.

'Definitely worth the 300 million years,' said Zoe.

'That,' Rob responded, 'is a find... a fuckin' ree-sult... the 300-million-year-old twig,' and he held the piece of pyritised wood to the light and its mineral surface gleamed subtly in the first sunlight it had seen for a very long time. 'I am keeping that.'

# TWENTY

I WONDER IF HE DID KEEP IT, THOUGHT LEE, HIS attention on an image of Rob holding the fossil stick as he sat on the beach. Lee looked to his mirror at the thought to check for passengers. The car was still empty, but there was latency. The music was coming from a memory stick plugged into the radio and not a tape. Lee settled to this reality, the fossil stick receding back to its place in his record and his attention now on the tunes and the road. ...*And satisfaction guaranteed every time...* called the MC over some laid-back garage flavour of bright piano... *Goin' out to the ladies in the place... Get up there...* and Lee found himself taken by the rhythm, shifting cheek-to-cheek in his seat, winding his waist as much as he could manage, his head rocking side to side. And now it really was a garage swing; he'd forgotten this part of the mix, or maybe at the time the flavour had been different for him. He loved the way music could do that, how it wasn't fixed, the

way it depended on you and where you were for its meaning...
and the vocal sang its love to him in the breakdown, the beat
coming back four-to-the-floor, deep, deep garage and driving
synth, vocal explanation, coming from nowhere, feeling
surreal, another one breaking cover. Classic tune, he affirmed
automatically but, he qualified, definitely house.

Interesting, thought Lee; he could see now that he carried
designations with him that he had not had at the time, that
had not been in the music for him then. Then it was just
rave music and a set would have different faces. It wasn't all
Hardcore mayhem; there were more laid-back and groovy
dimensions, there was real texture in a rocking early '90's rave
set he decided. He let the piano-house roll over him and it
encapsulated the uplift that was at the core of early Hardcore,
that sound was on the money, right on the button, the head
of the fucking nail, that was the nutshell it was in. Fuck, yes.
Then, genius on the ones and twos, incoming techno madness
over euphoric gospel. Boss horns blowing all over the place,
pulling at the knees, flexing the hips, and the mood goes
spooky. There's an edge now, dark corners, jagged dystopia,
peril, possession and paranoia but always a way through for
the Hardcore hero.

Yes, that is what we're talking about, thought Lee, and at
that point he said it out loud as if to passengers in the car...
'That is what we're talking about.' He noticed too how the edge
had come as he had reached and passed over the Charlie Brown
interchange, the place where the North Circular met the M11.
The bit of road he really liked – at least one of the bits he really
liked. The section he always noticed coming in or going out;
it was a good bit of road to drive. Both approaches put him
in a game; both were graphic, gritty, hyper-real. Lee found it
soulful, especially, he recalled, when coming home from a top
night; taking the elevated section, no other traffic, swinging

round north onto the motorway, dawn breaking over West Essex spread to the horizon on your right. Coming back from Labrynth, he would have approached it from Leytonstone and the Green Man – no A12 link back then – and missed the elevated section, the drive in the sky as he used to say to his mum when they went to visit Kitty and Ada in Barking.

He'd come this way a lot with his mum and his nan and his grandad; lots of family connections. Grandad Swigler would always go on about the old Charlie Brown's and The Roundabout pub, demolished for the new roads Lee loved. As he got older, Lee would look from the window and try to imagine the place Grandad Swigler knew, before the flyovers and dual carriageways. He would gaze at the scrubby wasteland beneath the ramps and passes, see odd paths winding through the grimy grass and mounds of bramble. Sometimes he would see a horse or a pony tethered there, still, alien and lost-looking; marooned on land cut off from the rest of the world; a world carried by struts and pillars and slabs of sweeping concrete which roared with the noise of an ocean all around them. There must have been ways to get to the places you glimpsed from the road, but you couldn't see them.

The journey for Lee now was becoming all the times he had ever driven this route; he felt them layered in him, one upon the other, all a part of the latest journey he was on; a journey that was telling him the story of his life, who he was, who he had been, where he was from. *Was that what was happening here?* he wondered, open to the possibility but uncertain about everything. He shook the thought away, together with the gentle vertigo it made in his head and the swooping sensation to his stomach that had returned. His eyes glanced to the road signs and he followed the path of the decision already taken, away from historical Essex, now London and into the open country of the modern home county. Lee smiled to himself as he thought again of Grandad Swigler and how he always came to life around this area; it's where he'd spent most of his young life; here and out and down the county towards Grays and Tilbury. Sometimes when Lee was in the van with him, he'd talk about those times, about the war and just after; about being a warden, trying to survive on scrap dealing in the years afterwards. He always talked like he missed it, hard though it was, like it was a time when he was certain about who he was and where he fitted. Lee found this world remote; the wagons, the horses, the bombs, the carnage, his mum living in a tent, and the litany hit with a gut-wrenching drop and the car filled with dark.

Sirens wailed in the darkness, animal and scared and the fear was in him; but he sensed determination too, determination to find a way, determination to protect his place. The siren wail was insistent now and a deep and menacing orange glow suffused the blackness with a silent roar. There were boomings and snappings, crashes of great noise, cascades of masonry and showers of sparks. He could see the skyline of London lit with fire and crossed and recrossed with searchlights. A deep pulsing drone from the sky was a bass note to an orchestration of terror, and he watched horrified as a bow of burning light spanned the city, rooted at one end in the Essex Docks and the East End and at the other to someplace way west of the City.

'Can you see that, Lee?' asked the voice of Grandad Swigler. 'Can you? That's what happened before this road, before we left it all.' The scraps of stories and memories that Lee had accumulated from parents and relatives over the years were merging and completing themselves before him. He saw a young woman... no, a girl really... maybe fifteen years old, dark-haired and striking-looking, a blanket wrapped like a scarf about her head and shoulders. Her face shone with fear and resolve. She held tight to a battered pram which she bounced on its sprung suspension from her place on a slatted bench. The outline of brickwork arched out of sight above her and a string of bare yellow bulbs passed over her head. Ellipses of light trembled on the walls and revealed other creatures, indistinct in the semi-dark, bundles of rags in the waxy gloom. The place reverberated with detonations and the bulbs shook shadows like cave paintings on the brickwork. In the spaces between explosions, a modulating wail of fear filled the tunnel, a counterpoint to the earlier sound of sirens. The girl's own baby, lying wide-eyed in the pram, added to the sound; but the baby's noise was low and quiet, a deep instinct to remain unnoticed.

*I know. I know.* Lee was not sure whether he had spoken out loud or whether he had just spoken inside his head. He felt compelled to answer the voice of Grandad Swigler, to let him, it, know that he was not ignorant of the things he saw, just unable to grasp them. He already knew this about his nan and his mum but they were still things alien and strange.

'Fear, determination and sheer bleedin' luck,' said Grandad Swigler. 'Sheer bleedin' luck, boy.' And the dawn after the night in the shelter came sour, the sky mottled skin like reboiled milk, patched with smuts and columns of oily flame. The fires still burned fiercely everywhere and the air was choked with dark smoke and the stench of soot and burnt fuel and water on hot brick and blood. Lee could smell it, like the smell of the chicken factory. He swallowed against the memory. Men in tin hats, blue uniforms, armed with ladders, shovels, wheelbarrows, moved amongst the destroyed and smoking buildings. The streets, where they could still be made out, ran with the water of fire hoses; water turned red with spent life. Where they were not extinguishing fires, the men in tin hats were searching for survivors; searching for survivors but mainly picking up the pieces of those who had not survived.

One man worked alone, shovel and barrow, and Lee knew him by the slope of his shoulders and his bowed gait. He would not have known then that Vancy, Lee's nan, would have been leaving the shelter, fatigued and hungry, alone and reliant on the kindness of strangers. Lee's eyes smarted with tears and his senses flashed in time-lapse the rebuilding of the East End and the Essex docks. He watched the peaceful destruction of houses, including The Roundabout pub, followed by the ramps and the flyovers and the new motorway. 'You've got your roads and you've got your family, Lee. Roads and family 'n' that's it, boy.'

Grandad Swigler's voice was in the car, coming over the music; the grey road sharpened ahead and made him start; the car took a shimmy left and right and he steadied himself against the wheel. A bass drone and fog-horn synth were all that was left of the air raid, and the music revived through the bones of his skull to incantation... the consequence of badness, eternal death promised the vocal, looped to the point of discomfort... The beat and the horn pounded, the chatter of alien machines answered by the MC... *and we don't believe in the 45s or the revive, Hardcore music all the time...* The vocal cut back predicting death from badness and alien voices closer, louder, closer, louder... until a whispering breakdown brings back the funk, locking and popping electro, Kraftwerk synth, scratching and porno samples. For Lee it was good. It was the mood of the jilted generation. It gave him energy and focus. But he lacked something now, and what he lacked and wished he had more than anything was company. It became very apparent to him that this was not a journey he was used to making alone.

The M25 junction came up quickly and he was on to North Weald before he knew it. The music had worked its magic and the view and the weather matched his mood. This

223

was the spot he had looked for on the map; that place where, just past the M25, the land on either side of the carriageway opens up to the eye and you can see the swell of the giant earth as it lifts fields and ditches and hedgerows, in long, riding wavelengths. The road rises and falls with the topography, a grey ribbon to a far ridge, tufted with woodland. The sky meets the land in a blue and white dome and shows distant weather; curtains of cloud, dark and striated with rain; gleaming spaces between thunder-heads; vibrant rainbows. At other times, from behind billows of haze cumulus, the sun splays onto fields. Today, the air was bright, keen with a stiff breeze. Squadrons of rolling white clouds scudded overhead. It was a picture of promise.

Lee felt this not because he had any particular link with North Weald – he had never been there – but because what you saw of North Weald from the motorway was the airfield, and Lee's life had been full of airfields. As the thought occurred to him and as he glanced across to the hangars and smooth grass around the runway, a voice to his left, next to him in the car, sang out.

'Power...' intoned the voice, extending the vowels in unison with the vocal on the tune. Lee glanced sharply to his left, towards the source of the word.

'Look,' said Zoe, pointing up through the windscreen to the blue and white above. Lee shifted his eyes to follow Zoe's finger and saw the gliders she had spotted. There were two of them, high up, making quiet, spiralling progress up a column of warming air, moving slowly on their outsized wings, dragging light and shadow as they turned.

'Must be off the airfield,' concluded Lee.

'Yea, all right, Clouseau,' said Zoe. Zoe sat, a well-reclined co-driver in the passenger seat, as she had on countless journeys home. On one level, in his head, Lee knew that the years of driving home after a night out were in the past, that he had a different point of origin but, at the same time, he knew he also had to admit these other journeys. He cautioned calm and remembered the way Zoe, on more than one occasion, had helped him through some tight spots when it came to gripping reality. *You have what you wished for,* he told himself: company on the drive, roads and family as Grandad Swigler would have said.

He glanced in the mirror and saw two more passengers. One, male, lay crumpled in the corner where seat met side of car, swaddled in a hoodie and an MA2 jacket, arms folded across chest, head to one side and slightly back, mouth slack, eyes closed. The other, female, sat neatly behind him as he drove, knees together with hands clasped lightly on top. She too was wrapped against the cold outside and the vagaries of the car's heating. She stared forward, eyes relaxed, as if reliving an enjoyable experience. In fact, that is exactly what she was doing, and the shifting scapes of the hardcore only added to her pleasure. Rob and Kelly. Lee shrugged and reached down for the half-smoked reefer that looked at him with a fat roach-eye from the ashtray. That would help, he told himself. That would help.

'Power,' sang Zoe, matching the vocal on the tune again. 'Syncopation,' she then said. 'It's all about syncopation.' Lee smiled. Business as fucking usual, he thought, took a third, deep and final toke on the reefer and offered it. She took it, nodding to herself and the music, in clear agreement with everything.

'Syncopation is everything in our music... it's the life force...'

'Zoe, Zoe,' said Lee. 'Listen, mate, can I ask you something? It might seem a funny question... but... how did we all end up in the car like this?' Zoe looked at him through slightly narrowed eyes for a moment.

'What you talkin' about, young man, Mister Danny-Lee? *How did we end up in the car like this?*' She repeated the words back to him, emphasis intended to make him see the ridiculousness of what he had just said.

'You fuckin' space cadet,' said Kelly, 'what you on?' Then, laughing, 'No, don't tell me. I already know... same as me.' She shouted the last bit like an excited toddler and Zoe and Kelly both laughed; but Lee needed information.

'Yea, yea,' said Lee, 'good one... but just tell me where we've been... you know, Lab, Roller Express, Tasco's, you know... and what happened... generally...'

'Generally? What happened generally?' she repeated, again with sceptical emphasis. 'What the fuck does that mean?'

'Lee, get a grip, mate,' chipped in Kelly from the back. Lee said nothing and waited, unperturbed by the derision. He knew she wouldn't be able to hold the silence.

'Right,' she said, 'we were at Desire, Bagley's, yea...? Came back through Leytonstone 'cos we gave a lift to that girl you met – Hannah...? The road protester. You met her last night; told you she had to get out of Claremount Road for a bit and let her dreads down.

'Okay,' said Lee.

'We had a cup of tea 'n' a spliff, looked up a tree they were occupying then went on to Terry and Michelle's.' Lee remembered Hannah. She had been quietly outraged by his lack of engagement with the roads protest; said that if he gave her a lift back home she'd show him around. Maybe convert him. Lee had laughed. He'd tried to explain he wasn't against what she was doing; in fact, he thought it admirable – he'd used that very word – but he had added that he thought the new road was going to be fucking wicked for getting out of East London. She told him he was part of the problem and that now he had to give her a lift home.

'Yea, yea,' said Lee, 'before that, though... how did we, you know, get ourselves on the road?'

'Lee, mate, are you all right?' asked Zoe.

'Obviously not,' offered Kelly.

'You're not gonna throw a weird one, are you?' and Zoe laughed at the question as she lined up the next thing she was going to say. 'You know, like that time you had to pull over 'cos you thought you'd forgotten how to drive?' Zoe pictured the car on the hard shoulder, parked at a slant, Lee holding the wheel tight, staring hard through the windscreen, talking in a half whisper as if revealing a terrible secret: '"Zoe... Zoe... I don't think I can remember how to drive anymore,"' mimicked Zoe as she looked across at Lee who stared straight ahead at the road, a smile wriggling out between fastened lips. He snorted a laugh despite himself and shook his head at the pitiful state he had been in. It had been all too real at the time, he thought.

'One of Zoe's favourites,' he said, with an attempt to sound superior. She never tired of the story and it clearly got better for her with each retelling. To be fair, thought Lee, he would have done the same in her position.

'No, mate, just tell me what happened... so I'm clear on the details.'

'The details...' Zoe said. 'Well, to the best of my recollection, this is how it went...' and as she spoke, Lee saw it all...

## //

The lights had come up in the main room but the music still played; the MC was urging them on to more and more. It was packed with people but had eased a little so you could, at least, dance. A couple of hours before, there had been so many bodies in the space that all you could do was sway and strain your neck, trying to see if there was a better place to be. Lee had found a sweet spot by a pillar and stood there with Hannah – the road protester he had met – and Kelly. He could see Zoe across the room, on a dance platform, white jumpsuit with Day-Glo piping, horn slung round her shoulder, bass pout on, arms going back and forth, dancing at the pointing fingers and raised arms of the ravers down on the floor around her. She was totally lost in the music and the dance; she was indivisible from them and they from her. She was pure clarity and vigour and, even from a distance, her celebration reached Lee; he knew there was no better feeling; the knowledge tingled and glowed.

Lee pulled his attention away from the dancing Zoe and turned to Hannah, who stood with him and Kelly by the pillar.

'Hey, Hannah,' he said, cupping his hand against his mouth and leaning down towards her, 'you wanna lift home then?' She turned to him, her jaw churning on gum to the pound of the bass, her face shining and oily with the effort of the night. She nodded enthusiastically. He looked back up towards Zoe. There was no reaching her for now, better just to wait, enjoy the last tunes and soak up the buzz. He looked at the scene; so different now the house lights were on; you could clearly see the people you had been dancing with all night, see the deep pits of their eyes and the fierce contentment in their faces. It reminded Lee of the big outdoor events and the raves in circus tents and aircraft hangars, where you could dance outside or just stand and wait for an epiphanic sunrise that would define the night; stand with thousands of others in the disclosure of the dawn, dish-eyed, loose but alert, and coming up on the last half of a quality pill dropped twenty minutes before. And, as the sun rose, it affirmed every emotion and revelation of the night. The first time Lee had experienced this it had been overwhelming; he felt he was physically and emotionally connected with everyone there and that he and they would be forever linked to each other by what they had shared. He still felt that link to those people, he realised, and it made him grin.

The grin attracted enquiries.

''Avin' a good one, mate?' Someone was shaking his hand and grasping his shoulder; he could see the shape of his own face in the dark mirrors of the bloke's eyes.

'Yes, mate, fuckin' wicked. You?'

'You know, mate, you know... safe.' And they bumped fists and nodded at each other, at the guiding principle that had brought them together. The bloke moved off, his Kangol bucket hat bobbing in the groove, approaching as many as he could to repeat the question he had just asked Lee. Lee watched him and remembered excruciating moments as a kid, in church with Granny Harker when the vicar would ask them to greet a stranger – say a blessing or something. This was alien behaviour for Lee but Granny Harker loved it; she would even get talking to complete strangers outside of church, much to Lee's discomfort if he was with her. Looking back, it struck him that the idea must have been to create the kind of energy and emotion he had just enjoyed with Mr Bucket Hat. He wondered if Granny Harker had experienced that kind of thing in church. He imagined her being with him now, right here, Desire, Bagley's, main room; her Sunday best marked with soot from the walls and her shoes stained with the liquor that formed from the fags, water, sweat and dissolved dirt that accumulated overnight on the concrete floor. He pictured her with her tinted and coiffed hair, like a lilac cloud, greeting all these sweaty, gurning, loved-up ravers and thought how she might well have loved them for their friendliness, for their enthusiasm, and for their generosity. The music stopped then but the crowd remained wanting;

they were shouting, 'One more. One more,' in what became a steady, roaring chant accompanied by horns and whistles. But the lights were up and the bouncers amongst them; it was plain that the night was over. Lee looked back up to the stage. Zoe was there, hugging the people around her and grasping hands. He tried to catch her eye but failed.

'Hannah, Kelly, stay with me and let's go get Zoe.'

'But I need to find Rob.'

'Where is he?'

'I dunno, I ain't seen him all night.' Lee had a vision of an energetic Rob standing with a small group in the outside area. Lee was too far away to hear but Rob must have been telling one of his embroidered stories. Every now and then there would be howls of laughter, fuel to the fire Rob had set. But that was hours ago... the outside area would have been closed down way before... he had to be somewhere in the main room, here with them. Lee scanned the crowd as the bouncers steadily ushered people towards the exit. It was slow work as people spilled back through the shepherding arms of the bouncers into parts of the room that had just been cleared; here they would idle around and strike up conversation with any others who had slipped through the net before being caught by a further sweep and moved incrementally towards the exit.

'Just stay together, Kells, we'll pick him up outside.' Kelly was open to suggestions that made life easy and all three of them began to move towards the door out. He could see Zoe now; she was off the stage and heading in roughly the right direction but her focus was clearly not on home.

'Right, let's just pick 'em up outside,' said Lee, making a decision under pressure in the field, and he and the two girls allowed themselves to be carried by the slack tide of ravers towards the door. Lee hung on to Kelly and Hannah to make sure they stayed together; so many things could upset a plan to meet outside.

Once outside, Lee stood and scanned the exit to be sure he didn't miss Zoe leaving, while simultaneously keeping tabs on Kelly and Hannah so they didn't wander off or, inadvertently, get swept up in the stream of people leaving the venue. Zoe appeared eventually. She was in the process of saying goodbye to every person that had been in the main room, that and letting them know what a great night she had had and checking on the quality of theirs. She was also with Rob. Result, thought Lee.

'Zoe, Zoe, Rob,' Lee shouted, and finally got their attention and a chance to get them out onto the road and into the car.

'Yea, thanks for that,' said Lee, once Zoe had finished her resume of Desire at Bagley's; he had been only half-listening to Zoe, so immersed had he been in the flood of his own recollection. 'Just checkin' someone was paying attention, you know.' He felt completely present now and full of the lucid ease that is the residue of a top night out.

'Look,' said Zoe, pointing up through the windscreen. Lee saw the gliders again, higher and darker in the sky.

'Must be off the airfield,' said Lee.

'Yea, you already said that,' mocked Zoe, but the airfield had Lee's attention, the airfields that had figured so much in his life. That was probably down to his Dad and his Dad's dad having been in the forces, Lee thought. He supposed that meant he came from a military family. Funny that, thought Lee, although he wasn't sure why it was. Yes, he came from a military family, he decided, and wondered whether his dad would have liked to see him join up. Lee paused in his thoughts and felt his awareness shift in a way that gave him *déjà vu*. He shivered. *Obsessed*, he pronounced to himself in his head, *obsessed*.

'My dad,' he said to no one in particular, 'is, I think, obsessed... you know, my dad, Zoe?... Kells? He's fuckin' obsessed, ain't'e...? Has been my whole life... all those historic sites and military history... it's a fuckin' obsession.'

'Yea,' said Zoe.'I mean, I don't really know him... only met him a few times ... but... you know... who am I to say...?'

'Well, take it from me, he's obsessed... in fact, I'd call it addicted,' and he nodded as a block slid perfectly into its place. This gave Lee a sense of command and he began to survey the huge catalogue of battlefields and monuments, museums and historic sites that he and his sister had been dragged around by his dad. It seemed that whenever he and his sister stayed with their dad for the weekend, or in the school holidays, that that is what they did: visit these boring places. Lee recalled a fragment of the boredom and horrified himself by thinking of all the other places his dad must have gone to alone, filling more huge catalogues. No wonder mum left him, he thought; that'd drive you round the fucking twist after a while. He laughed at it now but, at the time, it had been a torture. His dad always dressed it up as a day out for him and his sister: I know what you kids'll like, he used to say when they came over, a nice spin out to Shitsville-on-the-Wold so we can look at the site of where, now, nothing is actually visible. Him and Angela in the back of the car, metal detector in the boot, thermos in a carrier bag on the front seat with sandwiches pinched up in a sheet of tin foil, a few bags of Hula Hoops and a couple of Granny Smiths. Lee pictured his dad's Cortina pulled over at the side of a wet country road, parked on a scrap of verge where the hedgerow opened for a gate that gave access into a field beyond. His dad sat in the front, his tagged-up history books piled on the passenger seat with the packed lunch, and a map open on his knees, head down, scanning its signs and symbols, then up, staring out over the tussocky field, trying to overlay onto the wet green world outside the map's printed abstractions in such a way that it would confirm, to his satisfaction, that this was where two antique armies had come together to cut each other to pieces with swords and pikes and to fire exploding balls of metal at each other's bodies. There was sometimes a post with a plaque on it by these places and it would tell you that this was the site of the Battle-of-Waste-of-Fucking-Time, fought in sixteen-forty-who-gives-a-shit, between two similar groups of men with no real idea what they were there for and which led to the formation of some piece of nonsense we're still stuck with today and to the loss of umpteen hundred lives and a slightly smaller number of arms and legs.

I bet they didn't see us coming, Lee thought, as he looked back on the sight of a slightly frantic, gangly, middle-aged man pacing round a field with a map in his hand, a couple of books stuffed in his pockets, watched by two defeated-looking children in orange kagouls, mindlessly eating Hula Hoops. As far as Lee could remember, the only trip that wasn't like this was the one they made to Harwich. He must have been quite young, as Angela had only just started school. They had driven to Harwich in whatever car his dad had owned before the Cortina and then just stood there on Dovercourt Beach, looking out to sea under a blank sky. Lee wasn't sure what they were doing and he asked his dad what they were looking for. His dad said that they weren't looking for anything, that they were just paying their respects. That was when Lee learned about Grandad Harker; learned he was not around anymore because the destroyer he was serving on had been sunk by a mine during the war, somewhere off the coast near Harwich. It was the only time Lee had really heard his dad talk about anything personal and they never went there again. Lee could still see the sadness of the three of them standing on the sand and looking at the restless water.

Maybe he was being unfair, he thought. After all, his dad had taken him round most of the T2 hangars in Cambridgeshire and Norfolk years before he went raving in them. If nothing else, that was a good story to tell when you were out.

'Hey, Zoe, you remember them Coventry Eclipse raves in the big hangars?'

'I should reckon,' replied Zoe.

'Remember that first one, Knettishall, near Thetford?'

'Fuckin' 'ell, Lee,' said Zoe, laughing, 'I never knew where it was to start with… remember the night, though.'

'Yea,' said Lee, 'top memories… those hangars, though, they were fuckin' mental.' He had all the flyers in his collection, the one with the war planes in silhouette his favourite. He'd done a few sketches for that one. Carl Cox, Grooverider, Fabio… they'd all been at the T2 events… but no tapes. Top Buzz had been there too, Lee remembered as the mix invaded the car like a mighty wind, filled it with the spirit of crazed steam-organ stomp; it came rushing in, vocals over and over to breakdown then every noise, full-on, measured, liquid. Nice, thought Lee.

'Those old hangars must have wondered what hit 'em…' he said, '…probably thought the fuckin' war had started again – worse than the bloody Blitz,' he added, imitating the voice of Nanna Swigler. 'Must have been a shock, though,' said Lee '…on your own for years in the middle of nowhere, nothing going on but chicken shit and tractors and all of a sudden, bosh, Top Buzz in the place.' Laughter.

'Didn't you go there with your dad or something?' asked Kelly.

'What…? Yea, yea, that's what I was gonna say,' said Lee '… that first Knetishall one… yea, so when I could see what was going on the next morning, I realised I'd been there before, when I was a kid, with my dad… I told you, he was fuckin' obsessed… military sites, the war, battlefields… so, we went on this holiday to Norfolk with him one year, me and me sister, spent most of it goin' round old airfields, him takin' pictures and talkin' to old geezers he met about what they could remember.'

'Yea, I remember now,' said Zoe, 'you said the hangars should have plaques outside saying this was the site of a Hardcore night; a top rave went off here; many minds were lost.' They both laughed.

'Yea, man, commemorating the history of rave – people need to know.' Lee paused before saying with mock-seriousness, as if doing a documentary voiceover: '…a significant role in the development of rave music and culture, contributing to one of the most influential youth movements of our time.' Laughter. Top Buzz thundered on and Lee conceded that the idea for commemorative rave plaques had come from his dad. All through that holiday he had kept on about commemorative plaques for the T2s and the old airfields, like they had for some of the old battlefield sites. He said that these places had saved our freedom; that the people who manned them were heroes; that they don't make men like that anymore. Those words had stuck with Lee. He thought about what he was doing now, a man of conscription age, compared to the young lives of both his grandads. He supposed that they just did what they did at the time they were doing it in, just like he was. He digested that idea for a few moments; thought of Grandad Harker killed by a mine. That, he thought, was more of an accident than an act of war. Maybe, all of it was accidental. Those men just happened to be born when and where they were; a war came and they fought it. If we had been born then, we would have fought the same as them. And, if they had been born in the '70s, they'd be out raving at the weekends like us. That's what's so sad, Lee concluded, the accident of it all, the randomness, like the poor fuckers sliced to shit in a forgotten field.

'D' ya think your mum and dad, or your nan and grandad, or whoever, would have been into raving…you know… if they were young now?' said Lee, out loud, to the car.

'I reckon my mum would,' said Zoe.

'Yea, mine too,' said Kelly.

'Mine fuckin' wouldn't,' said Rob, who had just woken up.

'Morning, camper,' said Lee, 'no, mine neither… just wonderin'…' and he thought of how his mum, doubtless with Malcolm's encouragement, had chucked him out to go and live with Nanna Swigler after that second Knetishall Eclipse; she said he was wasting his life, was a bad influence on his sister and that she thought he'd joined a cult. Less of the bad influence, he thought; Ange was well clued-up… that's why she'd laughed at *E please Bob* on *Blockbusters*, nothing to do with his influence. The only bad influence about it all was the one it had on his finances. No mistake about that but serving up a bit of speed on the side helped ease the pain. Otherwise, it was pretty sweet at the Swigler's Arms. No more creeping around the gaff and no more Malcolm in his face. Nanna Swigler was sound. She might have been a raver, he thought, and Grandad Swigler definitely would have been; he'd have been a fucking MC, thought Lee, and Mad P, once again, hit the cue '…*who wants to fly, who wants to be on top of the world? Let's go… snap, crackle and pop… shout going out to the nut-nut crew in the place… and it happens to be the Technics extravaganza…*' and the tape finished and hissed to silence.

# TWENTY-ONE

The silence in the car seemed sudden to Lee and, as the tape cut, frames jumped across his field of view. Vertigo and a nano-flash of pure energy caused him to lurch from the plexus; he felt he saw the world from the furthest reaches of his head, as from high above through a small aperture, as looking back down at your house through a hatch in the ceiling while you stand in the quiet air of the loft. It might have been worrying in different circumstances; in different circumstances in different times, it might have made him anxious that he'd really overdone it this time with the drugs and the lack of sleep; but, as it was, Lee was beginning to understand how this pattern operated; he noticed how the intermittent lurches and swoops, whatever they were and why, were becoming familiar, that the fear and confusion in them was subsidiary. He was beginning to see that when he had taken his discoveries and his visions and Zoe's words

237

and music into the car that morning he had signed up for the sudden drops and brake-turns of the roller coaster he now found himself on. Those extremes of sensation, he thought, you wouldn't want them all the time, or for too long, but you definitely do want them; they are integral to it all; they define experience; they are the thrill. He was actually enjoying this, he realised, and the zoom reversed, a frame-jump and he was driving again. The road and the music became his primary focus; the motion of the car and the progress of the music one headlong movement; Lee, the crest, pulled from the chest, acceleration pushing shoulders and stomach back into the seat.

Lee, alerted by the compression, looked to his mirror, checked peripheral vision on his left-hand. The same set of passengers are on board but there are differences – he thought – variations in the way they are dressed, the way they hold themselves. He couldn't be sure. Every time he has checked for detail it has seemed right for that moment, even when there is something telling him it's not. What he could see now, for instance, matched the music perfectly, corresponded with the passing landscape, hit the mood of the moment but, there were subtleties, gentle spaces on the edge of his blind spot, subtleties he couldn't put his finger on, little wrinkles that differentiated what he saw from what he had seen; specks in the sunlight that you knew were always differently arranged even if you couldn't pinpoint how. Lee took a frown and slightly narrowed eyes back to the road; he wasn't certain where they had been and where they were returning from; it might have been another Labrynth, another event at Bagley's; had they come careering away from The Astoria or a mad one at Raindance; from rocking out The Rocket, rolling Roller Express or maybe it was a long haul – World Dance, Dreamscape, Helter Skelter? It might have been any or none, it might have been all or one; Lee was relaxed. Points in time, coalescing, merging, now had a point that was persuasive; persuasive and beguiling. He thought about asking again; calling out to the car, to one of the others for the low-down – where, what, when? But he decided there was no need; either it would emerge or it wouldn't; nothing would be lost or gained either way. The direction of travel remained the same whatever the answer. He was content to wait and see.

Hastingwood, Junction 7 was coming up; exit here for the Harlow Hardcore, thought Lee, but before he could say anything, Zoe, without warning, took the moment and spoke:

'Syncopation,' she said. 'It's all about syncopation; it's the heartbeat of our music—'

'…speaking of which…' Lee cut in, '…'nother tape on, Zo?'

'…er… yea… yea…' Zoe agreed vacantly, still wondering at the heartbeat of the music. Lee smiled; this was Zoe's time. This was the point in the journey that she liked to hit her stride with some topic or other. Lee predicted to himself – assuming it was the same journey – that it would be about the kitchen chat they'd had earlier at Terry and Michelle's; the one with that bloke in the cap.

'Hey, Zoe, is that what you were bangin' on about in the kitchen with that bloke at Terry and Michelle's?' asked Rob. Zoe said nothing. She was leant forward now, her top half in the footwell, reaching out to find the box of tapes waiting in the darkness by her feet. 'She was,' Rob replied to his own question. 'Classic fuckin' Zoe, bending this geezer's ear right off… but then he came back with as good as he was getting… fried my nut… that's when I found you in the garden, Kelly, you know, when we tried to get the birds to whistle back at us.' Kelly gave a little bird whistle and Rob answered with one of his own.

'I wondered what you were doing out there,' said Lee, 'you fuckin' fruit loops… I dunno what their neighbours must think,' he added. This was answered by a rattle and a sigh from the passenger seat as Zoe collapsed back into her seat, having successfully located and retrieved the tape case.

'Steady, Zo, you can do this,' said Rob.

'Fuck off, Rob,' said Zoe automatically as she unzipped and flipped open the tape case on her lap and gave its contents her full attention. The case was full and the spines of the plastic cases and the lettering on them seemed to march up and down across her lap. She hated reading in the car, especially with her head down. She flipped the lid back over the tapes and held the case over her shoulder.

'Kelly, Rob, you do it, it's messin' with my head.'

'Here, give it to me,' said Kelly, and took the case.

The car filled with the noise of tyres on the road and air on fast-moving metal. Kelly let her finger follow the stack from top to bottom, reading and registering the information on each case, but, for most, immediately forgetting it as she moved on to the next. The words on each tape case sparked a thought or an idea or an association with something that once happened or something someone once said, and she kept following herself down the slope of her wandering attention. The rhythm of her thinking escaped from her mouth in fragments of vocal and melody, almost sung, partly hummed. Kelly quickly forgot where she was and what she was doing, and her finger, shortly after reaching the bottom of the last stack of three, returned to near the top of the first, where it hung motionless over the cases in the box. 'Uh, uh umm, Uh, uh, umm, take me away, take me away.'

'Someone'll take you away in a fuckin' minute if you don't choose a tape,' said Rob. 'C'mon, what you doin'? People are waitin''

'Yea, Kells, c'mon, get some tunes on,' chipped in Lee.

Kelly came to abruptly and surprised herself with her own presence which her temporary mental absence had taken elsewhere and, unthinkingly, took out the tape case which her finger was on, removed the tape, leant forward, exchanged it with the out-coming tape which Zoe held over her shoulder like a relay baton. Zoe clickety-clacked the tape into the slot while Kelly returned the other to its home. Kelly zipped the case and gave it back to Zoe, who plunged it into the darkness of the footwell to wait some more.

'Teamwork,' declared Kelly as Shaggy and Breeze, Groove 2-Eclipse Dance Festival 1992, took over from the empty roaring of the road noise.

'Selection,' said Lee as he walked across the middle of a farmer's field in the Fens near Ely, towards a marquee that had once been home to The Royal Ballet and the Circus World Championships; it looked resplendent and the music was loud even at a distance. The drive had been full of tension, he remembered; they'd heard that the Essex police were out that night pulling ravers and making life difficult as they tried to go about their business… *police officer, leave us alone, we don't want no trouble in the Hardcore Zone…* he sang to himself at the thought. They had taken the long way and been wary all the way; and the Fen landscape on the last part of the journey, illuminated by a pearlescent pink glow produced by the diffused light of the sun setting behind broken rolls of charcoal clouds, had filled them all full of a strange sense of foreboding. The earlier tensions and attentions of the police probably hadn't helped, Lee reasoned but, he thought, the Fens were weird if you weren't used to them. They were still weird the next morning but the sense of threat had gone and the place became just glorious. He saw himself dancing outside the marquee as the sun was coming back up on the other side, buzzing like a bastard on some of the best pills he'd ever had, a menthol inhaler up his nose, blowing hard on an Acme Thunderer, top off, covered in sweat and dancing like he was made of cool tubes of articulated mercury. *Fuck me*, thought Lee, as the memory intersected with the chemistry of the previous night and rippled through his entire body. *Fuck me*, he said to himself again, *that was a wicked night.* When the rave had finished no one wanted to leave. They had stood in small groups beneath the immense sky, its limits defined by a horizon that went for three sixty degrees round the ends of the earth. They had stood there and talked quietly, hushed as if in a library or a church, the music still singing in their ears, sharing fags and trying to build spliffs with damp papers and fingertips like prunes, already reminiscing.

'I was thinking of that event last night,' said Lee, 'how we stood outside the tent as the sun came up. I'll never forget it.' Lee's words took them all to the field in the Fens as Shaggy and Breeze filled the car with sub-bass and euphoric synth. The music inspired Zoe and reminded her where she had been before the tape case hiatus. The ideas she had been chewing over with Lee and that bloke with the cap at Terry and Michelle's.

'Syncopation,' she said and, without pause, launched herself: 'Beats and rhythm enclosing space, framing samples, carrying melodics. You know what we've done, we've not only made our own soundtrack – every modern generation has done that to an extent – but we, we've done it from the bottom up. We've twisted together a twisted sound for our twisted times. It's the shape of the noise and the culture of noise that's been pouring into the UK since the war – especially London and the cities. It's like separate streams that have joined together in a mighty flow. Yea, a mighty flow, together stuff that before was separate; we've fused into this mad monster that just wants to fuckin' dance and party; it can't stop itself;

it cannot be stopped, it has to run its course. Yea, the way I see it, there's the Hip-Hop thing – looping the best beats, lifting funk motifs and soundtracks; there's Balearic synths and Euro beats – the euphoria, the sun-drenched innocence; Detroit techno and Chicago house, the jack and the groove; there's the final bounce and spin of Acid; and, underlying that, is roots and reggae – sub dub and bright up-strokes; there's 70's MOR and Disco – super production values, crystal vocals and orchestral backings – and there's New Wave Synth Punk – moody, minimal and sinew basslines. We've taken all that and the noises goin' on in the background, and we've put a mine under it, a technology bomb… and as the pieces fall, we're reassembling in a way which makes our sense. I tell you, man, this music is monumental… we'll look back on it as pure gold.' Zoe didn't care whether anyone was listening or not. She was in a groove and she loved it there. Lee let the words wash around him, enjoying the way Zoe had sharpened her talk since earlier at Terry and Michelle's. 'Pure fuckin' gold,' Zoe repeated.

'Yea,' said Lee. '…yea, definitely the technology, that's crucial; but don't forget the drugs; drugs need to be there – drugs are defining; and ya know what else… what else is defining?' Lee left it hanging for a moment; he hadn't made this point in the kitchen at Terry and Michelle's and felt he had a clincher. He glanced at Zoe. She looked back, brows raised in question. 'Cars,' said Lee finally.

'Cars?' Zoe questioned.

'Yea,' said Lee. 'Cars… this time is the first time that the youth have really had cars on a big scale, had their own transport. Think about it. When I was little there were tons of families on the estate that didn't even own a car. Now pretty much everyone has a car and as soon as you're seventeen, you get your test done and you get yourself a motor. And if you can't manage that, you have a mate that can. We couldn't have done it without the cars. Think about all them car park meets, all the drivin' we've done, the hours we've spent in this car and others, making it to and from raves, chattin' shit and listenin' to tunes.'

Zoe was thoughtful. 'Yea,' she said, agreeing the thesis, 'cars and ravin'… d'ya think the Mods went for scooters 'cos of their budget as well as for style, or did it suit the drugs they were doin'…? And what about Punk… the youth culture that went by public transport… you never saw a Punk on a scooter, did you…? Maybe a Goth on a moped…' Zoe laughed to herself as by now she was her main audience. Lee had returned his concentration to the roads and to the music; the music which broke on the wing-dam of foghorn techno, then came up a breathless vocal leading on a rough-neck break. In the mix, the signs for Junction 7 bounced by, counting down on the verge; Lee drove to their same pulse and, in his left-hand eyeline, took them on the punch of the beats, acknowledged departure with a full-throat reedy warble of big layered Hammond, white on blue, primary school font. Lee sang at the signs as he passed, before they could wave back; he was rolling now; this was a journey that was underway and he sang out to the car, sang to the road and to his companions, sang his heartfelt desire that he did not wanna lose their love, did not wanna lose their love…

Zoe saw the Harlow sign too. 'Rish was there last night,' she said, leaning her head back round the seat so they could hear in the back.

'Yea, saw him,' said Rob, 'should get some studio time next week or the week after.'

'Is Baz doing stuff with him now?' asked Zoe.

'Yea,' said Rob, 'but not as Clever Boy, they're doing something else. Jag and Josh, too… but they were already with Pace from way back.'

'Aye, aye,' said Kelly, 'Jag and Josh, bish, bash, bosh.'

'That was mental, that night,' said Kelly.

'It was the start,' said Zoe.

'It was part of the start,' added Lee, who always liked to dissect the genesis of a story.

'It was part of the start,' needled Rob, and Zoe joined in.

'And it started,' said Kelly, ''cos that dancer set her arm on fire.'

'...and that's not a sentence you hear very often,' said Lee, laughing. 'There's plenty of things about that night,' he continued, 'that I won't forget in a fuckin' hurry.' And, the music detonated deep munitions, breaks hip and taut, plucked strings thunked across a percussive piano breakdown and sped-up vocals. It was dark and Lee watched a pair of white gloves, strung with flashing lights, cross and chop right before his eyes. They were turning this way and that, making shapes with the dark spaces, describing angles and planes, tracking lights across the fields of his hyper-sensitised retinas; firing flares across the galaxy of his brain through the wormhole of his optic nerve. He had seen the girl with the flashing gloves dancing on the stage earlier and now she was down in the crowd, sauntering around in a Day-Glo patterned top, flying cyber-dreads swinging down her back, trying to spin people out with her illuminated gloves. For the most part she was succeeding and Lee was enjoying the show. To be honest, he thought, any kind of well-intentioned stimulation in the state I'm in is going to have a pleasing effect. Kelly and Zoe were dancing next to him and were egging the girl on to more and more complex shapes and energetic figures.

But Lee could sense something else alongside. Another flavour of stimulation that jarred, that didn't quite fit the harmonics of the night; something that pushed itself forward over the dancing girl's display and the dancing of Kelly and Zoe, inserted itself between them and the lights and the music. It was like melting; like cheese on toast; no, more like a wasteland bonfire, smouldering plastic and degrading chemicals; a thick, rasping smell. What the fuck is that? thought Lee. It had pushed its way fully into his head now and was demanding attention. It reminded him strongly of the time he had gradually become aware that the mad visuals he could see flickering and jumping about on the wall at the back of the hangar at one of those Norfolk raves had been firemen putting out burning hay bales. Shit, he thought, interrupting himself, something is on fire.

He mentally pulled himself out of the dance and looked now, focussing as hard as he could manage. The stage, the walls, the roof, the crowd, all looked fine. The backs of the heads in front of him looked as they should and – he turned and looked over his shoulder – so did the fronts of the heads of those behind. He turned back to face the stage and the dancing girl's arm was there, right in front of his face, the white gloved hand wound with lights, up at an angle, her eyes behind it wide with smiling mischief, and her wrist and forearm, just where the glove ended and some wires emerged, a flicking tongue of blue-yellow flame. Lee stared at it and sniffed, trusting his nose more than his eyes; there was no smoke that he could see but he could smell the product of combusting flesh and battery chemicals.

'Your fuckin' arm's on fire,' shouted Lee, pointing at the flames. At first, the girl thought he was dancing with her again but the look on his face must have been sending a clear and different message. She followed the line of emergency in his eyes and looked at the flames without being able to understand what was happening. Kelly too had followed Lee's urgency and was shouting:

'Fuck, your fuckin' arm. It's burning.'

'Shit,' said Zoe, 'your fuckin' arm!' The girl then understood and reacted, initially starting back as if the flames were not part of her and then reaching around her wrist with her other gloved hand to smother them.

'Shit,' said Lee, 'what the fuck is goin' on?' and the three of them led her, still holding her wrist and looking confused, to where Rob and Baz were sitting, part of a sprawling chatting, smoking and chilling group of punters.

'Fuckin'ell,' said Baz when they updated him and Rob and everyone else about what had just happened. 'Hard fuckin' core. How'd ya manage to set your arm on fire?' The girl sat and explained, quite matter-of-factly, to the audience before her, that it must have been sweat getting into the nine-volt battery taped to her wrist to power the homemade lights on her gloves. They all had a good look at the wires and the seeping, blackened battery casing that she had by then removed from her arm; they looked too at the seeping and blackened skin of her burned arm. The girl seemed nonplussed and to not share the consensus view that she had sustained quite a serious injury. She was, she said, now that the fire was out, ready to rejoin the rave and get back on stage, which she duly did.

'That,' said Rish, who had been sitting and chatting with Baz, 'is one of the most mad fuckin' things I have ever seen... and I've seen a few.'

'She was on fire, tho,' said Jag. 'Talk about time to make the floor burn.'

## //

Three or four hours after the incident of the girl with the burning arm, they were loading themselves into the Polo on the way to Rish's place near Harlow.

'This,' said Rob, 'could be a fuckin' moment of change. Things may never be the same again.'

'Yea, all right, Rob, calm down,' said Zoe, 'it's only Pick Up the Pace...'

'This one, Zoe?' said Lee rapidly.

'Yea, yea, here, here...' Zoe cut back as Lee altered his line into the roundabout.

'But it could be what we've been lookin' for...' said Rob.

'If it is, then it is,' said Zoe. 'Don't fuckin' sweat, geeze. Just go with how it is. We're goin' for a chill and a fuck about.'

'High Wych, Zoe, is that the one?'

'Yea, High Wych,' said Zoe, 'follow that.' It was early morning, mid-winter and still just about dark, with the sun beginning to make ghosting shadows in the clouds. Zoe was haphazardly giving Lee directions to an address just outside Harlow neither of them had been to, on roads neither of them knew. Rob and Kelly were, intermittently and unhelpfully, involved in the co-driving but fully involved in distracting Zoe. Although Harlow was definitely in Essex, thought Lee, it was, nevertheless, a land that was as nearly foreign to Lee as South London. He considered it to be more Hertfordshire; its canals and swampy river valleys; its closeness to Stortford, Welwyn and Stevenage. The way the thick blue line of the M11 on the map cut it off from the rest of Essex strengthened this idea in Lee's mind. Maybe it was also Grandad Swigler and the way the motorway always provoked him to say, with a sharp sucking of teeth and shaking of the head, that the M11 ended one thing and began another. Lee could see his Sherpa parked early one morning on a bridge of the Birchanger roundabout, a very young Lee and his grandad were looking north at the earth movers and trucks sat on the orange scar of the early construction of the Cambridge section of the road. 'One thing ends and another begins, Lee,' he had said. 'There's no stopping time, no more idling,' he had added. Lee wasn't sure what he had meant but maybe it made more sense now than ever as he explored these unfamiliar roads on the other side of the motorway, assisted by Zoe's reading of a map by torchlight, supplemented with occasional excited interjections from Rob, based on dim knowledge gained from helping Baz with work somewhere around here. At one point, when they had found themselves going the wrong way down the 414 towards Chelmsford, Lee realised he should have just gone the way he knew, even if it was longer. Still, he told himself, they were back on track now and hopefully on the way to Rish's house; Rish, co-founder of Pick Up the Pace records with his mate Marcus, whose fascination with the burning hand incident had led to them being where they now were and who was the cause of Rob's excitement.

'There's a High Wych mix of that Jag and Josh tune. You know, the one they dropped last night,' said Rob.

'What, *Turn of the Screw?*' Said Zoe.

'Yea, what a tune,' said Rob. Jag and Josh had also been there to witness the girl with the burning arm. Rob could see opportunities for him and Zoe to get on the radar with their own tunes; they were big on ideas, he knew, but small on gear and access to a studio. For Rob the Pick Up the Pace crew were like a beacon and had been testing the ground when the girl with the burning arm had appeared. Rob saw it as a good omen, like the burning bush, or a rainbow. 'Tell you what,' said Rish, when the dust had settled and Burning Girl had returned to the dance. 'Why don't we go back to mine after this, chill out, chat some more, play some tunes, listen to some samples, bladi fuckin' blah...?' Addresses and numbers were scribbled onto fag packets and it was a plan.

They finally reached the house of Rish in High Wych, somewhere just outside Harlow; the combined effect of the effort to do so, the time of day they were doing it and the continuing exhilaration of the preceding night made it feel like Shangri-La. They approached the PVC front door, top half frosted glass, bottom moulded white plastic, like it was the entrance to a secret land few had ever seen before and not a new-build semi, part of a development of many such, along with a smattering of entry level executive homes that was adding to the creeping edge of Harlow New Town. The lowering morning was cold and still and the estate they were on perfectly quiet, at rest, as it should be so early on a Saturday morning. They bundled through the front door in a spray of stage whispers and poorly suppressed laughter. The kettle was on and someone could be heard upstairs moving furniture and bringing machines to life.

'Right,' said Rish, coming down the stairs, a breakbeat kicking into life behind him as he did so, '...this is a special day because me gran is away and so are the neighbours; and that means we can make noise.' The news prompted a brief outpouring of sound from them all as if to test the theory, which Rob followed with:

'Can we smoke in the house, Rish?'

'Smoke away, mate,' he replied, 'but let's get up the fuckin' stairs to the bat cave.' Rish turned on the bottom step and headed back up, two stairs at a time, towards the swelling beat, now with sci-fi bassline taut against a battery of whooshing synths. Everyone followed.

'This,' said Rish, gesturing expansively, 'is the studio. This is where it all fuckin' 'appens.' Lee, Rob and the others were in what must have been the second bedroom of the three-bedroom semi, but there was little in it to identify it as a bedroom. One wall was taken up by a pair of decks and a mixer; alongside that, another desk, supporting a much bigger mixing desk, an Akai Si 50 and a computer. Above, on a rack fixed to the wall, a DX 7 keyboard. Another wall hosted tape machines, amps, modules, thick monitor speakers, a shelf of cables, a bass guitar and mics. The music was coming from one of the tape machines and the monitors. Under the surfaces and around the room were crates and bags of records, including, in one corner, a couple of small stacks of unstamped white labels. There was a small sofa in one corner and besides stools at the desks and work surfaces, a couple of armchairs. Zoe looked around the room, taking in the equipment and the vinyl and simply the fact of house space dedicated to making rave music. She had seen home set-ups before, decks and a mixer in the bedroom, or, maybe, in a shed outside, like Lee's cousins. Rob had a computer and a deck in his shed now and said he was getting a sampler through Baz but she had never seen anything like this. She was in awe of what she saw and looked around and caught Lee's eye with hers, full of wonder and infused with spirit. They walked to the decks while everyone else found a seat and began skinning up or rabbiting. Zoe stood at the mixer and they surveyed the other gear assembled around the room while her hands rested lightly on the platters, lay on the slipmats in the glow of the active power lights. She moved one platter gently back and forth and whistled soundlessly at what she felt.

Zoe turned to Lee and nodded silently then round to face the rest of the party and looked directly at Rish. She grinned widely. 'Wicked,' she said. 'This is fuckin' wicked.'

'Go on, Zoe,' called Rob, 'spin us some tunes, you fuckin' bad gel.' Zoe grinned back and made a scratching movement with the platter on which her right hand still rested while self-consciously pulling a face. 'Yes,' said Rob, his hand in the air beating out the rhythm of the music that was already playing over the monitors. Rish joined them and pointed out some of the equipment but it was just names and numbers. Zoe said so but said she also wanted Rish to write them down for her. She told him that she wanted what he had.

'You make the tunes here?' she said to Rish.

'More or less, mate, yea,' said Rish, looking round the equipment and paraphernalia spread around the room. 'We've put out two so far, but we've got plans to take over the fuckin' world and this is where it starts.' As he finished the sentence he moved across the room and took a record from each of the piles of white labels and held them before him, one in each hand. Zoe gazed at the two discs and then again around the room – the bedroom of a three-bed semi just outside Harlow – and Lee could see her face change as a bright, warm light flooded her brain and unfolded there for her a view of extraordinary clarity. He knew what she was thinking because he was thinking the same; *never before have we had the power of the music directly in our own hands like this.* And Rish, with everything he said about how he and Marcus – the other half of Pick Up the Pace, who was still on his way home – made tunes, was confirming it all for them. 'We're getting a bit more serious now,' he said, 'but, yea, we basically just get together with a bag of samples and try and make something we'd wanna hear when we're out. It's that fuckin' simple really. We're just makin' it up as we go along but that is a first and that is real power.'

This was enlightenment. It was that direct, thought Lee. Something he had always felt instinctively, was finally revealed. He tried to explain this to Rish. He explained it badly but Rish got it. Of course he got it, Lee had said afterwards. Of course he fuckin' got it, he was doing it. This must be what it feels like to be religious, he'd said to Rish in the course of his explaining, like when someone says they've seen the light.

'Well, I've seen the fuckin' light,' said Zoe, 'and there's no turning back. This is ours for the taking. This is ours.' This moment ranked right up there; first big rave, first pill, that time he'd done acid on the beach and that night at the illegal in Thetford Forest. It ranked right up there.

'You know what?' said Rish, 'not many people see it like that...' Rish paused here to smartly address a long straggling line of coke that Josh had presented to him on a small shaving mirror. Having done so, he looked up from the mirror, tilted his chin to the ceiling, closed his eyes and shook his head in a series of small shudders while using his thumb and middle finger to alternately open and close his nostrils while rapidly sniffing. He made a sound like a distant helicopter. 'Yea,' he said, 'not many see it that way... or not many bother to think of it that way... and why would they... why should they...? But I've always seen it like that... always thought about it like that. My mum and dad were fuckin' hippies... ya know, in the 60s 'n' that, radicals, free love, dismantle the system, put acid in the water, free the people, break the chains of oppression, no more isms and schisms... so I've always seen it like that... it's a natural progression for me...'ere, look...' And as he said this, Rish raised the two records in his hands up into the air and turned to face the room. 'Oi,' he shouted, 'who thinks these can change the world?' There were general shouts of encouragement. 'Right,' Rish shouted at them again, waving the records about above his head, 'who thinks ravin' is political?' This time he got groans and 'Fuck off... we don't want that shit...'

Rish turned back to Lee and Zoe, laughing. 'Fuckin' dipsticks,' he said with affection. 'They don't know what they're doing. Don't realise the power... don't know this is major... tell you what...' he said, putting his face close to theirs and slowing down his delivery, '...tell you what for fuckin' nuthin'... this is the biggest thing there's ever been.' Lee began to think of him and Zoe and Rob up a ladder on a balcony on a farm somewhere near Cambridge, of Zoe talking about flyers round the world, and of both of them talking about streams of influence and technology. 'There has been nothing like this before,' Rish said with complete conviction; then, straightening up and bringing more energy to his words, he fired at them, 'Punk, punk, punk... people always go on about punk and how it changed shit. Yea, well fuckin' wicked 'n' all that and I loved it too, yea, loved what it did, although the music was shit, but I'll tell you somethin', no favours asked, what we're doin' is gonna piss all over punk. Anarchy? Revolution? Look at this,' and he held up the records again. 'We made this a few months ago, mainly in this room right here; then we got it pressed, then we jumped in a van and took it straight to the record shops, shops run by ravers for ravers, and we put it personally in the hands of DJs we knew would do the business. Within a month of finishin' the tune and within a week of pressin' it, you,' and he pointed at Lee and Zoe here, 'were dancin' to it; off your nut in a dirty warehouse, or a muddy field somewhere, dancin'.' He paused to let the words settle and to lick his gums and the inside of his lips, dry with the talk and the Charlie.

'The means of production,' he continued, 'distribution and consumption, are in the hands of the people, more specifically, in the hands of the ravers. The people are takin' control, there's moral panic in the papers, questions in Parliament, special police units, changes in the fuckin' law to outlaw beats and dancin'... for crying out fuckin' loud, they're changin' the law to try and shut down celebration of our music.' There was genuine outrage in his voice, but he calmed as he inhaled deeply and sniffed sharply before adding in measured tones: 'But that battle is already fought and we won. Yea, the old parties and the acid thin', splendid as it was, shot down... but that was a sacrifice for a bigger prize... we just went licensed and they had to change the licensing to let us in... makes it look like they're in control but the pressure to party was too much for 'em... the pressure from all massive, all crew, creeds, races and fuckin' religions... just too much pressure.' He nodded, satisfied, before adding, 'for the time bein' anyway.' Rish collected his thoughts then said, 'Look at that white label,' and pointed at the label on the record visible through the hole in the sleeve. 'That's what punk could only dream about. But we're doin' it. We're doin' it all ourselves. That is politics and it don't come more political than that... control your resources and you will control the fuckin' world.'

'Wow... yea...' said Lee and Zoe together, mesmerised but also out of their depth.

'Tell me this,' demanded Rish, 'how many different people have you met since ravin'? How much has your fuckin' mind been expanded by that, by the drugs as well, by the music 'n' all the rest of it, yea, yea, but how many people have you met that you would never have met before...? Yea,' he said, nodding at the acknowledgement in their expressions, 'it will change you, it will change us all. You will look back on this as the most amazin' fuckin' time. We believe in somethin' so hard right now that we're makin' it happen without even realisin' what we're doin'. It's like the fuckin' big bang. It was all there, buildin' potential but looked like nothin' was going on. Then, spontaneous eruption. Acid, ravin', Hardcore, jungle...' He paused. 'I'm tellin' you all this for nothin' by the way.' Rish laughed and they laughed with him.

'Where's it gonna go then?' asked Zoe, fired by his words but not really sure what she meant by the question.

'Oh, don't get me wrong,' said Rish, 'I weren't born fuckin' yesterday. They will possess it back one day. One day you'll wake up and it'll be gone... except up here,' and he tapped his head, 'except up here.' Both Lee and Zoe were taken back to similar words they had heard coming from the mouth of Baz as he drove them home from an illegal rave in Thetford. Lee wondered whose idea it was, Rish's or Baz's, or perhaps they had fashioned it together in a moment such as they were in right now, inspired, coked to fuck and on a roll.'But that don't matter because it will have been. It will have left its mark. The world will forever after be just a bit fuckin' Hardcore,' and he nodded with satisfaction as he reached into a drawer of the desk and pulled out a medium-sized freezer bag full of glowing green bud which he held before Lee and Zoe and said, 'right, who wants to build a spliff?'

# TWENTY-TWO

LEE SAT IN THE CAR AND SMILED TO HIMSELF AT the response he had made to Rish's question – a perfect three-sheeter baseball bat of a spliff, loaded with the stinky weed from the freezer bag. He could almost taste its sharp pungency and he licked his lips. The road was drawing him now, reeling him along, pulling him on to Junction 8 and the Birchanger interchange. The music stabbed percussive organ, bass-thumps, a dry snare, tambourine; drops back for master bass, rub-a-dub style in the flat spaces of the break. The road signs and markings on the tarmac split the road, offering the airport and the A120 off to the left. The signs told Lee what he already felt; they told him this was the modernised and developed Junction 8, not the Junction 8 of his trips home from the rave. The signs told him that he was on his own; that he was heading back to Essex on a quiet Saturday morning; they told him he had made discoveries that morning while attempting to clear out the loft, they told him there was something he needed to sort out. This road, thought Lee, this new version, this twenty-first-century A120, changed the journey for him, it was like it showed him he was in another time now; just as the coming of the M11 had changed the times for Grandad Swigler, that something had ended and something else had begun. Lee decided then that he would take the old road, the road that originally had taken him east and west, outbound and home, in that other time.

The choice made, Lee let the music and the mix and the silence in the car accompany him. The sheer character of the sound sat with him as a presence. A Hardcore character, super energetic, super empathetic, tuned to the headstrong, irresistible to the dance floor; just to listen to it even all these years later got you buzzing. The breaks and stomps, the marches and steps, the screams, the squelches, the whirrs, the roars, the soars of strings, piano riffs, off-beat rhythm guitar, dancehall dubs, wobbling bass, fat and swaggering, and the boisterous menace of the pipes of a twisted steam organ. The music was company and rude proof of sentience.

Lee became vibrations of dust, original matter freshly combined, a complex organic machine, conscious and enlivened by sunlight, electricity and chemical process, hurtling at 120 feet per second in a metal box on wheels spinning across a hardened surface of oil and tar, and rock and chalk, and sand and gravel. A bag of chemistry and flesh, blood and water, fibre and bone, precious metals and exotic salts, all making chemical signature, taking account, deriving through a narrow range of highly processed external perception a sense of the shape and the nature of the universe. A moving metal box on a ball of rock and iron spinning on its axis at 1,000 miles an hour, round the sun at nearly 70,000, rotating in a galactic arm at half a million, at over a million in a galactic spiral. Lee intuited the impossible magnitude of speed and space and time and it was stillness; the space was so big and spread over time so long, it became stasis. Like looking at a continental desert from a low-flying jet, the enormous distance travelled belied by the unchanging sameness of the landscape and the barely trembling shadow thrown by the craft onto the sand. The stillness lay at the point where the silence and the movement and the music and Lee's consciousness met; a point where Lee became the flow of active enjoyment of his own awareness; a point repeated over and over, frame by frame, a life passing through the shutter gate, each point unendingly connected and part of those before and those to come. Lee recognised the state and he held it like a cloth of delicately woven fabric; billowing, alive, an arrangement of replicating threads that rippled with all possible connections.

Lee went with his flow and took the slip off the motorway and eased round the many lanes of the roundabout to take the car east by the old A120. Without thinking or asking, he immediately indicated left and pulled onto the forecourt of the petrol station that idled amongst the trees just beyond the junction. This garage, this point of the journey, right on the Birchanger interchange, was always a way-marker for him, located on the very joint of the A120 and the M11 where, whether going to London or coming back, the journey articulated. It was a last port before destination. There would have been nothing here prior to the motorway, thought Lee; nothing but the road through the fields and the woods that lay between Dunmow and Stortford. If you went back far enough, it would all have been forest, like Epping, like Hatfield, like Hainault, the old Forest of Essex that stretched from London to the sea, quiet, lost, a road running between banks crowded with trees. Then, he might have stopped at an inn for the night, or changed horses but, as it was, he stopped by way of tradition, from habit, for the sake of old times, for the sake of the journey, to pay homage to his own story; to his own history that stood like a ghost by the roadside, looking at him, looking through him.

Lee pulled the car around the pumps to leave it parked nose-first, facing the glass of the kiosk. As he stopped, two more cars seemed to arrive on the forecourt as if materialised there out of the crisp air. One was bound east, the other west. Lee watched as the two cars drew up, stopping within seconds of each other, one at the further line of pumps nearest the road and the other alongside the pumps nearer to Lee. Lee watched all this in his rear-view mirror, stretched in epic CinemaScope. The cars, both white Polos, looked identical; they appeared to be versions of the same car; one on the outward and one on the homeward stage of its journey. Lee looked hard at the cars now, his concentration deep; his intuition that both cars were the same car each occupying a different leg of the same journey was not a source of unsettling confusion as it might have been a day before, and he was no longer fased by the shutter slip, stuttering dual exposure, the swoop of his guts and the flutter of the plexus. The flow and counterflow of the journey he observed took charge.

In the car going east, he saw Kelly, snuggled warmly in her nest in the back of the car, shopping needs being passed to Rob and Zoe through the gap in the headrests; he saw himself, the person he was then, get out to busy himself with the petrol cap.

'Lucozade Original, ten Benson 'n' blue king skins,' he heard Kelly recite without thought, and watched the car empty with no sure sign that anyone had heard or taken any notice of what she had said. Kelly, unconcerned, ruffled herself back into the security of her coat and the solidity of the back seat, relaxed about what might come back to her, if anything.

He saw his ghost, the young Lee, take the pump from its slot, turning as he did so, to absently watch Zoe and Rob move across the forecourt and disappear inside the glass kiosk to wander amongst the shelves of crisps and sweets and biscuits, looking for something to fit the niche of their rave-contoured appetites before they got home, or somewhere like home, that could offer tea. Lee maintained his gaze across the forecourt via the mirror, keeping his ghost-self, which held the nozzle of the pump in the tank of the car, centre stage. Lee blinked into his mirror as his young ghost turned his eyes from the kiosk to stand and stare squarely in his direction. The gaze was unseeing; it passed through the car in which Lee sat in front of the kiosk and registered nothing, before moving again to settle on the other white Polo across at the next line of pumps.

Lee saw a barely perceptible nod of recognition from his ghost; the plate of the Polo was out of his sight but the young Lee could immediately see the car was the same or similar to his own. There were signs of age and wear across the right wing of the car that matched those on the car he was filling with petrol, and even the muffled hits and kicks of music coming from inside had a familiar vibration. There were shapes of a driver and three passengers inside, matching the complement of his own vehicle, and young Lee would be thinking that he might well be looking at himself and the rest of the crew pulling into this very garage last night on the way out, heading into town. They had stopped here last night, he would have reminded himself and, he would have added, there had been four of them in the car but, he would have shrugged, take your pick, he would have said to himself, offered up casually, this was a routine that had played out with a similar car full over most weekends of the preceding three-odd years. Nothing to see really. And, as Lee viewed himself in the stretch of the rear-view mirror, pumping petrol years ago, he felt the scan of

261

his vision turn and begin to lock with that of his past self and the second white Polo, the one heading west towards London, which was now in his eyeline.

He stared at this second car and as if responding to the intensity of his gaze, the weak white light of early morning receded, deepened, and the familiar shape of the vehicle took on deep shadows beneath, and its upper surfaces shone with the artificial light that fell in angled blocks from the garage canopy. The car shone grubbily on the forecourt, framed by the lines of pillars and pumps; the canopy and kiosk were set like a flare against the insect-flicked gloss of a summer night filled with yellow-white stars and a slice of moon. He looked hard at the west-bound Polo and for a few moments the view inverted and he saw his own car small and distant, wobbling in the lensing circumference of an inverted telescope. The view reverted and he saw the shape of the driver, his own ghost-self, turn and talk to the shadowed passengers in the back seat. He recalled the very moment from the night before, felt, completely knew, that he could transfer his perception across to the other vehicle with the tick of an eye; and with that sensation of possible transference came a realisation, an understanding of the chain of perfect linked segments that had brought him here in the pale light of early morning, that had brought him to the pumps opposite in the warm dark of the previous night, that would bring him back many years later on a Saturday afternoon to remember and to see it all again. He saw the chain looped and looped around, every piece perfectly placed back through journeys previous and lying ahead along the road of journeys yet to come.

Lee was dazzled by the revelation and looked to where the links of the chain met with his self at the pump; then back along the chain, a short rewind to view the perfectly placed pieces that had brought him and his raving crew to the garage forecourt the night before. The first frames came broken and intermittent, cutting to black and white and disappearing altogether as he caught glimpses of his car, the white Polo, in Colchester earlier in the week, somewhere round the back of World Class Records. The reel settled and there was Zoe, dodging across the road towards him as he waited, parked up. She had a stack of tickets in one hand and a bundle of flyers in the other. Somewhere in a pocket, he thought, he had a roughly made list of names on a torn half-page of orange craft paper – stolen from Ange – that would account for each of the tickets in Zoe's hand. That was how it went. Cut next and he and Zoe were outside Clive's, a ten-minute drive from World Class, a quiet, grand-looking Victorian terrace in a hushed, leafy street, warm with sun-baked tarmac, just off the main road. They were outside before going inside to pick up some hash. A cup of tea and a smoke later and they were back on the road.

'Nepalese,' said Lee thoughtfully. 'Wow… I was well stoned in there.'

'Me too,' said Zoe. 'I can see why Clive said it was a bit of a treat. Good shit, man,' she said with a laugh.

The film cut and buzzed grey and white before stabilising to show the way up the garden path of a '50s-built semi. Lee was on his own and about to pay Brian a visit to pick up the weekend's speed. Thirty grams, uncut and staying that way; twenty grams were spoken for – see torn orange paper for details – the rest he would shift in the venue. A cup of tea while one of Brian's scrawny urchins retrieved the gear from somewhere in a field at the back of the houses and he was off again. White static buzzed across the film. That was the tickets and drugs sorted, thought Lee. The next frames spun and slipped, finer details of who was being picked up from where, who was working a shift and couldn't make it until later, blurred and blurred around until a final decision, made on the night, confirmed the London link-up. As the car sat on the garage forecourt covered in light and surrounded by night, there was only one more piece remaining; just one more scene to perform that would take them to the brink. At that point everything would have seemed open to circumstance, the point charged with the probable and planned for, edged with the unlikely and the possible. The promise of the night infinite. And, afterwards, there was perfect poise and sunlight, chasing home the promise of before into the new day.

Lee shook his head at the vision in a vision, and as he steadied his gaze, his eyes again found themselves viewing the wraparound screen of the rear-view mirror. The feature was playing out and he watched the two white Polos, mid-'80s plates, brake briefly where the forecourt met the road, left and right, then accelerate away, echoes of each other, one into the night towards the roundabout and the M11, the other into the sun of the morning, off down the A120 towards Dunmow and Braintree. Once the air had settled, Lee reversed his own car and followed the course of the east-bound Polo, twitches of vertigo becoming a comfort now. The memory of the car he followed would take him to Rob's garage; Rob's garage bristling with decks and other audio magic, some of it Zoe's, some of it his; Rob's garage where they would install themselves and spend the rest of the weekend playing tunes, messing with samples, abusing whatever substances they had left and entertaining the crew from Cambridge and Clacton and Colchester and Witham and who knew where else, until the day faded from the sky and they had wrung themselves dry.

# TWENTY-THREE

As Lee followed the road and the time travellers, out of sight but inexorable, the music again filled the emptiness of the car; splashing wet snares on the loose, running off of edgy keys under and over a staccato of speed-pitched vocals. He felt the heavyweight kicks, placed in open space, reverb in his guts as much in memory as in straight physical action and reaction. The sounds elbowed into his thoughts, chest to chest, chins up, jostling with the information coming in from the signs and marks on the land that, patiently and unchanged, inscribed the route. The one enhanced the other and demanded Lee's attention; demanded full recognition of his intimate knowledge of this road, right down to its final instalment. When it was still the "A" road east he had sat in its stubborn traffic too often as passenger and driver, and had become familiar with every tree and hedgerow, every idiosyncratic outbuilding and eccentric sarsen it had to offer. As a kid it had carried him part or all the way almost everywhere he went and, once he started raving, he travelled back and forth along it in all those other hours he had not yet given to it; in his heightened states, he reviewed and renewed his closeness to the way and apprehended its dream-time significance. He squared himself now to this old investment and the inevitability of its course; took the lumpy line it made on the map and accepted the insistence of destination. He prepared himself to pay his respects to the places of mystery that lay along it; he prepared himself to meet his culminations, to take on the points of inflection, to roll round the recurring loops where the road passed through Dunmow and met the way to Easton, where it finally and repeatedly, relentlessly, reached Rob's garage.

Lee eyed the road before him but saw also the Polo which travelled the same route and which he had seen leave the garage just ahead of him; he could see its journey forward and back and watched it bounce in abbreviated stop-frame from Takeley to Dunmow, past Felsted and Stebbing, Saling and Rayne; saw it materialise in a slap of matter perfectly aligned to its own shadow on the precise measure of its dimensions on a square of roadway outside Rob's; he saw the stopped vehicle, puffed and wheezed with journey, gently yawed on its shocks and suspension by the bass which reverbed inside. He saw himself hold the door and watched as bodies bundled from the car into the garage, flicking switches, licking Rizla, picking tunes, nodding rhythm, singing synth, upending the mash of the night before to take more than was really there. He saw it all on that morning as he'd seen it so many times before.

Lee pulled back on the lens of this vision and returned himself to his readiness and to the road which worked its way east in real time; he wanted to experience the journey fully, to take in the litany of landmarks and follow the line of it on the map of his awareness and memory. He effortfully turned and tuned his focus to this as he approached the little right-hander, the little road, no more than a lane, that bumped along to Hatfield Broad Oak. It was a bead on his rosary and he smiled as he passed the junction. Its prospect was beatific and calming and he briefly allowed his attention to wander down the road as it heaved up the humpback over the dismantled Dunmow-Stortford railway to reach the sequestered patch of antique Essex forest that, protected, survived there. The forest had always been refuge for Lee, a place of escape, and he heard his own words sound in his head:

'Come on, this party's pony... let's go to the forest and do some trips...' He'd addressed the people thus and urged them to seek the sanctuary of the trees. 'It's a fairy tale in there and the moon's nearly full tonight.' The words rallied them and he saw their dark lunar-patched shapes limber through the fence and pick their way by the moongleam that shone out and fell reflected from the underside of clouds. The escapees settled in a silvered, sylvan glade, took their acid and spent what seemed like much time looking for hats and putting the hats they had with them on trees and bushes.

Lee took the loop further back, back to his forest origins, to his first experience of the old woodland and its big trees. Even now, he could still find response to the pure aura that had enfolded him during that first childhood visit to Hatfield Forest; the sky-reach of limbs and the bulked trunks that seemed arrested mid-movement, slow striding like mega-fauna, were deeply imprinted upon him; the trees, then, far bigger and more full of the earth than he could have imagined; the creepers, twisting from the ground to the high branches of awed canopy, through spots of shadow and sun, themselves as big as any tree he had seen before. A place of fairy tale, he'd suggest years later, a place scary with supernatural hazard, made safe only by the presence of adults and the trodden ground of the path. It had amazed him then and he realised how that amazement had inhabited him, like a bird nested in the high heart of a tree, ever since.

Back in Rob's garage, the birds were screaming alarm in the hedgerows. Lee could hear them now, shrill and panicked in the weft of the bass and the breaks, weaving through the smother of the smoke. They repeated the calls and the messages left by his mum and by his sister, adamant and terse. Rob said they were either never made or their importance never made clear to him. But Rob was protective of his parties; Rob liked to possess events and make them his own, extensions of himself. It was the same with the tunes that they'd made together; their nativity was in collaboration, but as Lee's calamity pushed a wake across the stream, Rob assumed proprietorial rights and took possession. It was true that intrusions of the real could badly skew a vibe but Rob protected what he saw as his creations ferociously and to the exclusion of all other concerns. Lee had an indelible picture in his head of Rob's mum at the door of the garage, half-in, half-out, her head cocked like a bird that had come in from its unheeded screaming in the hedgerows. Mrs Murgan looked at him from a far place; he could feel the bead of her eyes and her attention upon him but couldn't intuit her meaning, so far was it from where he was, or, maybe, like Rob, he just didn't want to admit the intrusion, warned off by the angle of her body. But Lee could remember wondering about it; he could remember little rags of darkness at the edges of his vision.

'Hey, Zo, d'ya see Rob's mum come in then? What's up with that?'

'Dunno, Danny boy, dunno, but it's bound to be trouble,' she'd mocked, the irony fierce now.

'Hey, Rob, what was that then? With your mum.'

'Ahh, just *your* mum, mate,' Rob had said, 'trying to find out where you are.'

'Yea?' said Lee. 'Bit weird, innit? Why would she do that?'

'Dunno, mate, but she knows now and I've told you, so let's get on with it...' Lee continued briefly to question but rejected his own questions as not worth following up and gladly took the reassurance offered by the no-consequence manner of Rob's explanation. Something still pulled even then at his sleeve as he moved on and away from the strangeness of the message but he brushed it away, batted it to the corner with the back of a hand. Lee followed Rob's direction, concurred with him and roused the assembled by announcing that there were drugs to take, tunes to play and shit to chat.

## //

Lee wrestled his attention back to the road ahead. Takeley approached. *Takeley I'm Yours*, he sang under his breath, and as he passed without pause the Jubilee Hall, he paid tribute to unlikely venues in nowhere places. Some of the best parties, he thought, in places unremembered and unaccounted for save in seldom-visited memories amongst a few. Lee could laugh now as his head filled with the outrage and altercation, the confusion and the rumour that shut down the last event he had been to at the Jubilee Hall. Yardies dealing crack from the Gents' bogs had apparently been the claim. Lee always wondered whether the informer on that night might have been his dad. He'd definitely been living in Takeley at the time; shacked up with that weird biker girl, the one he was with before he married Julia. Lee had picked Angie up from his dad's the weekend following the shut-down. Both his dad and Pat – was that her name? – had seemed flintily satisfied with the police intervention. They had banged on about hooligans and druggies and respect for property and neighbours. Lee had ignored it; that and everything else they said, and got himself and Angie out of there as fast as possible back out onto the road he was taking now.

As then, the road kept moving its way, implacable, barely raising itself to go over the stream of The Roding, turning itself through Canfield and then on past the red and dusty brick of the Easton Lodge Gatehouse. Lee winced at the sight of the old building. It was decrepit, abandoned and boarded, squat and gloomy, and oversaw the old Roman road of its past with resentment crumbling to indifference, deaf to sad echoes of royal hunting parties and hedonistic Edwardians. As a very young kid, Lee had wanted to live in the Gatehouse, alone and feral; it was the haunt of a catweazle and, at that time, still looked like a liveable place. Lee knew that the ghost of his young self, the self that drove the car he had followed from the garage at Birchanger, would come alive at the gatehouse. Even if nothing was said to those he was with he would be moved; he was, after all, returning from his own Secret Garden, returning from what would become his last hardcore rave. Of course, the young Lee would not know it was his last, would not know that journey amongst all others was so selected, but he did know he had just been to Double Dipped; he did know he had enjoyed The Secret Garden. Young Lee's head was full of the rave and its jungle backdrops and as he passed the old gatehouse to the Lodge it would fire memories of other secret gardens in that place that were maybe even more potent for Lee than Hatfield and its forest of spirits; memories set years before on visits with his dad to fish the four ponds of the estate. Lee had never been back there since, and the gardens and ponds were a precious fragment in his brain, hidden and hard to reach, vague like a gene-memory of endless prehistoric woods. As Lee passed the old building, he would understand that he could never go back there; understand that even if the place were unchanged – which it would surely be – it would never again be the childhood memory of monster dragon flies – an insect he had never seen before – huge gunnera and ferns; tall, tall trees, lengthening old and unimpeded straight to the sky; and still, dark ponds scaled with leathery lily pads and stacked with enormous silent, gliding carp.

'Gatehouse to Easton Lodge,' he heard himself say to the car as the old brick structure passed by. '...used to go fishin' there with me dad. Wicked place. Like a fuckin' jungle to a little kid... a secret garden.' Lee laughed at the link he had made and no one else really got.'No tigers, though...' he added, thinking of the huge painted backdrops in the club that he had enjoyed and discussed with someone he met on the night '... but I did once see a white stag there and there were green and blue dragonflies as big as ya face.'

The synth tracked the iridescent insects as Lee's focus returned to the present and the sound lifted him to points of expansion, the beats settled and grooved and the bass wobbled and fuzzed at the limits of his ears, forcing other senses to contribute. Lee calculated the progress of the Polo as he passed the site of the old paint and polish factory, sniffing disdainfully at it as Grandad Swigler always would; the car ahead of him on the road would already be in Dunmow, taking on the early morning roads with the energy that came with the final stretch. Lee saw it clearly, a moving spot of hot, wild energy on an empty Sunday morning. He saw too the lights of the ambulance coming the other way through the cutting of the old by-pass and heard Rob as it passed the Polo in a Doppler smear of colour and sound:

'Bit early for all that,' Rob said.

'Just keepin' you on your toes,' added Zoe, unconcerned. Lee continued to drive the Polo forward, unconcerned too.

It must have been the one, Lee later figured, triangulating the time and the space and the coroner's conclusions. It must have gone up to the roundabout then back towards the town before turning hard down Rosemary Lane, the chassis dipping low on the wheels as it did, taking the dip behind Foakes Hall, the downs, the Rec, the Clockhouse, the school. Then left through the water meadows of the Chelmer, before taking the airfield road towards the Perryfield Ponds, towards Eastern Lodge.

Lee's recall of the rest of that day spun him back to the garage; the calls and the messages left by his mum and sister, Rob's deflection his own complicity, the sanctity of the chill-out; Rob's mum at the garage door, the drugs to take, the tunes to play, the shit to chat.

He had stopped revisiting it. It would never add up, or make sense, or any difference, but for a long time he had done little but pick at the details, tie and untie the ends and drive and redrive the last part of that journey, as he followed, in his head, the ambulance.

Lee was through Dunmow now, over the floodplain of the Chelmer and heading up towards Felsted. His brow was furrowed with the long-neglected story of that day. He tried to reconnect with Shaggy and Breeze but the phase shifts and breakbeats only took him back the way he had come, and he let the story take its own course as it spent several more hours at Rob's before taking him back the way he had come more than once. He was the last to leave Rob's that night, him along with the Clactonians – Ian, Faye and Mark. The goodbyes were full of hugs and grins and vibes and pride in the achievements of the weekend and the resolve to see it through, hardcore to the end. Lee took this spirit with him as he walked through the late evening dark, cooling into night, to the car. But as he stood and slammed the door shut and turned to face the front door of Nanna Swigler's just minutes later, he deflated. He became a husk. A fragile shell. A creeping brittleness spread over him like the rapid ageing that always eventually overtakes the overreaching undead who think they can cheat mortality; in mere moments, he thought, he would collapse to dust like a cinema vampire exposed to light. He was an empty vessel; he would ring hollow like a gong or a bell if he was struck, provided the blow didn't shatter him first. Lee gathered himself and opened the door quietly and with deliberate and contrived innocence of action. He heard the TV and could see its blue-grey light spilling out of the door of the front room, patches of cold yellow where the radiation bounced from Nanna Swigler's brass plates and ornaments.

'That you, Lee?' Nanna Swigler's voice, croaky with night and hours of non-use. Lee flinched at the demand for interaction.

'Yea, Nan. Just gonna have something to eat and then bed,' said Lee with as much casual normality as he could muster from the bottom of the over-scraped barrel of his conscious self.

'You need to call ya mother, Lee. She's been after you all day. It's ya dad,' said Nanna Swigler. Her tone was flat and ominous.

*What, Malcolm?* thought Lee. No, his mum wouldn't call Malcolm that, and neither would Nanna Swigler. What was going on with his dad then? Lee stood in the hall and looked at the living room wall and Nanna Swigler's slippered feet that he could see through a slice of open doorway. He felt a long way from the room and the TV. He looked up into the dark corner of the distant living room and saw Rob there, looking at him from the garage doorway earlier that day; it seemed a lifetime ago, the memory faded and worn by age and recurrence.

'He's 'ad an accident, Lee. A bad one. He's in the 'orspital.'

Lee fell far and deep, bouncing off damp, crumbly brickwork in long swooping arcs. The pit of his stomach lurched and tried to ready him for action, but his body was dull and unresponsive. In his head, he tried to deal with the phone call he couldn't make and the news he knew he probably couldn't bear. He saw the ambulance they passed that morning in Dunmow, an emblem of emergency, and it jabbed painfully significant at him, breaking the heavy surface of his fatigue.

'Oh, okay, Nan. I'll give her a call.' His voice was still in the mode of crafted innocence he had used earlier. He could hear the inadequacy of the words; the bland inappropriateness of tone in response to the understated gravity in Nanna Swigler's voice. Could he make the call? Could he? Could he handle not making the call and picking up the broken pieces tomorrow? Better to call now, he advised, do it now and disperse the danger. He called.

His mum was at home. His sister Angela was at the hospital. His dad had had an accident. It was bad. He would probably not survive. He was mostly unconscious but he had asked for Lee and Angela. Where had he been all day? Didn't he get the messages left with Rob's mum and with Zoe's? She had rung everywhere. Angela had rung on Rob's mobile too. Think, think, think, slapped Lee at his own face.

Lee schemed. His car was parked outside but his mum didn't know that and neither did his nanna and she wouldn't check. Just say you've been drinking. I never drink, thought Lee. They might offer to pick me up. Just say you're going and don't go. What would you do if you were normal? If I was normal, if I was normal... I'd go, uncertain and confused because I never saw the bloke anymore, but I'd go nevertheless because he was my dad, because we did dad stuff in the past and that's what you did when someone was dying, even if you never did it when they were living. Lee realised he wasn't helping himself. He tried to start again. Right, he managed, I'll go. Just got to sort a few things out. Lee pushed himself upstairs to his room and stood in the doorway staring at the flyers on the wall and ceiling. He marvelled at them and they moved, kaleidoscopic. He shook the flyers from his attention, closed the door behind him, rummaged in his pockets and, without thought or pause, emptied the powder from the wrap he found there and sniffed it up through a tatty fiver, breaking all the rules he didn't have about that kind of thing.

## //

Lee saw them from a distance framed in the vanishing lines of the hospital corridor: Amy, Angela, Julie, Jim too, Dad's brother. They were sitting and standing, comforting; there were arms, tears, tissues, a nurse and a doctor to one side, mouths compressed with the delivery of bad news. Lights were bright, notices laminated and the lino floor was shiny and went up the wall in a generous curve so it could be properly mopped. Lee slowed his approach and tried to read the scene, an art expert reading an old picture. In his head he could hear that nun with the glasses and the teeth explaining what it all meant, and it all meant that Teddy Harker had sunk out of sight, that the sea had washed over the forecastle deck and taken him down to the silt and the shells and the sand and the still debris that continually gathers beneath the moving, moving surface. Lee stopped. They hadn't seen him, he didn't think. He turned and went back the way he had come.

After that it was a blur. His head scrambled. He was being carried on a flood; his status fixed but his position changing rapidly. Sometimes you can't help the place in which you find yourself, he reassured, but you can help what you try to do about it and how loud you shout. But he did nothing and he shouted nothing and he let himself spiral away with the debris. He stayed with Jim and Sandra, he stayed with Billy and June, he tried coming back to Braintree but it didn't work out. He ended up with Graham and Pat in Loughton. They had no kids. They had a spare room. It was near to London. He assumed an insulating anonymity and stayed that way, disguised and hidden until fortune brought him Marianne. Marianne was Swedish; she was new to London and new to England; there was no history to coordinate, there were no strings to connect them but the ones they made for themselves and she was moved – God knows why he continued to wonder – to bring him back to a version of himself. Lee's mum moved back to Dunmow and Lee continued to avoid Braintree; he removed all need to go back there, he reasoned his absence and airbrushed the road from the map.

Yes, every fucking chance I had, confirmed Lee ruefully as the widening screams of Blame mixed to an acid squelch, hands high piano and housey vocal, revived him. He was in Rayne now and took in the squat party there that followed the Prodigy at the Embassy; then past the site of the Braintree Barn and there was Baz and Rob in the car park that first time, tracked to a field and a photograph desaturated with time, and now he was in the town. He committed himself and drove determinedly through the old estate, past the place he'd lived for so long with his mum and Malcolm, past too Nanna and Grandad Swigler's old house. It all looked the same; if he ignored the cars and the fashion, he might have been driving the old Polo; the absence of change was unsettling and he hurried the car on until he reached Rob's mum and dad's. Once there he sat across the road, quiet in his parked car, and watched himself hold open the door of a white Polo from which, in procession, came Rob and Zoe and Kelly, like rabbits from a magician's hat; MA2s, baggy jeans, caps, dancing trainers, sweatshirts tied round the waist, water bottles in one hand, a stack of flyers in the other, oiled and anointed by whatever sweaty rinse-out they had been to, straightening up from time crumpled in the car and bowling up to Rob's garage, on their way to squeeze every last drop from the weekend.

Lee worked out later that his dad must have arrived at the hospital about the same time as they had pulled up outside Rob's after The Secret Garden, the car swaying and ready to burst. When the ambulance crew had found him, Edward Harker had been as close to dead as you can be while still, yet, alive. Blasted and bleeding, he had lain in a field near the Lodge for several hours. A fisherman and estate warden had found him early Sunday morning, thinking the bundle of rags, the mound of earth and concrete in the corner of the field, was the result of fly-tipping. Later enquiries revealed that people living nearby thought they had heard an unusually loud gunshot, or a gas gun, late Saturday evening but thought nothing of it. This lack of thought was unfortunate for Lee's dad, as it was also unfortunate that the noise was neither a gun nor a bird scarer but a very live and very unstable bomb; a Luftwaffe SC 50 on a degenerated LZZ long time-delay fuse. Teddy Harker had been using his metal detector around the old airfield site at Easton Lodge, searching, as he liked to do, with the help of old maps and photographs and the memories of locals, for artefacts, aircraft parts, mess hall utensils, dropped coins and personal effects. That Saturday evening, he unhappily made what was probably the find of his life; only one bomb exploded but there was a cache of several. The ambulance crew had reclaimed him from the field and taken his broken body to the hospital at Broomfield. Lee saw now the accident of it; the act of war that began the chain had long expired by the time his dad got there; despite the so many ways it might not have happened, it had.

# TWENTY-FOUR

Lee continued to sit until the ravers had vacated the pavement and disappeared inside before he got out and approached the familiar glass front door. He could have been coming for a smoke with Rob, he thought, as he pushed the button on the bell and shapes and colours moved behind the glass in response. Lee knew that Rob's mum and dad still lived there; they weren't the moving type; they were clean-living, quietly fit and active, and how they had been responsible for producing Baz and Rob was still a mystery to Lee. Lee managed a smile at the thought as the door opened.

'Hello, Mrs Murgan,' said Lee.

'Oh hello, Lee, dear. Please come in.'

'I can't stay, Mrs Murgan,' said Lee as he followed the old lady into the house. 'I just wanted to come and say hello as I was in the area.'

'I know, dear,' she replied as if she were comforting an upset child. 'Look who's here, Wally,' she said to an old man sitting at the kitchen table routinely scanning the local paper. The man turned and stood as he saw Lee.

'Lee, son, so good to see you.'

And Lee could see Rob in both their faces; his death was there too in the lines and shadows on their skin.

'Hello, Mr Murgan,' said Lee as the old man reached out and held Lee's hand with both of his. With few words they went out to the garage and stood before three boxes on a workbench. Lee, at the direction of Mrs Murgan, began to look through them. One of them was much like the box he had opened in his loft earlier that day: tapes, a bag of records, flyers, photographs and – this unlike his own box – a piece of fossilised stick. There was also, perched on the top, added later than the other stuff, thought Lee, a two-channel mixer, Vestax, black cables wrapped round the silver body. A black Technics 1210 occupied each of the other two boxes. One had a grubby cracked cover, the other had no cartridge; they were both dusty and bore the marks of frequent use.

'Baz said we were to give these to you when you came,' said Mr Murgan, hovering by the door. Lee looked at him and then at Mrs Murgan.

'Did he?' Lee pictured Baz at the funeral handing him his card. He had said nothing about this at the time. 'How did he know I was coming?' asked Lee.

'I don't know, dear. He didn't say. He did say he wasn't sure when you would come but that he thought it would be soon.' Mrs Murgan paused and organised in her head the next thing she was going to say. 'He just said to give you all this when we saw you. He said to say that it's yours now that Rob's gone.'

There was a pause full of silence, and dust moved in the light slanting through the garage windows. 'I'd really like it gone if I'm honest, Lee,' and she touched his hand lightly with her own. 'You do want it, don't you?' Lee felt played, manoeuvred, but in the way a genuinely surprised recipient of a surprise party feels played. The shock and even fear of the deception quickly turning sweet and affirmative. Lee nodded at Mr and Mrs Murgan and under their oversight shifted the boxes into the boot of the car. As he pulled away, Lee looked to the rear-view mirror and saw Mr and Mrs Murgan, together on the front step, looking quietly at him, hands held up in farewell. He raised his own hand above his head as they receded and then they disappeared from sight as the road took him right and away.

Lee took the old road back and he selected DJ Ratty, Universe, Big Love '93 for the first part of the drive; it was sweet-spot Hardcore; Lee knew the score with this mix and he judged that it would take him to Birchanger, at which point he would select a pirate radio mix – he'd seen plenty of them on the memory stick. He had it mapped; an Eruption maybe, Pulse, Weekend Rush, Pressure, Kool, Don… He nodded at the road ahead and it responded only quietly. The route was muted for him now, the drive gentle; he could recognise its places and its histories as he passed but then they were left behind. He luxuriated in the easy movement and let the fibre-optic stable and the sound of the basement bass restore him.

Lee stopped again at the garage at the Birchanger interchange. He filled up, bought a coffee and stood drinking it, leaning against the bonnet and watching the road. How will it all be remembered, he thought, on into the future? An unfinished article in Zoe's folder asked the same question. Will it just disappear and fade away, slip from memory and recollection, like the Beatniks, like the Jazz scene of the '50s? Or Teddy boys, or even Mods and Hippies? We maybe remember the fashions, we still have the music but what about the people, the real people, the real things that happened and who they happened to? Who remembers that, who will remember that? There's a few books and films, some ageing enthusiasts, but by most, the energy and the people are mostly forgotten.

Lee thought of all those he had been with when he had been raving. It had only been a few years and he'd stayed pretty local to his own area, but there still must have been thousands and thousands of contacts. All those times, all those lives. The sheer numbers, he thought, must make it different to what went before but was it? Will we lose them too, what they did and how they did it, who they were, what they felt at the time and what they thought about what they were doing? Where will all that go? What happens to those thousands of points of light; will they disperse, deconstruct, fewer and fewer clusters, individually blinking out, the darkness patched between them growing, creeping around, consuming slowly over time the faltering, fading, flickering remnants until nothing more remains but the abstracted music and a few shaky video recordings?

What then? A researcher comes across old newspaper reports or footage of events and is taken by the excitement and energy and scale of what they discover; by the horror and sense of crisis on the part of the authorities and the establishment; they dig and delve and assemble the material they can find and try to interpret it, to reconstruct the way it was, like archaeologists reconstructing Pompeii from fragments and pieces of culture uncovered in the petrified ash. Would the reconstruction reveal Lee and his mates, sat foursquare in his Polo, hammering down the M11 in a cloud of spliff smoke, socks full of drugs, buzzing their tits off listening to Labrynth tapes or tuned to Pulse FM on the radio, points of light converging? Would the research show the put-together-in-a-spare-bedroomness of the time, the phone number on the bottom of a flyer, the mate who knew someone who knew about a good party going off wherever it was; show them heading out wearing whatever they happened to be wearing, meeting in a car park, reading the map with a lighter? Would they get the surging, defiant, instinctive freedom and abandon, the lack of uniform organisation and structure, the urge to have a party because a party is the best thing to have, the total commitment to be at the rave as completely as you could possibly be, to invest all of yourself in the abandon of the night and to take the residue of that total commitment away with you into the next day, into the next week and into the rest of your life? Would it pick up the soul-shifting moment when the hit of the music coincided with the lift of the drugs and your physical and emotional being bonded in shared experience with everyone you could see around you; when you knew that your rush was the same rush being ridden by thousands of others who had committed, like you, to make this night the night that it was and to make it a time that would add forever to the bedrock of who you were? Would this come through? Would it?

Lee doubted it would come through. There may be some glimpses in a photo, in a video and, most definitely, in the music it was there to be found; but the whole knotty junction of time and space and energy could surely only be understood as a shared, lived, experience. *Might it be passed on, though?* he wondered. Perhaps, he thought, perhaps it was a mystery, shamanic and secret; maybe it could be transferred by the positive vibrations it had generated and which endured. This appealed. This felt like it might be a way. Maybe that was part of what was happening here, maybe that was part of what was happening back then; we were receiving spirit magic, who knows how old, kept alive over centuries, passed down as part of ceremony and ritual, a sacred flame. Is it our duty now to keep that flame alight?

He genuinely considered all this, and in the wondering of it, he saw how it would be as he arrived home in East London in no more than a couple of hours. He saw himself come through the front door bright-eyed and buzzing with the pirate radio mixes he had been playing in the car on the way back. Marianne and Eva would look up as he came in and ask where he'd got to. He'd confuse and amuse them with talk of Hardcore Bizzness. They'd help him unload the stuff from the car. They'd ask about the stuff he'd left on the table. He'd tell them that nothing would change but that nothing would be the same again; that he'd had to go on a little trip and now he was back and here they all were for the first time, because we are always here and now for the first time. Then he would say that they were going to set the decks up in the front room and that *you*, pointing at Eva, had some real education coming your way. And *you*, he would say looking at Marianne from head to toe, taking her in completely with his eyes as she stood, one of his notebooks in one hand, the other hand on her hip, steadily observing him, *you*, he would say as he waved his arm towards the flyers and the tapes and the records, are going to help me do something with all this stuff.

Lee's smile was broad as he saw all this and he flicked through the contents of the memory stick looking for an old pirate radio mix to get things started. He hit play and pulled off the forecourt following the ghost of a white Polo as the sun set into a wooze of synthesised strings, low frequency oscillation and crisp typewriter snare. The kick boomed flat and dry around a hissing high-hat, a rubbery bass driving the funk forward. The music opened a horizon of possibility for Lee now, as it had done back when it first aired and voices of the old radio filled the car and spoke to him.

*Takin' it nice and easy... takin' it nice and cool... Big
shout going out to the ones like Rob, Zoe and Kelly...
To the bad-boy crew... live and strong... to the one like
Baz, out to Danny and the Cambridge Massive, to Ian
and Faye and the seaside hardcore...
Big shout going out to the man like Terry, the one like
Michelle... Hold tight...*

Lee turned the car onto the M11 slip and the sun slid
round to his right, slanting gold across the carriageway.

*Check one. Sounds of the Crucial D on the 1s and 2s. All
massive... Big up, rude gel in the place... going out to
Donna, to Trish, to Vikki and the one like Caz..
Listen... now listen... All massive and crew...
Big up the DJ, big up the DJ, DJ on selection comin' on
through...
DJ on selection know what to do
Rockin' for the Hardcore in the venue
Bad-boy DJ on the 1s and the 2s
Coming on strong for my ravin' crew...
It's the fashion, it's the style... Rinse out the style...*

The road sped on under Lee's car; the rolling green of Essex
flowed by on either side and motorway bridges marched
towards him. It was like he was stationary and the ground was
spinning beneath.

*07654 256 763 time to get busy. Crucial sound... mix
up.
Shout going out to the gaffer... the main man... let's
have a bigger fan in the studio...
Oh, I can feel the rush coming over me, I can feel the ecstasy.*

*Takin' you higher on Saturday afternoon... keepin'*
*you on ya toes...*
*Big tune and that's coming from the man like Scott.*
*Going out to the one like DJ Phizz, bumped into him*
*earlier. Sorry, mate, didn't have it on me... get it for*
*you later.*
*Respect to Mum in Enfield... Niceness on the FM*
*dial... You know...*
*Love to the up-for-days crew... Oh, the vibes are oh so*
*nice...*
*Shout to Jason on the pager. Don't think we can do*
*that one. No way, brother. Shout to TP on the pager...*
*biggin' up the studio crew. Thank you, sir, big up*
*yaself... big up ya chess...*
*And this one for the Essex crew – get on the case,*
*sounds of the weekend, sounds of the rush...*

Lee nodded and looked at the sky and the fields, the ribbon of road, the other cars and their unknown occupants. It had been so good, it was still so good, it was present and vital; he felt he could inhale it. Lee gripped the wheel with purpose and broadcast his state.

*To the east and the south and the north and the west... the*
*rain, the moon, the sun and the stars... bassline... huh...*
*Time to move your mind, your body and your soul...*
*Maximum boost. Going just like this. Who's hardcore*
*in the place, big it up, big it up.*
*Goin' out to the Patrick, the one like Jamie... big up*
*Mike; big up Steve; out to the Wayne.*
*It's the FM style, deep, deep as we get*
*All Hardcore Junglist... all massive... wide-awake*
*crew, hold tight.*

*Kitchen Crew comin' on through... tea in the garden,*
*enjoyin' the sunshine...*
*Everybody loves it...*

Ahead to the south, homeward, across the chalk basin and along the line of furthest visibility, Lee could see the boxed outline of the city; he turned up the music and settled back in his seat.

*And you know we're started now...*
*Rockin and jumpin' through...*
*Saturday afternoon bizzness...*
*Keepin' it sweet, keepin' it simple...*

*Easy does it now, Easy as we go,*
*Sound just rollin', rollin', riddim follow riddim...*
*The roughest the toughest the highest the great,*
*Going out to my raving crew each and every time.*